For Elif, Fatma and Mithat

"I had also a commission from the Sultan of Turkey which called for immediate action, as political consequences of the gravest kind might arise from its neglect."

Sherlock Holmes in *The Adventure of the Blanched Soldier*, Arthur Conan Doyle

Chapter One

You could have knocked me down with a feather, as the saying goes. When Mr. H summoned me on that grim November morning, I was quite expecting to be assigned some chore, or else have again to listen to a new complaint. My poor maid, Phoebe, drives my lodger to distraction with her general ineptitude, so I was wondering, as I climbed the stairs to his room, what new outrage she might have perpetrated.

I found Mr. H standing by the window, looking out over Baker Street, grey and gloomy in the drizzling rain, while Dr. Watson, seated in his usual chair, raised his eyes from his newspaper to give me a wink. Whatever could it mean?

"It's the kind of day, is it not, Mrs. Hudson," Mr. H said languidly at last, "that makes one hanker for the Mediterranean."

What could I reply to that? I said nothing.

Without turning to look at me, he continued, "I understand from Watson here that you have shown some aptitude for helping out in certain delicate situations."

"I beg your pardon, Mr. Holmes?"

He sighed.

"Dr. Watson has informed me that, in recent times, you have been instrumental in clearing up a crime or two."

His scepticism was evident from his tone.

"I have managed to get to the bottom of a few mysteries, right enough," I replied.

I glanced again at Dr. Watson, who was giving me a quizzical look. Mr. H turned swiftly to face me. "A case has arisen," he said, "where I find myself at an insuperable disadvantage." He paused. "In short, Mrs. Hudson, I am a man,"

"I never doubted it," I replied, biting my lip to stop myself from bursting out laughing, sure that my lodger would not appreciate levity.

"Have you heard," he continued, "of Abdul Hamid II?"

"Well, now…" I racked my brains. "He sounds like an oriental gentleman."

"He is the Sultan of Turkey."

"Ah!"

"And he most graciously shows some interest in my activities. Indeed, in the past I was instrumental in helping him out of a difficulty, to the extent that he wished to confer on me the Order of the Medjidie. I demurred, convincing him that it would call unwanted attention to the reason for my visit to his country."

"You are too modest, Holmes," Dr. Watson said. "Mrs. Hudson, were it not for our friend here, the very foundations of the Ottoman Empire might have been shaken to the point of collapse."

"Some might say and a good thing too," Mr. H continued. "However, Sultan Abdul Hamid was then certainly the lesser of two evils. Anyway, he has contacted me again today through the embassy here, after finding himself again in dire need of assistance, and not trusting those around him to provide it." He gave me a long hard look. "In this instance, it is impossible for me to intervene directly. I need someone – a woman of discretion – to act as my intermediary."

"I see."

"I hardly think you do, Mrs. Hudson, without more details of the case. So let me enlighten you. And do sit down…"

Really, I thought, he could take a leaf out of the Sultan's book, and be more gracious. I sat at the table, as did he, across from me.

"What do you know of Turkish customs?" he asked.

"Very little. And what I have heard is somewhat… unsavoury."

A bloodthirsty, unchristian race, that murders its enemies, and forces its women to go around with their bodies, and their faces too, almost completely covered up.

"Certain it is that they do things differently from us, although who can say in the end, who is right, who is wrong?"

"Well, as to that…"

"Anyway, the Sultan is worried about his wives."

"His wives! He has more than one?"

"He has… how many, Watson?"

"Thirteen, I believe."

"Goodness gracious!"

"And these ladies, do you see, live separated from society in a closed part of the palace where men are not permitted to enter. Apart from the Sultan himself of course."

"A harem," interpolated Dr. Watson.

"Oh, I have heard of those," I said, nodding. Indeed, I had seen paintings in the National Gallery of London illustrating such places, peopled with plump girls usually in a state of partial or complete undress.

"I said no men are permitted to enter," Holmes continued. "There are exceptions, however. The wives are protected by eunuchs."

"Unfortunately," Dr. Watson was grinning broadly now, "Holmes and I are not willing to undergo the necessary operation."

Mr. H gave him a withering look.

"Do you know what eunuchs are, Mrs. Hudson?"

"Well… I suppose I do."

"They are men who pose no threat to the virtue of wives, having…er…had their manhood removed."

"Yes," I replied hurriedly, hoping he would not feel the need to explain further.

"Do not forget the concubines." Dr. Watson folded his newspaper, and then folded his arms. He was enjoying himself enormously.

"Thank you, Watson," Mr. H continued. "I was coming to that. You see, Mrs. Hudson, as well as his official wives and eunuchs, the Sultan's harem contains quite a number of concubines... as well as slaves to serve them."

I was glad to be sitting down. Eunuchs, slaves and concubines! This was barbaric indeed.

"You have no doubt heard of concubines, Mrs. Hudson." Dr. Watson was grinning broadly.

"They are mentioned in the Bible," I replied primly. "King David..."

"Yes, yes...: Mr. H was drumming his fingers on the table, patience not being one of his virtues. "You see, Mrs. Hudson, several sudden and somewhat mysterious deaths have occurred within the harem among the concubines. The Sultan is concerned for his own safety, as well, as is to be expected, for that of his wives – none of whom have so far been involved, thank goodness. I should add that Abdul Hamid is a ruler preternaturally nervous about possible assassination attempts upon himself."

"So how can I be of help?"

I already suspected what his reply would be.

"We need a woman possessed of sharp wits to visit the harem incognito, as one of those European ladies fascinated with the exotic East. Once there, to keep her eyes and ears open and report back."

"A spy," I said. "And you thought of me, of course." I gave Dr. Watson a reproving look.

"You seem to fit the bill," the latter said, somewhat apologetically. "From what I know of your previous activities, you have shown yourself to be a discerning woman, Mrs. Hudson, and not afraid to put yourself in – let's not say dangerous – but awkward situations."

"Let's call a spade a spade," I replied, "and say dangerous, doctor."

For, on at least two previous occasions, my very life had been threatened.

"Very well." He nodded. "Dangerous, it is."

"The danger to yourself in this instance, Mrs. Hudson," Mr. H remarked, "would be very slight. Negligible, in fact. Look upon it, indeed, as a holiday."

My most recent "holiday" staying with my daughter in Kent had turned out to be anything but.[1] An adventure, more like, and one I could well have done without.

"Of course, you don't have to agree this very moment," Dr. Watson said, observing my frown.

Mr. H gave an impatient grunt.

"On the contrary, Watson, we need an answer urgently. The Sultan has impressed upon me that there is no time to be lost."

He waited, fixing me with an intense stare.

"I hardly think I can be of assistance," I said finally. "I don't speak Turkish."

"But you speak French."

It is true that my command of that language, while by no means fluent, at least enables me to get by.[2]

"Well, yes," I told him. "After a fashion."

"Good," he replied. "French is the second language of the Ottomans. All educated people speak it. But, as well as that, you would have an interpreter with you."

He had anticipated all my objections.

---

[1] See *Death in the Garden of England, A Mrs. Hudson Mystery* (MX publications, 2023)
[2] See *Mrs. Hudson goes to Paris*, (MX publications, 2022)

"Then explain further if you please," I said, "what exactly would be involved?"

This was more to Mr. H's taste. He leaned back in his chair and made a steeple with the fingers of his two hands.

"We will all travel to Constantinople together – Watson and myself incognito, though I hardly think it will be necessary for you to assume another name. I will introduce you to the Sultan, who will then lay the full details of the situation before us, since, at this moment, I have only the vaguest information on the subject, the Sultan fearing to commit particulars to writing. You will then take up temporary residence in the harem and, as I have said, keep your eyes and ears open and report back to me. That is all." He gave Dr. Watson a look. "There will, as I have already said, be no danger in it for you."

It was hardly the full description I had been hoping for. Nonetheless, I have to say that I was tempted. To be immersed in such a strange and exotic culture! I smiled to myself. How astonished my dear late Henry would have been at my recent doings, and this would most certainly top the lot.

Chapter Two

When Dr. Watson informed me that it would be necessary to travel first to Paris, and from there to take the train for Constantinople, I was delighted. It would be a chance for me to meet up with old friends from my time in that city.

"I know a very acceptable hotel, not expensive at all, but well situated and very clean," I told him, thinking of the Hotel Lilas, where I had stayed on my last visit to the French capital. It would be most pleasant to see Madame Albert again and find out how she and her son were getting on.

To my astonishment, Dr. Watson burst out laughing.

"My dear Mrs. Hudson," he said, "in the first place, we will not be lingering in Paris at all, agreeable though that would have been. I am afraid, given the urgency of the situation, we need to make all possible haste to get to Turkey, and so we will simply be staying overnight, but certainly not in some cheap little hotel. The Sultan has made very different arrangements for us, all at his expense, of course."

Thus it was that, just two days later, and after the familiar crossing from Dover to Calais and onwards, I found myself staring up at the immense façade of the Grand Hôtel du Louvre. I remembered it, of course. In fact, it was in the extensive shops on the ground floor of that establishment that I had purchased the cerise silk dress that had served me so well both in Paris and Kent, even though I had little occasion otherwise to wear such a splendid outfit. Once again, Clara had packed it for the present sojourn.

"For when you'll be meeting with royalty," she had said, while folding it carefully.

Phoebe's eyes, meanwhile, were out on stalks.

"Kings and queens," she exclaimed awestruck. "Oh, Mrs. Hudson, m'm!"

"Well now…" I decided not to confuse her further with talk of sultans and sultanas, the latter which she only knew of from adding them to scones, sneaking a few into her mouth when she thought I was not looking.

If my servants were impressed with what was ahead of me, it was surely nothing to what I felt myself as I entered the Grand Hôtel. We took what Dr. Watson informed me was a steam-powered lift – most elegant, spacious and smooth, to boot – to reach the first-floor lobby. I could not help gasping as we came out into a huge space that dazzled all the way from its pale marble flooring, up walls painted with frescoes of mythological scenes, to gilded galleries, and, pendant above all, great glittering chandeliers. Elegantly constructed return staircases led to upper floors for those who did not wish to avail of the lifts. People of all shapes and sizes, each one clad in the height of fashion, crowded the space, while liveried attendants hovered near, awaiting instructions. They even bowed to me, right, left and centre, as if I too were a member of the aristocracy. How much more comfortable, I could not help thinking, I would be in Madame Albert's cosy parlour, and I was glad of Dr. Watson's arm to lean on amidst all this unaccustomed splendour, Mr. H, having scurried off I knew not whither, and knew not to ask. "Have courage, Mrs. Hudson," the Doctor whispered to me. "You are as good as anyone here, if not better."

The initial formalities took place at a great reception desk of wood so polished one could see one's reflection in it, where a young man who smiled rather too much with his teeth and not at all with his eyes, took my name, and checked it against a register, finding it there somewhat, I think, to his surprise. He then summoned a page, who could not have been more than twelve years old, to conduct me to my room. I pressed some coins into the boy's hand, Dr. Watson having informed me that I would be expected to reach for my purse on every similar occasion, for the purposes of rewarding those doing for me things I could just as well do for myself.

My trunk having preceded me to my room (or rooms, for I had a separate bathroom all to myself!), I was astonished to find there a pretty russet-haired girl, not much older than the page, engaged in unpacking for me.
"Please don't bother," I told her in my simple French. "I am only staying for one night and can remove the necessities for myself."
"But madame," she replied. "I must do it. I am your slave."
"What!"
She giggled.
"My name is Madeleine and I am to be your slave."
"But I don't need a slave."
"You will need me in Turkey."
Most taken aback, I sat myself down on a very fancy chair upholstered in pale green silk, with a gilded wood frame, and elaborate carvings that poked painfully into my back, awaiting further enlightenment.
"I have been hired to accompany you as your interpreter," the girl continued. "You see, madame, I am half-Turkish and I speak the language."
"I see. But, my dear, I wouldn't be at all comfortable calling you a slave. Can you not just be my maid?"
"The ladies of the harem will understand that I am your slave, so that is what I must be."
I smiled back at her then. "Well, I will try not to be too harsh a mistress."
After the long journey, I felt myself to be in dire need of a rest and, informing Madeleine that we would speak more later, sent her away, so that I could lie down and shut my eyes for a while. Of course, the minute I did so, jostling thoughts crowded my head making sleep, nay even relaxation, impossible. Whatever had I let myself in for? I soon got up from my grand four-poster bed, and sat at the window looking out over a Paris that seemed very different, in the dull winter weather, from the sparkling city I had known in

the summer. My room was warm, but I could tell, by the way people outside were bundled up and scurrying for shelter, that the day was cold and wet, much like London, in fact. Would Constantinople be warmer? I thought of turquoise seas, waving palms, a cruelly bright sun that rendered colours so much more vivid (recalling those "impressionistic" paintings of the south that I had viewed on my previous visit to Paris). But in the palace, I supposed I would be locked away with the wives and concubines. Would I even get to see the sun?

Mr. H had already warned me, as far as he could, what to expect from my stay in the harem, and what he expected from me.

"You need also to know something of Abdul Hamid II himself," he had said. "He is a strange mixture, a pitiless autocrat whose unlikely hobby it is to make rather exquisite pieces of furniture from wood. A man of some culture, he has composed operas and written poetry, yet he relies on his secret police to put down dissent. He believes in educating the masses and has set up schools and universities…"

"For women too?"

"Alas not, Mrs. Hudson. But let me finish. You need to know this. In latter years, fearing reprisals particularly from the Armenian community who are seeking their independence, he has become increasingly reclusive, retreating from his palace on the shores of the Bosphorus, inland to the fortress of Yildiz, and seldom goes out, nor permits his entourage freely to do so. Nevertheless, you will find plenty to enjoy within the precincts. The palace is surrounded by lovely gardens, which doubtless you will be permitted to enjoy, as well as a theatre and opera house."

It was hardly reassuring. A prison, never mind how well-appointed, remains a prison.

Dinner that evening was a quick and quiet affair, despite the best efforts of the waiters in the lavish restaurant of the hotel to tempt us to linger, brandishing menus and wine lists. No doubt they laughed behind their white-gloved hands at the lack of *joie-de-vivre* of the *ros-bifs*, as I believe the French like disparagingly to call the English.

Mr. H, never one for his meals – eating to live rather than vice versa – and particularly when it was not what he was used to, merely played with his food. Dr. Watson, however, tucked in with more appetite. I had been tempted by the lobster, remembering other occasions in this city where I had partaken of that succulent crustacean. However, even though the Sultan of Turkey was paying the bill, I settled for a modest chicken chasseur, thinking it would prove more digestible, especially after the rich chestnut soup.

I was, in fact, feeling somewhat at a disadvantage, used to serving my gentlemen rather than sitting down with them to dine, especially in such grandiose surroundings, and conversation was stilted. However, I had to ask about Madeleine.

"The girl says she is to be my slave. That the Turks will expect me to have one."

"They will not be surprised," Mr. H replied. "The benefit to you, Mrs. Hudson, is that Madeleine is fluent in Turkish. Although people will speak French to you, there are sure to be occasions where they are not forthcoming. Madeleine will be able to tell you what they are saying..." He paused. "Need I add that they should not know that she understands them?"

"I see. She is to help me spy."

He wiped his mouth with his napkin. "Precisely, although I dislike the word. You see, Mrs. Hudson, because she is a young girl and a slave, they will not take her seriously. Tongues are more likely to wag in her company."

I slept badly that night. Perhaps, after all, the food had been too rich for me. Perhaps the heavy fabrics surrounding me on my bed proved too stifling. Perhaps the wind hurtling round the Place du Théâtre-Français reflected my disturbed thoughts. Perhaps after all I was filled with foreboding regarding the forthcoming mission.

Early the next morning, before the sun had even risen, if it were ever planning to do so on that gloomy day, a very light breakfast of hot chocolate, buttery croissants and brioches was brought to my room by the same page who had shown me there in the first place. Should I give him some more centimes? I did so. It seemed the correct thing to do, for he left me bowing deeply. Madeleine soon joined me, and shared the abundant fare.

"I am a lucky slave," she said, licking her lips.

I suspected I would get to like her a lot – I already did, in fact – and would be glad to have her as a companion.

Over the croissant crumbs, she told me more about herself, how her father had been a French diplomat who had spent some time in Constantinople before bringing his Turkish wife back to Paris with him. He had died young, soon after Madeleine was born, but Fatma, his wife, had got used to the freedoms of the French capital, and was not inclined to go back to the stifling atmosphere of her native country, despite the urgings of her family.

"She doesn't worry about you travelling there, then?" I asked.

"Madame Hudson," the girl looked at me with tears in her eyes, "Maman is dead also. I live with the nuns in the convent, and let me tell you, I am very glad to escape from them, kind enough though they are."

I wondered who had found her for me.

"Why, M. Holmes of course," she said. She knew no more than that.

"Well, Madeleine, I am happy to have you come with me. We will be friends, I think."

"Oh no, madame. I will be your slave, and you must speak to me sternly at all times."

"Not when we are alone, surely."

She took a big bite of a brioche and chewed it thoughtfully.

"Perhaps not," she conceded.

The train was not due to leave Paris until the evening, but if I thought that, despite what Dr. Watson had told me, there would be time to visit my old acquaintances, I was soon to be disabused of the notion. Moreover, if I thought my wardrobe good enough for the Turkish court, I was wrong again.

"The ladies of the harem will expect you, as a rich English lady, to be dressed in the heights of Paris fashion," Mr. H informed me. "You must look the part."

He had not come alone to my rooms. "Let me introduce Madame Celestine," he said. "She will attend to your needs."

He moved aside to admit the newcomer. Madame Celestine proved to be a very thin, very elegant, very elderly French woman, with something of a stoop, and a sharp little nose that poked out in front of her, reminding me, in her grey silk gown, of one of those herons standing at the edge of the lake in the Regent's Park. She looked me up and down, and remarked, not encouragingly, 'Ha! Well, we will do what we can."

Now I know that my figure is perhaps fuller than a Parisian would consider stylish. However, I am comfortable in it, and thus rather resented the attitude of this dresser.

Mr. H left us together – with relief, I think – and Madame ordered Madeleine to open my trunk, examining my wardrobe with frequent exclamation of "Tsk!" much to the girl's amusement. The woman even despised my cerise silk.

"This will not do," she said. "Come. You too, girl."

So, a very large part of that exhausting day was spent in the fashionable shops of the Grands Magasins du Louvre selecting outfits suitable for a lady of my supposed status, amid many more sighs on the part of Madame.

"Of course, these will have to be altered to fit properly," she remarked.

"But we are leaving tonight," I protested.

"Not a problem, madame. They will be ready. And at least," she continued, "you will be travelling to a country where they admire excess flesh on women."

She sniffed. As for me, I was far too amused to be offended.

Madeleine, too, had to be fixed up, since, slave or no, it seemed she could not be dressed shabbily. Even clothes which are normally not on view had to be acquired, shifts and all, from the skin out. I tried to protest.

"Who will be interested in my undergarments?" I asked.

"The ladies of the harem, presumably," replied Madeleine. "They won't ever have seen the like."

Thus, heaps of lacy linen and silk were added to the sum of purchases.

The establishments we visited being far too grand to display prices, I was relieved to discover that the Sultan was paying for all this as well as everything else. Thank goodness, for the bill must have been enormous.

I debated with myself whether to tip Madame Celestine when at long last she was satisfied that I had enough fashion for the trip, but her abrupt manner was not that of one expecting anything from such as me. It was with considerable relief that Madeleine and I were able take the lift back up to my rooms, having bade farewell and thanks to the woman, whose only response was yet another sniff.

"Well, I never," Madeleine said, throwing herself on to my bed. "Did you ever think!"

"No, I didn't," I said, "and please get up, for I need to lie down after all that."

Apparently, my existing wardrobe was to be held at the hotel until my return, while the new clothes, altered and packed in a new trunk, were to be sent directly to the station, to be put on the Constantinople train. I would not know myself, I thought, rather sorrowfully, for the selection had been all Madame Celestine's and none of mine. However, I had gained at least one concession. I was to be permitted to travel in my own comfortable dark blue woollen gown and jacket, for which I was most grateful. With that in mind, I dismissed my slave, laid myself down on that grand bed and slept most soundly until the time came to get ready to leave.

Chapter Three

If I had been overawed by the Grand Hôtel du Louvre, how much more was I at the sight of the train that was to take us to Constantinople. My experience of such travel hitherto was of mildly inconvenient seating in cramped carriages, even when one paid extra for first class. Now, having arrived at the Gare de L'Est, our little party was conducted to a gleaming vehicle that seemed to stretch on forever. We were early, with plenty of time to settle in before the Orient Express, as our conveyance was called, was due to depart.

A liveried attendant welcomed us on board our Pullman car and showed each of us to our private cabin. Mine proved to be a small but well-equipped compartment, panelled in amber-hued wood, and complete with a wash basin. I was even more astonished when the smiling young man, whose name, as he told me in French, was Jules, indicated that the seating would, come night-fall, be turned into a bed.

"I shall return then, madame, to prepare it for you. Meanwhile, of course, you can also visit the saloon cars, the ladies' withdrawing room and the restaurant. You see here on the door a plan of the train for your information. The Orient Express is designed for your pleasure and comfort. If you have any questions or requests, I am here for you."

He bowed, about to take his leave. Once more, recalling Dr. Watson's instructions, I attempted to press some coins on him.

"Many thanks, madame, but no. I will leave the train at Vienna. You can reward me then, if you wish to."

If I had made a *faux pas*, he was discreet enough not to make me feel it. I sat down, more bemused than ever.

There soon came a light tap on the door. It was Madeleine. She entered, looking round herself with as much amazement as I had done.

"How beautiful it is," she said, turning the tap on the wash basin and watching steaming water gush out. "Oh, Madame Hudson," she added quickly, "I should have asked permission…"

She gave me a saucy smile, turning the tap off.

"And where are you staying?" I asked.

"In the carriage with the poor people, of course."

"But where will you sleep, my dear?"

"Sitting in my seat, I suppose."

"For three nights! Oh no, that will not do." Who knew what unpleasantness she might be subjected to, a mere child. I looked about myself. "Perhaps," I said doubtfully, "there is room here."

"No, no. Impossible, even if I sleep on the floor."

"I shall talk to the attendant about it."

I rang the bell to summon Jules. But when I asked about a cabin for Madeleine, he looked sorrowful, shrugging his shoulders, simultaneously opening his hands in the French manner.

"There is no place," he said. "And anyway," looking the girl up and down with something of a sneer, "she is your maid, no?"

"Maid or not," I replied forcefully, suddenly annoyed at his snobbery, "I need her near me."

Once again, I reached for my reticule.

He sighed. "Let me see, madame. I will think on it."

After he left, Madeleine busied herself unpacking the necessities for the journey I had placed in a carpet-bag. I should rather have done it myself, but I could tell the girl wanted to justify her position as slave, or, at least, maid.

Another tap on the door. This time it was Dr. Watson and Mr. H, checking how I was settling in and suggesting a move to the saloon car. I stepped out into the corridor, since the little space could hardly accommodate us all.

"I should rather prefer to wait and see if Jules can find a cabin for Madeleine," I said, explaining what I had done.

Mr. H frowned. "It might have been better to leave things as they were," he said.

"Why? I do not want a young girl like that crowded in with possibly unsavoury types. She is my responsibility now."

"Yes, but you see if there are spies on the train, as well there might be, it will seem very strange that you favour your 'slave' so much."

I was most taken aback at the mention of spies, and suspected, not for the first time, that our expedition was rather more perilous than Mr. H had previously indicated. However, that was beside the present point.

"If Clara or Phoebe were travelling with me, I should do as much for them," I replied. 'Let the spies think what they like, that it is an old woman's English eccentricity."

If I were expecting one or other of them to dispute the "old" description, I was to be disappointed.

Mr. H merely looked at Dr. Watson, who shook his head.

"I fear our Mrs. Hudson will not be moved," he remarked.

"Maybe she will when she hears how much a berth costs," Mr. H said drily. "I doubt the Sultan will consider his money well spent on a servant."

At that moment, however, Jules returned, all smiles.

"In another carriage, I have found a berth which is empty as far as Budapest," he said. "Not quite like this but private. After Budapest, perhaps there will be another, madame. You will have to ask the new steward."

I smiled back and thanked him. Given Mr. H's last remarks, I decided not to ask the price. Let them give me a bill later, if they so wished.

Calling to Madeleine, I told her the good news.

"Oh, madame," she said. "You are so good to your poor slave."

We all laughed a little uneasily.

"Come," Jules told her. "I will show you."

He led her off, while the rest of us made our way to the saloon car to await our departure.

To say it was luxurious hardly did the saloon credit. I could hardly believe I was on a train. There was even a baby grand piano at one end of the compartment, while our final destination was foreshadowed in the soft oriental carpeting, and lamp stands of an exotic design. Carved mahogany panels lined the walls; deep, leather-covered armchairs were bolstered with golden velvet cushions. More golden velvet was evident in the draperies at windows that looked out over the platform of the Gare de l'Est, where latecomers were even now rushing to board.

Many of the seats in the saloon were already taken, but we managed to find three together. A waiter sprang at us almost immediately with a tray of glasses filled with a greenish liquid.

"Mint tisane," he told us. "Although of course you can have whatever you desire, madame, messieurs."

Somewhat dubiously, Dr. Watson and I settled for the tisane, which happily proved most palatable, refreshing and sweet. Mr. H requested a coffee, "For you know," as he told us, "the French don't know how to make a proper cup of tea."

In due course, whistles were blown, flags were waved and slowly, slowly the leviathan that carried us, moved out of the station, to the accompaniment of a soulful melody on the piano, played by a poetic looking young man.

Goodbye, Paris. Hello, adventure.

Chapter Four

The outskirts of Paris, in a twilight rain that was now pouring down, provided as dismal a prospect as that of any other big city, and I was happy to turn my back to it. But how to fill the eighty long hours that the journey would take? I had brought with me a supply of novels, including, *Jude the Obscure*, the latest by Mr. Thomas Hardy, whose earlier work, *Tess of the D'Urbervilles*, I had very much enjoyed, despite it being so sad. Dr. Watson had most kindly presented me with the letters of Lady Mary Wortley Montagu, who, as wife to the then-British ambassador to the Ottoman Empire, had made it her business to attend the Imperial harem. Of course, her visit predated mine by almost two whole centuries, but, as Dr. Watson remarked, things were not likely to have changed that much, and I thanked him most sincerely. Indeed, her letters were to prove an entertaining and informative distraction.

To brush up my French, I had also with me a charming little volume titled *Lettres de mon Moulin*, by M. Alfonse Daudet, which I had read some time before, but which would repay another look. As well as reading matter, for, after all, one cannot spend all one's time with one's nose in a book, I had brought with me plenty of wool to knit outfits for my latest grandchild, my daughter Eleanor's Henry. Enforced idleness goes against the grain with me, and I hoped that I should not feel too confined.

Just then, apart from the pianist, who continued to treat us to the melancholy airs that Mr. H informed me were works by M. Chopin, a measure of entertainment was provided, unknowingly, by some of the other people I observed around me, the newly-wed couple with their foolish smiles, the grim older couple who spoke not a word to each other (would this be the fate of that young couple in years to come? I hoped not), the fashionable very young woman and her gentleman companion of an age to be her father although I do not think that he was, the solitary men buried in their newspapers. I studied these latter closely to see if they might be the spies mentioned by Mr. H. None of them appeared very sinister, although, in order to conceal their intentions, I supposed they would not.

Since luncheon at the Grands Magasins had been a hurried affair, Madame Celestine not having wished to waste good shopping time upon such irrelevancies as food – eyeing my *croque monsieur* with disapproval while she had partaken solely of a cup of black coffee – I soon found I was getting hungry, and thus was pleased when, after about an hour of travel, an attendant entered the saloon to announce that dinner was being served in the restaurant car. It seemed everyone else was waiting for this news, too, because there was a general flurry of movement towards the door. Mr. H, however, remained seated.

"I do not think we need to go just yet, do we? The second sitting will do for us. It will be quieter."

He returned to the Turkish grammar he had been studying.

I sighed.

"I think Mrs. Hudson would like to eat now," Dr. Watson said.

Mr. H reluctantly raised his eyes.

"Is that so, Mrs. Hudson?" he asked.

"Well," I replied, "I should perhaps prefer not to wait too much longer."

"Hmm."

"Actually, I am of the same mind, Holmes," Dr. Watson added, nodding to me. "I am already missing the tremendous spreads that you provide for us, Mrs. Hudson."

"Then let the two of you go off and dine," Mr. H allowed. "I shall wait for later."

"Don't forget," Dr. Watson told him. "I know what you are like when absorbed in something or other."

Mr. H, without raising his eyes from his grammar, waved a dismissive hand at us, and we duly made our way to the restaurant car.

Fond as I am of both my lodgers, it is with the good doctor that I feel the more at ease. Mr. H, with his brilliant mind, wayward habits, and his frequently aloof manner, can be quite off-putting. As for indulging in small talk, it is quite alien to him, while the doctor is happy to chat with me on trivial subjects.

"I wonder," I said, as we sat down at our table, decked with spotless linen and silver cutlery, "how young Madeleine will eat."

"You must not think of inviting her to join us here, Mrs. Hudson," the doctor said. "That would be going too far. She has been provided with a basket of provisions that will serve her until we reach Vienna, where there will be time to leave the train and purchase more supplies."

"You have done this journey before, then?"

"Yes, indeed. When Holmes first went to meet the Sultan, I accompanied him. Now," he picked up the menu, "what will you have?"

Once again, I was astounded at the sheer lavishness of the arrangements. An elaborate four-course menu was on offer from soup, through fish and meat to dessert.

"Do they prepare this on the train?" I asked Dr Watson.

"I hadn't thought about it," he replied. "But I suppose they must."

"They must have an enormous kitchen."

I should have loved to visit it, but I suppose, in my role as a rich widow, such activity would be inappropriate.

We feasted lavishly, the doctor, waggishly, proposing a toast in an excellent wine to the Sultan of Turkey who was paying for it. I refused the doctor's offer of a post-prandial liqueur with my coffee, and excused myself, pleading weariness. It had been a long and exhausting day, and I was ready to sleep.

I took myself back to my cabin, passing Mr. H on the way, still engrossed in his grammar. Knowing him, he would be fluent by the time we reached Constantinople. As for myself, I hardly thought it worth trying to master, in just a few days, a language so alien to me. In any case, my complete lack of Turkish would be part of my disguise.

Back in the sanctuary of my cabin, I found that, in my absence, Jules had prepared my bed, silk sheets, woollen blankets, and all. He had pulled down the blinds and left a small jug of water, a drinking glass and a packet of biscuits on a shelf over the foot of the bed. I locked my door with a sigh of satisfaction, and prepared for sleep, which overcame me swiftly, rocked as I was by the gentle motion of the train.

I awoke with a jolt and the sounds of voices and for a moment was quite confused as to where I was. The train had stopped. I peered out through the blinds and found we were at a station, with people getting off and on. Strasbourg. How fast we were moving across the continent! From my schooldays geography, I reckoned we would soon be in Germany. Dr. Watson had assured me that I should not be disturbed in the middle of the night when borders were crossed, that Jules dealt with all the formalities, so I turned over and went back to sleep again.

As morning broke through the blinds on my window, I was roused by a light tapping on the door. It was Madeleine. I let her in.

"Did you sleep well, madame?" she asked politely.

"I did indeed. Did you?"

She smiled. "Not at all. Katy and I chatted all night."

"Katy?"

"The girl in the other bunk."

"Oh, you are in a shared compartment, then."

"Yes. Katy is such a baby. I had to take the top bunk because she was afraid that she might fall off."

"Now, Madeleine," I said severely, "I hope you haven't been telling Katy about our expedition. Mr. Holmes is very firm that we must not discuss it with anyone."

"Oh, no, madame. I told her I am maid to a nice English woman going on her holidays to Turkey."

"Good."

"You *are* nice, madame. That part was true."

"Thank you, Madeleine."

She then informed me that Jules, the steward, wanted to know if I wished to take breakfast in my cabin. However, since Dr. Watson had intimated the night before that we should breakfast together, I declined the offer, rather tempting and self-indulgent though it was.

"But what about your own breakfast, Madeleine?" I asked.

"Oh, I have lots to eat, thank you, madame," she replied. "For now."

Having ascertained that I needed no assistance in getting dressed, she was off, back to her new friend.

Eating, as I soon discovered, was a big part of the experience of the Orient Express. The chefs clearly prided themselves on their elaborate and extensive menus, and if you were not fully satisfied at breakfast, luncheon or dinner, you could order extras from the stewards, to be brought to your cabin or delivered to the saloons. For my part, if I am not active, I do not care to consume too much, for it lies unpleasantly heavy on my stomach. Mr. H, as I have remarked, has no great interest in what he is eating. The good doctor, however, made up for our shortcomings on this occasion with a hearty and appreciative appetite.

"I am delighted," Dr. Watson remarked, wiping his mouth with his napkin, after consuming a heaped plate of ham and eggs, "that the caterers on this train haven't succumbed to the French notion of a good breakfast."

As for me, I rather liked the morning habit of fresh croissants and hot chocolate, having acquired a taste for it while in Paris, and so was delighted that this was on offer, too.

Mr. H, after consuming several cups of strong coffee, a small piece of toast and a boiled egg, expressed the intention of returning to his cabin and continuing his Turkish studies, while Dr. Watson indicated that he was planning to go to the smokers' compartment to peruse the latest copy of *The Lancet*, the medical journal to which he subscribes. Clearly, neither of them wished for my company, which suited me well enough, too.

Returning to my cabin, I consulted the plan to see where the ladies' withdrawing room was situated. It proved to be in the opposite direction from the saloon and restaurant car, towards the rear of the train, and I duly made my way thither, armed with a book and knitting.

Several ladies were already established there – chatting, or playing cards, or leafing through magazines – in a saloon no less sumptuous than anywhere else, although the décor here favoured pastel shades of pink and pale blue, presumably thought to be more suitable for the gentler sex. Nodding politely to the other ladies who had all turned to look at me on my entrance – some of them returning my greeting, while others merely stared back blankly – I found myself a comfortable chair and took out my knitting, a jacket for baby Henry in white wool.

"What a good idea!" This from a lady who must have just entered, positioning herself in front of me. "Why didn't I think of bringing some knitting?" She paused, and then chuckled. "And why did I assume that you must be English?"

I nodded. "Well, you are correct in that."

"Of course, I am." Lowering her voice to a stage whisper, she added, "These foreign women wouldn't bother with any occupation so useful. May I?" She indicated the seat next to me and, without waiting for me to express agreement, plopped herself down.

The newcomer was a stout, florid person of about my age or a little older, into her fifties. Her pepper and salt hair emerged in crinkly curls from under her cap, and her dress was plain and serviceable.

"Eliza Dodds," she said.

"Martha Hudson."

"Very pleased to meet you, Martha."

So we were to be on first name terms immediately.

"Likewise," I replied

"Well, this is very comfortable, I must say." She stretched her short legs out in front of her and looked around.

"It is most delightful," I replied.

"So different from the trains in England, dirty, smelly things. Have you travelled this way before, Martha?"

"No. It is the first time for me. How about you?"

My companion chuckled. "Goodness no. I have hardly ever been out of Norwood…"

She fixed her eyes upon me.

"I can see," she said, "you are just dying to know what brings a woman like me on the Orient Express, travelling to Turkey."

"Well…" Truth to tell, my curiosity was not that great. However, she enlightened me anyway.

"I am on my way to be governess to a little boy in Constantinople."

"It's quite a change for you then."

"A change is as good as a rest, as they say. What about yourself, Martha? What are you up to?"

I paused to pick up a stitch.

"Me? Oh… I am just a tourist," I said.

"A lady of leisure. Lucky you." She paused, then added, "Surely you are not travelling by yourself? These are dangerous countries, we're passing through. Full of bandits, you know."

"Mm…" I did not feel inclined to expand, and instead busied myself with my knitting.

"No, that's right," she went on. "Didn't I see you in the restaurant car with your husband, a tall, good-looking man. Actually, were you not with two men? Husband and brother, perhaps?"

Despite her nosy impertinence, I had to smile. Dr. Watson or Mr. H as my husband! It was not impossible, of course, since they were both only a few years younger than myself. But the very idea!

"Neither is my husband," I explained. "They are just friends." Then, when she raised her eyebrows, added, "I am a widow, and they are old friends of the family."

"Ah." She digested the news thoughtfully, perhaps wondering what else she could find out.

"And you?" I felt she expected me to ask. "Are you venturing across Europe alone, Eliza? Despite the bandits?"

Now that she had reminded me, I had a vague notion of seeing her in the restaurant car as well, in the company of another woman.

"My sister is with me," she replied. "You are right. Like yourself, I should not feel comfortable travelling on my own. Just now, Cecelia is taking a rest, but she might join us later."

I was not sure that I wanted permanently to be stuck in a threesome with the sisters, but only remarked, "Cecelia, that's a pretty name."

"A pretty name for a pretty young girl," she replied.

At that moment another woman entered the withdrawing room, one who could not be more different from my present companion, a vision in silks and furs, of indeterminate age, thin as a needle, pale-skinned and black-haired, her face exquisitely painted on. She reminded me of one of those Japanese women you see in those popular woodcut prints. A chubby, sulky-looking girl scurried after her.

"Oh, thank God!" the vision exclaimed loudly in French, causing everyone to look up, and an old dowager who had been dozing, almost to jump out of her skin. "No men at last."

She threw herself into the seat next to Eliza Dodds. "Ha! I have been up and down this damnation train for hours hunting for this sanctuary."

A surely unnecessary ordeal. She only had to check the plans that were displayed everywhere, or ask a steward for directions.

"Sit down, Yekatarina, do," she ordered.

The girl, who had been hovering nearby, staring at her feet, sat down at a distance with a thump, and, with her back to us all, pressed her nose against the window. She was a decidedly plain child of about twelve.

The newcomer opened her reticule and took out a cigarette case and a long ivory holder.

"I am not sure," Eliza Dodds said reprovingly in English, "that people are permitted to smoke in here. There is a special compartment reserved for smokers."

"Full of men!" the other replied, also in English. "I hate men, don't you! Although," she added, fitting a pink cigarette into the holder, "they are useful when it comes to matches… Has anyone got a light?" She called out, looking around hopefully.

No one replied.

She repeated the request in French. Again, no response.

"Damnation! Ah well." She regarded us properly for the first time, the cigarette holder still hanging between her lips, despite its

28

present lack of purpose. "I am Valentina Muratova," she announced, and then paused, as if we should know who she was.

"Martha Hudson," I said. "I thought I detected a distinctive accent, madame. You are Russian, I suppose." It was hardly difficult to guess her nationality, the name being rather a big clue. And yet the newcomer looked astounded at my perspicacity.

"Yes, yes, I see you are a true detective," she replied, somewhat to my discomfiture. I am sure she meant nothing by it, but I caught Eliza Dodds looking at me closely. "Assuredly I am Russian." She threw her arms wide in an expansive gesture. "Full of Russian soul… Have you read Dostoevsky? Remorse, repentance…" We shook our heads, disconcerted by the mysterious question. "But sadly I am chained to a French clod, without a sensitive bone in his body. Marriage! What an institution! Nothing but the enslavement of woman… Ha! But only for now, mesdames, only for now…" She inhaled as if her cigarette were indeed alight. Then gave a gesture of frustration.

"And might I suppose that is your daughter, madame?" I indicated the child at the window.

"Yes, indeed. That little frump over there is Yekaterina, who unfortunately takes after my husband, in both looks and manners."

The poor girl pressed her nose even harder against the glass pane.

"Now, madame detective. What else do you have to say about me? Go on. Tell me, please."

She had asked, so I obliged, studying her. "You are dressed expensively, flamboyantly, presumably to call attention to yourself, and I am sure you love the attention of men, however much you deny it." I smiled to take away the barb in the words. "You are used to people knowing who you are, so I suppose you must be famous, an actress or an opera singer, perhaps… I suspect the former since operatic divas tend to be built on a more substantial scale than you are. Perhaps you are travelling to Constantinople to take part in a play for the Sultan, since I have heard that he loves the theatre to the extent of having one specially built for his own entertainment." I considered further. "You say you have left your husband in France, but quite obviously have been prevailed on, against your will and hers, to bring your daughter with you, which suggests to me that the break from your husband is already permanent..."

"Good heavens! What did you say your name is? You are a regular Sherlock Holmes."

Oh dear. I had got quite carried away, and now tried to laugh it off. "I hardly think so. I am sure Mrs. Dodds here would have done just as well with the evidence before her."

"Miss Dodds," the other said, tight-lipped. "And no, I am afraid I would not have had any such insights."

"Yes, indeed," La Muratova continued, ignoring her, and waving a thin, black-gloved arm in the air. "I am going to play Medea for the Sultan, a dear man who has heard of me even if you ladies haven't."

"You are Valentina Muratova!" Another woman had come over to join the conversation, a French woman, as I guessed, for she spoke in that tongue, though perhaps I had done enough guessing for now. "Oh my God! I saw you in Paris as la Dame aux Camellias. How I wept when you died!"

This was much more to La Muratova's taste, She curled back in her chair like a cat after lapping the cream.

"Yes," she said. "That was one of my triumphs. One of many." She gave Eliza Dodds and me icy stares.

The newcomer, a woman in her fifties, well-dressed and *soignée*, as the French say, now produced a box of matches from her reticule. "Allow me," she said.

La Muratova inhaled deeply, greedily. "Thank you... You have saved my life, madame."

"Hortense Devaux. Oh, when I tell my friends that I have met you at last..."

"How charming, quite charming…" the actress was all gracious smiles. "You know, Hortense, I have some photographs of myself in my cabin. I will sign one for you… Yekaterina, go and get them, will you."

The girl jumped.

"Get what?" she said.

"Oh my God. What are we talking about? The photographs from my cabin, of course."

The girl pouted and did not move.

"No hurry," the Frenchwoman said quickly. "We will surely meet up again on this long journey."

"Yes, indeed, we will… You are an angel, Hortense, so understanding. Did you hear that, Yekaterina? You can keep on staring out of the window since it fascinates you so much."

The actress sat back, and sucked some more on her cigarette holder, whereupon Miss Eliza Dodds, coughing and ostentatiously waving her hand in front of her face against the perfumed smoke, got up and excused herself from the company.

La Muratova watched her go.

"You are not accompanying your friend?" she asked me.

I shook my head. "I know her no better than you do. We have only just met here in this saloon."

"I am very glad to hear it. I do not like her."

She sat back in her chair and closed her eyes, still inhaling deeply, oblivious to the unfriendly looks of some of the other ladies. Hortense Devaux, however, remained beside her, staring adoringly, hopefully, at her idol. Then finally, realising that La Muratova was not about to grace us with more conversation, she got up quietly to return to her seat, leaving the box of matches behind.

I continued knitting peacefully, and soon became aware of light snores emitting from my new companion. Looking up, I noticed that the cigarette holder with its glowing stub had fallen on to the diva's gown, along with a trail of ash. Fearing combustion might ensue, I picked up the holder and moved it to safety. The slight gesture must have roused the lady, for she leapt up.

"Is it the cocktail hour yet?" she asked of no one in particular. Then, without waiting for a reply – which indeed would surely be in the negative since it was barely noon – she swept out, grabbing the cigarette holder but leaving the matches where they were, Yekaterina trundling after her.

Chapter Five

Over luncheon – another splendid meal – Dr. Watson politely asked what I had been up to all morning, trusting I had not been too bored. I started to tell him about my encounters with the ladies of the withdrawing room, and even pointed out Eliza Dodds, who was sitting not far off from us with her sister. I described her searching and somewhat impertinent questions – omitting, however, to add that she had taken Mr. H or Dr. Watson to be my husband – when the latter gentleman interrupted me with an exclamation, "Aha! So you have found out our spy already, Mrs. Hudson."

I laughed at the thought of the governess from Norwood engaged in such a sinister occupation, but Mr. H frowned.

"Please remember that no one, Mrs. Hudson, is to be trusted or taken at face value. No confidences are to be exchanged with strangers on this trip. We are travelling incognito and our true identities are not to be bandied about…" He looked at me severely, as if he suspected me capable of such bandying, adding, "and I hope you have impressed this upon Madeleine as well."

I assured him that I had, but resolved to remind the girl again, in case she had forgotten.

Meanwhile, Mr. H had been studying Eliza Dodds and her companion.

"You say the woman claims to be travelling with her sister. That is already a patent lie," he remarked. "The two are quite unalike, and the supposed sister is hardly older than a child."

I looked across at the pair again. This time, Cecelia was facing us, and she appeared, in truth, very young, though hardly a child.

"A half-sister," I ventured.

Mr. H glanced at Dr. Watson. "Hmm. Well, maybe, although I rather suspect the supposed family relationship is a cloak for an altogether different one."

Now I am not so unworldly as not to know to what he was hinting, being well aware of the Sapphic tendency among certain women. It had not occurred to me in relation to Eliza Dodds, however, and now I tried not to stare too much in the direction of the two ladies. Nevertheless, I noticed they communed little with each other, the younger one seeming only to reply to remarks by the elder, and not to initiate any conversation. She was a pale, frail little thing, with purple smudges under her eyes and fine hair that seemed almost white. If Eliza Dodds were traveling to Constantinople to look after a small boy, why ever was she taking this fragile flower with her?

Conversation soon turned to other matters of no particular moment, and then, luncheon over, the gentlemen elected to go to the smoking compartment, while I, not at all fond of a smoky atmosphere, particularly when Mr. H's pipe tobacco was involved, decided to spend some quiet time in my compartment. There I soon cast aside both book and knitting and gazed at the landscape which seemed to flash past my window, a trick of the eye because of course it was I who was moving, speeding through the German countryside towards Vienna, which, as I understood it, we would reach in the late afternoon.

The landscape presented itself as a pleasing spectacle of meadows, woods and distant mountains, the latter capped in snow. The river Danube came into view from time to time, not blue as in the famous waltz, but a streak of steely grey, reflecting the heavy clouds. There was little sign of human habitation: merely the occasional small farm or distant village with a church spire or onion dome, the only living creatures being cows huddling together against the cold.

I closed my eyes. After the lack of activity, I could hardly plead fatigue, but nevertheless was overcome by that drowsiness that afflicts travellers on long journeys, and was only roused by a tapping at the door. It was Madeleine.

"Yes, my dear?" I asked.

"I am sorry to disturb you, madame, but it's snowing." Her voice was full of wonder.

She pointed at the window. Indeed, the landscape, so lately a picturesque enough rural scene, was now transformed. How could that be? I was sure I had only closed my eyes for a moment. Now fluffy flakes of snow were dancing down, light was fading into evening, and grass, bushes and trees were wrapped in a lacy shawl.

"It's like magic," Madeleine said.

Truly it was, and my little maid and I regarded the scene with pleasure. How different it would be in London, I thought, where snow soon turns to a foul sooty mess.

We were travelling very slowly, and I hoped that this precipitation, however delightful, was not delaying us. However, it seemed, from the increasing multiplication of buildings, that we were approaching a city. It must be Vienna. I said as much to Madeleine.

"Yes, there was an announcement about it. We will stop there for half an hour."

"That's good. We can go out and buy some food for you there, then," I said. "You have probably finished what you had with you."

"Yes, it's all gone. I gave some to the girl sharing my compartment. She was starving. But," she added, "no need for you to go out in the cold, madame. If you give me the money, I can purchase the necessary."

I assumed what she really meant was that she would like to choose for herself what to eat. Whether it would be the most nourishing fare, I much doubted. but agreed anyway, and reached for my reticule to take out my purse. Then I was struck by a sudden thought.

"But I have only French francs and English money. I wonder will they take that."

"I will ask the steward."

Never mind about staying warm, I thought. I too should like to stretch my legs outside. Then at least I could tell Clara and Phoebe that I had visited Vienna, though I suspected that particular fact would mean little to them.

Meanwhile Madeleine had dashed off and soon returned. The steward assured her the vendors at Vienna would take any money offered.

"He told me to be careful not to be cheated," she said. "Well, madame, I'd like to see them try."

I had no idea how much things would cost here in Austria, so gave her a good handful of French francs, reserving a quantity to present to Jules, who, as I remembered, was to leave the train here.

I donned my warm coat and hat, put on my boots, and buttoned them up, ready to face the wintry elements. Then I went in search of the steward and found him going along the corridor, informing the passengers of the imminent stop, reminding them that a new steward would be taking over, and presumably hoping to receive a gratuity as a result.

I pressed the francs into his hand. "You have been very kind," I said.

"Thank you, madame." Jules bowed. "Perhaps I will have the pleasure of serving you on the way back."

I nodded. Whenever that might be, for I had no notion how long this investigation was supposed to take, and rather hoped it would speedily be done with.

By now we were pulling into the Vienna Hauptbarnhof. As I alighted, rather to my astonishment, our arrival was greeted by loud music emitting from a brass band lined up on the platform. If the passengers were dozing, this would surely abruptly pull them from their slumbers. Still, the musicians, in their dark blue uniforms, belted in gold and with gold buttons and braid, plumed helmets atop all, made for a pleasing sight, even if their music was rather too military for my liking.

Despite the cold – and it was very sharp – the stop drew more people from the train, some I recognised. The young married couple, for instance, holding tight to one another and still smiling their foolish smiles, the solitary gentlemen pacing the platform, smoking (though neither Dr. Watson nor Mr. H were among them). Valentina Muratova was out too, clinging to her daughter's arm as she shuffled and scuffed her feet in the drifts of snow that covered part of the platform, despite the best efforts of porters with brooms to clear them away. Eliza Dodds, who seemed to have an ability to creep up on people, was emerging just behind me, cautiously descending the steps from the train, and then waiting to help her sister (I would take that relationship as given, until proved wrong).

"You're here, Martha," she said to me, somewhat unnecessarily. "I suppose, like us you just had to escape for a while. The air on that train is so oppressive, don't you agree?"

"You could always open your window," I said.

"Yes, but then it gets too cold. Cecelia is very prone to chills, aren't you, darling?"

Yet you have brought her out here in the biting air.

"We were thinking to get some Viennese coffee." She cast her eyes to where several booths were dealing with the customers from the train. "I have been told it is very good."

"That's an excellent idea," I said. "Let us see if we can find some."

Soon the three of us were each sipping that same beverage from a glass rather than a cup, the way they seem to do it in these eastern parts, the dark liquid visible at the bottom, the top white with whipped cream, the effect rather mirroring that of the snow upon the land. Eliza also bought herself a cake made of some sort of fried dough, sprinkled with fine sugar, we other two electing to wait for the doubtless substantial dinner being prepared for us on our train.

"This bun is all right," Eliza said, adding with distaste, "but goodness!" She held the glass away from herself. "Please don't ask me to drink that. It is far too strong." Nonetheless, she slurped up some of the cream, a little blob finding its way on to the tip of her long nose. "You don't have to drink it either, Cecelia," she said. "Just because we paid good money for it."

"But I quite like it, Liza." The girl's voice was squeaky, and she spoke in a rather irritatingly whiny tone. I could see, right up close, that she was older than I had first thought. Still quite young, late twenties, perhaps, but certainly not the child Mr. H had surmised her to be. Sometimes even he got things wrong, I thought, with a touch of satisfaction. All the same, he was correct in that there was nothing that spoke of sisters in their two faces.

Suddenly the girl stretched out an ungloved finger and removed the blob from Eliza's nose.

"What?" the latter asked.

"Cream, darling," Cecelia replied, licking her finger clean.

Perhaps noticing my astonishment, and in a hurry, perhaps, to change the subject, Eliza turned to me. "So what has happened to your maid?" she asked.

"My maid?" I answered, surprised, "I sent her off to buy something for herself."

"You gave her money? Ha!" She laughed unpleasantly. "Well, you won't see that any of that again, even if she doesn't disappear off altogether."

"Whatever do you mean by that, Eliza?"

"Oh, we've had plenty of experience with maids, haven't we, Cecelia. Let me tell you, Martha, you need to keep those hussies on a tight leash, or they are off with the first man they meet, taking whatever they can carry away with them."

"I am sorry to hear it," I replied evenly. "That has not been my experience at all."

Eliza opened her mouth to speak further, but Cecelia squeaked, "I'm freezing to death, darling. Can we go back in. Pleeese."

"Of course, my pet." All solicitude suddenly, Eliza conducted her sister back to the train. Sister? I could not help but have doubts. And how did Miss Dodds know I had a maid for I certainly hadn't mentioned it? Perhaps she was a spy after all. Appearances could certainly be deceptive.

Glad to see the back of them, I sipped at my coffee. It was indeed bitter, but the cream helped offset the effect, and I thought I might even get to prefer it to the stewed pot on the hob to which I was accustomed. I walked up and down for a while, and even kicked at the snow myself, a child again for a moment. It was crisp and made a satisfying crunch under my foot. But the air was certainly very cold, and most of the passengers were already getting back on the train. Despite Eliza's warnings, I had not been worrying unduly over Madeleine – she was hardly likely to run off with the first man she met, or even the second! As for the money, I had not given her so very much. However, she might be flibbertigibbet enough to miss the train, and so I cast my eyes around for her. Soon enough I spotted her walking back with various packages hanging from her arm, and two glasses of coffee in her hands. One for me, I supposed, pleased at her thoughtfulness, even though I was not sure I could drink another. But, in any case, I was wrong. Without noticing me standing at a distance, watching her, she went over to La Muratova's unappealing daughter, Yekaterina, now standing alone, and gave her one of the drinks. Yekaterina? Katy? That was interesting. But why ever would that particular child be starving? Surely her mother would provide for her. Perhaps it was a punishment for some misdeed, or perhaps, more likely, Valentina had just forgotten all about her daughter's needs. Or maybe the plump child was just greedy.

A bell rang to warn us to get back on to the train. I placed my empty glass on a ledge with others, and, still serenaded by the indefatigable musicians, who by now had to be quite frost-bitten, I reboarded the Orient Express. The girls, however, were still standing on the platform sipping their hot drinks, but, before I could call out, I saw a conductor going over to them.

Madeleine said something to him and he shrugged. Then the giggling girls brought their half-full glasses on to the train with them.

I accosted them. "So you are stealing glasses now," I said reprovingly.

"No, madame, just borrowing them." Madeleine was trying to keep a straight face, while Yekaterina snorted with mirth.

"Well, it's too late to take them back," I said, for the train was already moving, the band music muffled by the sound of the wheels. "But I am disappointed in you."

"Sorry, madame." She looked down, penitent, then lifted her eyes to mine. "But you see, we didn't have time to drink them. They are still too hot, even now. Feel them." She held hers out. I shook my head. "Please don't be cross. We'll give the glasses to the steward when we've finished. He can return them when the train goes back to Vienna."

She smiled. It clearly seemed to her a perfectly logical solution.

"When you have disposed of your packages, please come to my cabin," I said, still stern. "I'll wait there for you."

"I'll come now," she said. "Katy can take these."

She passed the packages to her friend.

Once back in the cabin, she rummaged in a pocket and brought out a handful of francs.

"Your change," she said, proudly. So much for Eliza's warnings. "They tried to cheat me," she added, "like Jules said, but I was having none of it, madame."

She picked up her coffee glass.

"You know, I don't even like it very much," she added, but drained it anyway. "Waste not, want not, as the nuns always say."

"All the same, Madeleine," I said. "I don't approve of what you did. It could be judged as theft."

"No, I told you..."

"I understand you didn't regard it as such, but, in these countries, you never know how strict they are likely to be about the rules. Imagine you were taken off to prison."

She stared at me, large-eyed.

"Please be more careful in future, my dear."

"I will, madame. I will."

"Now Madeleine, I just want to ask you something else. There is a woman on the train who knows you are my maid, even though I didn't mention it."

The girl looked thoughtful. Then her face lit up.

"A cross red ball of an old woman?" she asked.

"Well..." I could hardly condone the description.

"She came nosing along when I was knocking at your cabin door, when you weren't there. She asked what I was up to, even though it was none of her business, and looked at me like I was a thief or something." She bit her lip and glanced at her empty glass. "I told her I was your maid, but she didn't seem to believe me. So I told her she could ask you."

So that was that. A perfectly logical explanation.

"Never mind her," I replied. "As you rightly say, it was none of her business."

I dismissed the girl, after assuring her, that there was nothing for her to do for me just then.

"Yes, I had better get back before Katy scoffs the lot."

I had to ask it. "Does her mother not provide for her, then?"

"Her mother! Have you seen her? Imagine having a mother like that! I'd rather not have one at all."

She hadn't answered me, and yet she had. That poor girl, I thought. No wonder she was sullen.

After Madeleine had gone, I approached the new steward, an Austrian by the name of Otto. Speaking in English, since my German is worse than rudimentary, I gave him the glass, explaining that my maid had accidentally brought it away with her.

He took it, without comment and without a smile, and I rather felt that he suspected it was I who had appropriated the glass, and was now shifting the blame on to my maid. Oh dear. I had clearly got off on the wrong foot with him. But wasn't part of his function to be pleasant and accommodating to all the passengers, no matter how troublesome they were?

Back in my room, as the light dimmed further, I watched the landscape of Austria fly by, accompanied by sparks from the wheels. The snow-covered mountains looked nearer now, a looming, slightly threatening vista. Perhaps it was then, for the first time, that I felt that I was truly venturing into places unknown.

After a while, Dr. Watson knocked on my door and we made our way to dinner, where Mr. H was already in possession of a table and a newspaper, an out-of-date *The Times of London*.

"All I could get, apart from some Austrian rag," he said.

"Did you leave the train in Vienna, then?" I asked. "I did not see you."

"Not me. No, the new steward gave me this."

"Otto?" I asked. "He doesn't seem very friendly."

"I don't expect these people to be my friends," Mr. H remarked.

There was no answer to that, and we left Otto to his devices, concentrating on our dinner, which was as substantial as before. If it continued like this, I thought to myself, I should not be able to fit into the fashions selected for me by Madame Celestine, even though altered to accommodate my girth. With that in mind, I refused the dessert, a sponge soaked, as Dr. Watson informed me, in rum and topped with the whipped cream these Europeans seem to like so much. Instead, I simply partook of a couple of almond-flavoured petits fours with my coffee.

Thinking of the long evening ahead and rather tired of my own company, I agreed to Dr. Watson's invitation to go with them to the saloon, if only for a short while. Well, if eating were the main occupation on board the train, then it seemed that drinking came a close second. The cocktail hour mentioned by La Muratova, quite obviously lasted considerably longer than sixty minutes, all evening, by the look of it. The actress, indeed, was the first person I noticed as we entered. Despite her alleged distaste for the sex, she seemed to be revelling in the attention of a crowd of grinning males. She waved her glass across at me, her eyes lingering on my companions, both of whom, I could honestly say, were fine figures of men. Perhaps I rose in her estimation as a result.

"Another new friend?" asked Dr Watson.

"That woman is apparently famous," I said. "Valentina Muratova. She was quite put out that I hadn't heard of her."

"Of course, it's her." He regarded the actress more closely. "She's no Sarah Bernhardt, but she is quite good. I saw her at Drury Lane once. A little too histrionic for my taste."

We found places to sit ourselves down. It was hardly peaceful or relaxing. Apart from the buzz of conversation – and I have noticed before that people's voices get louder and louder the more they imbibe – the poetic-looking pianist, accompanied now by a violinist, was entertaining with lively tunes. Soon couples were dancing, a strange sight indeed on a moving train, and I wondered how the dancers kept their balance. Valentina Muratova was having the time of her life, flitting from partner to partner. The elderly man led his youthful lady friend in a somewhat too vigorous dance for someone of his age, she laughing wildly with or at him. The newly-wed couple were waltzing more sedately – did they never stop smiling at each other? An old dowager clung to a handsome young soldier, who was looking over her shoulder at La Muratova. It was all most entertaining.

Meanwhile, the Doctor and Mr. H were drinking cognac, while I myself partook of a small glass of port, to assist me in sleeping. We conversed little – indeed, it would have been difficult with all the noise and bustle.

"Excuse me, Mrs Hudson, Watson," Mr. H said eventually, putting down his empty glass, "I have had quite enough of this Tower of Babel, and am off to my cabin to conjugate a few more Turkish verbs in peace and quiet. You may wish to retire as well."

For my part, however, remaining highly diverted by the antics of the crowd, I was happy to stay for a while longer, as, it seemed, was Dr. Watson. Rather amusingly, the minute Mr. H stood up to leave, La Muratova, abandoning her current partner, stretched out a skinny arm in its long black glove, and beckoned to him.

"Don't leave yet, handsome sir. The party is only beginning." He gave her a startled look, as she continued, "Will you not afford me a dance?"

He shook his head and hurried out, whereupon she addressed herself to Dr. Watson.

"How about you, sir? You won't disappoint a lady, will you?"

Giving me a rueful look, the good doctor acceded to the lady's request, and they were soon whirling around the floor, La Muratova stumbling somewhat, suggesting to me that she had started the cocktail hour quite a lot earlier, and had maybe even missed the dinner that would have soaked up the drink, and put a little flesh on those bones. Indeed, she quite hung off Dr. Watson, who extricated himself as soon as the tune finished.

"Goodness me," he said, sitting down beside me, but offering no further elucidation as to the conversation that had taken place.

He prevailed upon me to have just one more small port, himself apparently in need of another cognac.

"Well," he said after the waiter had brought our order, "how are you enjoying the trip so far, Mrs. Hudson?"

"Enjoying is hardly the word, Doctor," I replied. "But it is all most interesting."

We continued to watch the dancers. The grim middle-aged couple had entered and were sitting near us, still not talking to each other, their faces blank. Perhaps they preferred to be in company, any company, rather than alone in the privacy of their cabin. Other people, who must have joined the train at Vienna, were chatting loudly in strange tongues, La Muratova moving among them with an almost hysterical gaiety. At one point, she came over to us again.

"Tell your son to fetch me a drink," she burbled.

Dr. Watson my son! And he only a few years younger! I was most offended, but he laughed.

"You have had quite enough, madame," he said, "if you think me youthful enough to be this young lady's son."

She laughed too, and fell upon him.

"Not your wife?" she said.

He shook his head, smiling, but added nothing more. "Well, damnation take you," she muttered and stumbled away.

"I think maybe it's time to leave," he said to me.

I quite agreed.

While I was preparing for bed, which Otto must have pulled down and made up for me, pristine new sheets and all, the train started to slow. Where were we now? It had to be Budapest! I could not resist but raised the blinds to look out. It was just like another other station, as far as I could see. Only the signs, written in German, or perhaps Hungarian, were clues to the fact that I was in the middle of Europe and not back home in London. The spirit of exploration having left me, I had no inclination to descend on to the platform, although I lowered my window in order to hear better the band that was welcoming us. In fact, they looked and sounded identical to those in Vienna, blue and gold uniforms and all, military tunes and all, and if I had not noticed for myself that we left that other band behind, I should have suspected these to be the very same gentlemen.

We stopped for some considerable time before setting off again. I must already have got used to the rocking of the train in motion, for it was only then that I was able to fall asleep.

Chapter Six

I jumped awake, out of deep dreams. A horrible cacophony was coming from the next cabin, high-pitched shouts, punctuated by low gurglings. Was someone being attacked? It sounded very much like it. I looked at my pocket watch. Two in the morning. The noise continued. I rose from my bed, wrapped myself in my robe and opened the door on to the corridor. I was not the only one. Various people were standing there, unsure what to do next, among them, Dr. Watson.

He strode up to me.

"Mrs. Hudson, are you all right?" he asked.

"Yes, but..." I waved at the adjoining cabin. "Something's wrong in there."

Dr. Watson knocked on the door, to no avail. The noise continued.

Now Otto had joined us, sleepy in the uniform jacket he had evidently donned in haste, and muttering under his breath. After knocking some more, he drew out a master key and unlocked the door. I was able to see in, and, if I had not been cross at being woken so summarily from my sleep, would have laughed aloud. Valentina Muratova, clad in a black silky negligee, was standing in front of a long mirror she must have brought with her, emitting the strange sounds we all were hearing.

"What is it?" she snapped.

"Madame," Otto replied, in French. "The noise."

"Noise! I am doing my vocal exercises, you fool." And she resumed.

"But madame, you must consider the rest of the passengers, who all wish to sleep."

"Sleep! Sleep! Ha! They can sleep as much as they want when they are dead."

Dr. Watson stepped forward.

"Madam Muratova," he said, in soothing tones. "Valentina… I know that, with your immense talents, you are far above us ordinary folk with our tedious regular habits. But take pity on us, please. Be as gracious as I know only you can be."

His words and more importantly, his good looks, worked like a charm.

"Ah, Monsieur Jean…" she said. "Yes, you are right. I can be gracious. I will do my exercises later."

"In the morning," Dr. Watson urged, smiling at her. "When everyone else is up and about."

"Only for you, handsome one," she said, and blew him a kiss.

Her door was shut. Otto shook his head as he made his way back down the corridor, while Dr. Watson squeezed my shoulder, as we all returned to our cabins. So he and La Muratova were already on first name terms. I doubted Mr. H would be too pleased about that.

I settled back into bed, but now was wide awake. I took a sip of water, ate a biscuit, and sat up reading a little more of Jude's sad history, disturbed somewhat by the banging and thumping noises coming from my Russian neighbour's cabin. Whatever was she doing now? It was long while before I managed to fall asleep again.

A rapping on my door finally roused me. I tried to clutch at the remnants of my dream, but they slipped away from me as dreams tend to do.

"Who is it?" I called.

"Your slave, madame."

"Come in."

I looked at my pocket watch. Just after eight in the morning. Whatever was the girl thinking of? Surely there was no hurry to do anything.

I must now confess to an unforgivable lapse of memory. With so little to think about during the journey, you would imagine that I had not forgotten about Madeleine. However, it was only when she sought me out now to complain that she had been ousted from her bed in the middle of the night, in order to make way for a new arrival, that I remembered I was supposed to arrange alternate sleeping accommodation for her with the new steward.

"What did you do?" I asked.

"What could I do? I climbed in with Katy. But she's fat and there wasn't much room."

"Oh dear. I shall talk to Otto immediately."

All at once, I noticed that we were stopped.

"What station is this?" I asked.

"Nowhere, madame... It seems we are stuck."

"Stuck? Whatever do you mean?"

A big smile lit up her face.

"It's more snow, madame."

She raised the blinds. A dazzling whiteness faced me, a great drift banked on the side of the line.

That was surely bad news. Madeleine, however, was thrilled.

"May I go out?" she asked. "Other people have."

"I don't see why not," I replied, "as long as you don't wander too far from the train."

"Thank you, madame."

"And dress up warmly. You'll be no use to me if you catch cold."

"Yes, yes, yes."

She dashed off, perhaps before I could change my mind.

I arose from my bed, clad myself in my robe and went out into the corridor in order to use the facilities at the end of the carriage.

There I found Otto and asked how long we were likely to be delayed.

"I cannot say, madam," he said. "Not too long, I hope."

Which was no answer at all.

I then asked if another berth could be found for Madeleine, explaining her predicament.

His response initially was similar to that of Jules.

"For your maid, madam?"

"I would not feel comfortable leaving a young girl like that prey to strangers."

Suddenly his rather sour face was wreathed in smiles.

"You are a good woman to care so for your maid," he said. "I will see what I can do." He was suddenly much more friendly and I wondered if he harboured socialistic views under that stiff uniform.

"Would madame like breakfast brought to her this morning?" he asked.

I thought for a moment. Why not? I was rather tired of the formality of the restaurant car.

"That would be lovely, Otto. Thank you."

He bowed and added, "I hope madam slept well after the disturbance in the night."

I smiled. "I was just glad it turned out to be a trivial matter. I almost feared someone was being murdered."

"Murdered on the Orient Express? Never, madam."

Once I was dressed, I raised my blind again and peered out at the snowy scene. Many of the passengers had ventured outside, among them Eliza Dodds, but this time without Cecelia. She stood looking about herself anxiously, as if searching for someone. Suddenly she glanced up at my window. Could she see me? I would surely be in shadow. However, I raised my hand in a greeting. She did not respond, so perhaps I was in error.

There too was Dr. Watson, pacing up and down, smoking. To my amusement, he was suddenly set upon by La Muratova, and,

50

following her exigencies, he reached into his breast pocket and drew out a silver case. She removed a cigarette from it and fitted it into her holder, while he struck a match to light it for her. Then, shivering ostentatiously, despite her silver fox fur coat, she put her arm through his and the two of them paraded up and down, the feathers on her hat waving in triumph. Anyone not knowing them might have taken them for a most handsome couple, married or not. How I would tease him about it later!

I could also see Madeleine, accompanied by her new friend Katy, who was keeping well away from her mother. As for me, I felt no inclination to go outside just then, especially since snow was still falling, albeit lightly. Instead, I sat back down with my knitting which was progressing apace. If I were not careful, I would have used up all my wool before even reaching Constantinople.

When the knock came on the door, I of course assumed it was Otto with my breakfast, and called out "Come in." However, it was not the steward, but Eliza Dodds and she was in a highly nervous state, breathing quickly, her face more flushed than ever.

"Thank God, you're here," she gasped.

"Whatever's the matter?" I patted the bed so that she should sit beside me. "Has something happened to Cecelia?"

"No… at least, not yet. Oh, Martha. Isn't it terrible?"

"What is?"

"Being stuck here, a prey to all sorts of bandits and ruffians."

"Goodness! I sincerely hope not."

"But it has happened before, you know." She was staring close into my face. "The train set upon, and just here in Serbia, too."

"Is that where we are?"

"Yes, and it is bandit country. I hope your gentlemen are at least armed. You are so lucky having them to protect you. As for Cecelia and me, we are two helpless women… Oh, Martha, what if they should carry Cecelia off and ravish her."

I burst out laughing.

"My goodness, Eliza, you are really letting your imagination run away with you."

She looked offended, but added, "It can happen. I have read about it. Look."

She pulled a book from her reticule and thrust it at me. *Faithful even unto Death* was the title, while the lurid cover illustration showed a young maiden in white beset by swarthy villains. I flipped it open and read a few lines.

"But this is a novel, Eliza," I said. "You shouldn't take it seriously."

"It may be a novel," she replied, "but I happen to know it is based on a true story, Martha. We women are in dire peril."

There was no arguing with her, so I told her I was sure, in that case, the railway authorities would have provided the staff with the means to defend themselves.

"I hope so, Martha. I pray so."

At that moment, Otto arrived opportunely with a laden tray, and of course Eliza had to ask him if he had a gun.

"A gun, madam?"

"In case we are attacked by bandits."

He looked from her to me, puzzled, and I rolled my eyes and shook my head just a little.

"Oh, yes, madam," he replied, biting his lip. "We are… what do you English say?… armed to our tooths."

Eliza sighed deeply. "'Thank God,'" she said.

"In any case, I have good news, ladies. The line ahead is clear and we shall be setting off again very shortly… So I am afraid the bandits will be disappointed this time."

Eliza jumped to her feet, nearly upsetting my tray.

"I must go and tell the good news to Cecelia."

She rushed off, forgetting to take *Faithful even unto Death* with her.

"She is very nervous," I told Otto. "It is her first time to travel abroad."

I myself was hardly a seasoned traveller, but, unlike Eliza Dodds, whatever situation I find myself in, I am not in the habit of getting into a state about the worst possible imagined outcome.

He gave an understanding smile, then added, "By the way, madam, I have found a new berth for the lady who arrived from Belgrade in the night. Your maid can stay where she is."

"Otto," I said. "You are wonderful. I will tell Madeleine the good news."

"I already informed her myself, when she got back on the train." For, thankfully, we were indeed on the move again. Otto bowed, and withdrew.

I settled down then to enjoy my breakfast and take in the scenery that had become spectacular. We seemed to be passing through some kind of a gorge, with great cliffs rising on either side of us. Next, we were plunged into darkness, as the train entered a tunnel, before emerging again on the other side of the mountain.

Apart from the changing landscape, the journey was much as it had been the day before and I found myself increasingly eager to have it over and done with. In the morning, I read and knitted in the ladies' carriage, without, I was not unhappy to find, the company of the Dodds sisters. Hortense Devaux was sitting across from me, but I was clearly not famous enough to attract her attention. Some of the ladies were playing whist, little cries emitting from them from time to time, presumably as one or the other scored a trick. In one corner, a woman I had never noticed before, a fleshy woman with the broad face of a peasant, despite her rich apparel, was laboriously laying out cards on the table in front of her. Patience: I could do with some of that quality.

La Muratova did not join us. I wondered was she sleeping off her late night, or was she already regaling our corridor with her vocal exercises.

I joined my gentlemen for luncheon, more for the company than because I was hungry, partaking only of a light soup and an omelette with mushrooms.

"I hope you will not waste away on us, Mrs Hudson," Dr. Watson remarked.

It was hardly likely.

"Sherlock Holmes! Or I'm a Dutchman!"

A loud voice boomed across the restaurant car, as a large, handsomely bearded blond man strode up to us. Everyone turned to look, which was most unfortunate, since Mr. H had hoped to maintain his incognito. However, what is done cannot be undone, and my eminent lodger rose to acknowledge the man, though not extending a hand to shake that of the other, held out to him.

"Baron Maupertuis! I did not know you were on this train. In fact, I was not aware that you were already out of prison."

The other laughed merrily, replying in perfect English, though with an accent I could not for the moment place. "Ha! And I thought you knew everything, my friend." He looked at me. "If the lady will allow," gesturing at the empty seat beside Mr. H.

I nodded, not knowing what else to do, and the Baron sat himself down. His personality was apparently as large as his physique. He put his great arms on the table and leaned forward, still speaking to me.

"And where, might I be so bold as to ask, are you going, lovely lady, with these two rascals?"

"Clearly," I replied, "I am going to Constantinople, since that is where the train is bound."

"Ha, ha, ha. I see you have taught your lady discretion, Holmes."

"Presumably you are going there yourself," I continued.

"Well now." He pressed a finger to a slightly bulbous nose. "I may be and I may not. There are a few more stops, you know, before Stamboul."

Mr. H sighed.

"Wherever you are going, Baron, I am sure you are up to no good," he said.

The other sat up as if deeply offended.

"That is where you are quite wrong, my friend. You see, prison has taught me the errors of my past ways, and I am now bent on a humanitarian mission, the nature of which must remain, for the time being, under wraps. A well-kept secret, don't you know."

He clicked his fingers at the waiter and ordered "the best you can give me," at the same time pressing a coin into the man's hand. Big gestures were clearly second-nature to him. I was of course dying to know what crime had led to his imprisonment, and how far Mr. H was involved. Just now, of course, I could not ask, and none of them was telling. Instead, the Baron again fixed me with pale grey eyes, and smiled.

"Now, I know the names of these two blackguards, and you have heard mine. But your name, madam, remains a mystery. Might you vouchsafe it to this poor old renegade."

"It's no mystery, Baron. I am Martha Hudson."

"Martha… Marta…" He waved podgy fingers in the air as if to set my name to a melody. "Ah…" Then to our astonishment, and that of the other diners, he indeed broke into song, the famous aria from the opera by Herr von Flotow, taking my hand without a by-your-leave, and gazing soulfully into my eyes. I tried to snatch my hand away, but he held it fast, his unpleasantly moist.

"If we have all finished our meal," Mr. H said, interrupting, and regarding the nearly empty plates in front of Dr. Watson and myself, "we can leave the Baron to enjoy his luncheon."

"Not at all," the latter cried. "I hunger not only for food but for good company, intelligent conversation… Where are you all going?" For Mr. H and the Doctor had stood to leave, and so I did likewise, relinquishing at last the man's damp hold.

"Delightful to see you again, Baron," Mr. H said coldly. "And more than delighted to learn that you have mended your wicked ways."

"I shall see you all again," the man replied with an enigmatic smile, enhanced with a gold-capped canine. "You cannot hope to escape me on this train."

As we made our exit from the restaurant car, Mr. H remarked, "I could not stay for another moment in the company of that person. We will take coffee in the saloon. I apologise, Mrs. Hudson, that you had to experience his misplaced gallantry."

"It was nothing," I said. "The Baron has rather a pleasing baritone."

"Even though the aria in question was written for a tenor."

Trust Mr. H to know that.

"Strange we haven't encountered him before," Dr. Watson said.

"Not strange at all, since he wasn't on the train. We would otherwise have seen him, for he is hardly a shrinking violet. No, he must have got on in Belgrade in the early hours."

By now, we had reached the saloon, and, taking our seats, ordered coffee. Only then I asked who was this man and how had he and Mr. H crossed paths.

"Oh, Lord," Mr. H said, stretching out. "Tell her, Watson. I am weary of the whole business."

Dr. Watson then proceeded to recount the case of the Netherland-Sumatra Company, a colossal scheme to defraud the unwitting public, as perpetrated by this same Baron Maupertuis.[3] Mr. H had exposed it, as a result of which the Baron had been arrested, tried and imprisoned.

"I am surprised that you do not recall it, Mrs. Hudson," he went on. "It was quite a few years ago, but the complications so

---

[3] One of the Untold cases. See *The Adventure of the Reigate Squire* in *Memoirs of Sherlock Holmes*, by Sir Arthur Conan Doyle

overwrought Holmes here, that he was quite ill for a long time afterwards."

Mr. H stirred himself. "Don't exaggerate, Watson. It was a mild indisposition. Nothing more."

"I remember now," I said. "You were very poorly, Mr. Holmes. The doctor and I were quite worried about you."

"Clucking hens, the two of you," he said. "I recovered, didn't I?"

"However," I went on, "as to what caused you to be ill, I don't think I was ever told."

"The case was all over the newspapers," Dr. Watson said. "Although Holmes's involvement was kept out of it for reasons of diplomacy."

"So the Baron *is* a Dutchman!" I exclaimed. "Now I recognise the accent."

"Actually, Flemish," Mr. H corrected me. "A small difference."

Dr. Watson frowned, clearly concerned. "The worry is that though he seemed friendly, he doubtless bears a grudge. All those years locked away, thanks to you! You should watch your back, Holmes."

Without opening his eyes, Mr. H replied, "The Baron is a nuisance, nothing more. A stinging fly." He swatted at an imaginary insect.

"Hmm. That's as maybe."

"I am sure he will be far more concerned with his own devilment, than in trying to thwart our undertakings, even should he discover what they are. By the way, Mrs. Hudson," and here he opened his eyes again and fixed me with a stare, "I trust I can rely on your discretion in that respect."

"Of course, Mr. Holmes," I replied.

"Because, as I understand it, the Baron has quite a winning way with the ladies. I should hope you can remain impervious to his charms."

I was much offended, and remarked rather frostily that he would have no reason to doubt me in that or any other regard.

"Good," he said, lying back again and adding, "though, you know, you might like to stay in the ladies' carriage for the remainder of the day, out of the Baron's reach."

"Mr. Holmes," I had to say it. "If you feel you cannot trust me, you should have found someone else for this mission."

Now the Doctor intervened.

"Of course, we trust you, Mrs. Hudson. Holmes simply wants to protect you from an unpleasant encounter, knowing as he does, the nature of the man."

"Very well," I said, standing up, "I shall go and take sanctuary with the ladies, but only for your peace of mind, gentlemen."

"Please don't take umbrage," Dr. Watson further urged. "In any case, I can't imagine that the Baron's path, whatever it is, is likely to cross with ours. Isn't that so, Holmes?"

The detective nodded agreement, but under the cover of his apparent nonchalance, I was sure his mind was working at full spate to consider how this new complication might affect our mission. As it turned out, he was perfectly right to be worried.

Chapter Seven

Would this journey ever end! I was restless, sitting in the ladies' carriage, with nothing better to do than idly watch the landscape of whatever country we happened to be in at that moment flashing by. I had abandoned *Jude the Obscure*, abandoned knitting, for I could not settle to either activity. I craved the distraction of conversation, but none of the other ladies present, known to me only by sight, showed any inclination to include me in their discourses, which, in any case, were in foreign tongues. No one suggested I join them in a hand of cards. The lady in the corner was still fully absorbed in her game of Patience and I wondered if it ever worked out without her cheating. I was so bored that I almost hoped Eliza Dodds would join me, or even Valentina Muratova, who could at least be relied on to be diverting.

We seemed at that moment to be travelling through an endless forest of oaks and beech, which cleared only very occasionally to reveal a peasant dwelling of extreme poverty or the spires of churches in some distant village. The skies, moreover, were heavy with clouds, and never a glimpse of the sun. Hadn't Mr. H promised me the blue skies of the Mediterranean? That vast sea could not be far distant now, and yet the weather was as dreary here as November would be in Baker Street. I wondered what my dear Clara and Phoebe were about at that moment, with neither myself nor my lodgers to attend to. Clara would certainly have found out some useful task – she was almost as skilled as I in making pickles and jams. Perhaps she would have set Phoebe some straightforward chore, to wash down the paintwork for instance – not letting the clumsy girl anywhere near my cherished but fragile ornaments, of course. I almost saw Phoebe in my mind's eye, all set to clean windows but instead peering out of them, imagining the moment a handsome prince would gallop up on his steed to carry her away from her life of drudgery…

"You're in a dream, madame!"

It was Madeleine, all smiles. I was more glad to see her than she could know.

"Just thinking of home," I replied, patting the seat beside me for her to sit down.

"Would you rather be back there, then, madame?"

Would I?

"No," I said finally. "I am looking forward to our adventure."

"So am I," she replied. "And I hope never to have to go home again. Not to that convent, anyway. Can you imagine, madame, they want all us girls to become nuns like them!"

I chuckled at the thought of the irrepressible Madeleine confined by vows of poverty, chastity and obedience. Her lovely red curls cropped to her skull.

"Do you want anything, madame?" she asked. "Anything I can do for you?"

"Actually, my dear, yes, there is."

I put her holding a skein of wool between her two hands, while I wound it up into a ball. When that was done, she asked me to teach her how to knit. I was happy to accommodate her, and that little occupation passed the time most pleasantly, Madeleine proving a quick learner. In her company, my mood lightened, especially now that a watery sun was peeping from behind clouds that were becoming ever whiter and fluffier. The scenery too seemed more picturesque. Now we were travelling alongside a river on whose banks stood quaint little wooden houses, painted in fading pastel colours. We passed, slowly enough, a woman in a wide brown skirt, holding the hand of a mop-haired child who waved at the train, a small dog beside them barking and jumping up and down in excitement.

"There's that horrid man again!" Madeleine exclaimed.

I looked away from the window, surprised to see the Baron, peering into our carriage. Did he not know it was reserved for ladies?

"You've met him?" I asked.

"Yes. He came to fetch Katy away from our cabin, saying her mother wanted her. If it was me, I wouldn't have gone with him."

"Why not?"

"I don't like him. He smiles too much and has wet hands."

"Goodness! How do you know that?"

"He patted my cheek."

The Baron was still standing there, taking in the scene. Then he caught my disapproving eye, tipped his hat, and flashed that gold canine in a smile. He even beckoned to me, but I shook my head, so finally he turned and went away.

"You see," Madeline said. "He smiles like a crocodile."

I doubted she had ever seen one of those sinister creatures, although maybe in the Paris Jardin des Plantes, which I seemed to remember featured such a stuffed creature. However, she was quite right. The Baron's smile was certainly reptilian.

"Yes, I have also met the Baron," I replied. "And, Madeleine, Mr. Holmes insists we are not to tell him any of our business."

"I wouldn't anyway. I wouldn't even tell him my name.... And look, madame, he's made me drop a stitch."

We continued with our knitting lesson. I wondered at the Baron beckoning to me. Or perhaps it was to someone else for the patient lady had got up and, collecting her cards together, went out. She almost collided at the door with a waiter coming in to take orders for coffee or tea or something stronger. I ordered coffee for

Madeleine and myself, since the tea they served on the train had no taste.

"How does it compare to the Viennese coffee?" I asked her.

"I hoped you had forgotten about that, madame." She grinned. "Better. Less bitter."

Eventually the long afternoon drew on into evening, and it was time to get ready to dine on the train for the last time. Madeleine went back to her compartment and I to mine, musing that the little maid seemed to have a good instinct where people were concerned.

The chefs had excelled themselves for this final feast, four elaborate courses, good French wine and even champagne. For once, I decided to indulge myself. Who knew what strange dishes I should be required to eat once in the Sultan's palace? So this night I partook of foie gras, lobster bisque, roasted beef and an orange souffle, sprinkled with chocolate.

"Cheese, Mrs. Hudson?" Dr. Watson offered. I could see he was highly amused at my renewed appetite, where Mr. H was perhaps a little shocked.

"Goodness," I replied. "I couldn't eat another thing."

"Not even this fine Camembert? Or this Roquefort. Mm," he said, "smells like Holmes's socks." He cut himself a sliver and I have to say I was tempted. Unlike poor Mr. Wilde, however, I can resist everything, even temptation.

"Well, Doctor," I remarked, "I see your fickle lady friend has abandoned you." I could not resist countering his teasing. He followed my gaze to where Valentina Muratova was sitting facing a gentleman whose bulky back was already become all too familiar. The Baron Maupertuis.

"He is welcome to her," Dr. Watson remarked.

Mr. H's eyes however had narrowed at the sight of the pair, locked together, as they were, in an intense conversation.

"Where is that woman's poor daughter?" I said. "Really, it is shocking how neglected she is. Her mother doesn't even make sure she gets fed."

"Really?" the doctor asked.

"Katy has been sharing Madeleine's food."

"Interesting," Mr. H said. "I wonder…"

But we were not to find out what he was wondering, for the train braked suddenly, violently, sending many of the lovely crystal glasses, the porcelain platters flying in all directions, some of them shattering on the floor. I was jerked right back in my seat, as was Dr. Watson. Mr. H, opposite us, was thrown forward, his ribs against the edge of the table. It must have been painful.

The train had ground to a stop. However, the nonchalant waiters, after an initial pause, resumed serving, while others swept up the shards of glass and plate. When asked what had happened, they just shrugged.

"Maybe some animal on the tracks," one said. "An ox, perhaps. A deer."

I spotted Eliza Dodds, at a table a few places in front of us, turning her head from side to side in alarm. No doubt, she imagined bandits taking over the train, robbing, pillaging and raping as they went. However, after few moments, the train resumed.

"Probably some idiot pulled the communication cord," Dr. Watson said, tucking in his napkin and taking another slice of cheese.

For his part, Mr. H was thoughtful. He turned in his seat to check something.

"The Baron left a while ago," I told him.

For the first time he looked at me with something like appreciation. Then he rose to his feet and left us also, without another word.

"Well!" said Dr. Watson. "I must apologise for Holmes's manners or, rather, his lack of them, Mrs. Hudson."

"Goodness, doctor," I replied. "Am I not used to his little ways by now? I presume he has gone to look for the Baron to find out if he was responsible for stopping the train."

"Where Holmes is concerned, I never presume," he replied. "But you may be right. Still, Valentina has left us as well. I imagine the two of them might be together in the saloon."

"Shall we go and see?"

If he was taken aback at my eagerness, he did not show it. "Why not?" he replied.

However, neither the Baron and La Muratova, nor yet Mr. H were to be found in the saloon. We then tried the smoking compartment, a place I had so far not had occasion to enter. Through the fog of smoke, it was soon evident that our quarries were not there, either.

"I'm foxed, Mrs. Hudson," Dr. Watson told me. "Where else could they be?"

"In their cabins, I suppose," I said. "Unless Mr. Holmes has donned one of his many disguises and is in the ladies' withdrawing room."

Dr. Watson guffawed. "Holmes might get away with it in a dim light," he said. "But I doubt the Baron could carry it off, not with those whiskers."

He invited me to stay with him, while he smoked a cigar, but I declined, and instead returned to my own cabin. Otto had not yet made up the bed, and in any case, it was far too early to retire, so I picked up *Jude*, with some reluctance, since I found his tragic history lowered my spirits mightily.

A brisk rapping on the door therefore proved a welcome distraction. I assumed it was most likely Otto and was most taken aback when it proved to be none other than the elusive Baron.

"Oh!" he exclaimed, as if surprised. "You are not Valentina."

"No, I most certainly am not," I replied. "She is in the next door cabin."

"Aha!"

Instead of retreating, he advanced, his bulk forcing me backwards.

"You are the friend of Sherlock Holmes…" He clicked his fingers in the air. "Marta."

I hoped he was not about to break into song again. However, his next move was more intimidating. He pushed the door closed behind him. Then he smiled.

"Dear lady," he said, "Fear not. I am not about to take advantage of you." He twirled his moustaches. "Unless, you too…"

"Baron," I interrupted, "please leave my cabin at once. If you are looking for Valentina Muratova, she is next door."

"Ah yes. As you already told me." He was still smiling, the light glinting off that gold-capped canine. "But first, dear lady, I should like a little chat with you."

"And if I am not inclined to chat, what then?"

"You can scream, madame, and the steward will come running. But how will it look? A man in your cabin. And such a man." He preened himself. I burst out laughing.

"I think I can defend myself well enough," I said. "In all respects."

He looked into my eyes. "You know, I like you," he said. "I like you a lot."

As if I could care whether he did or no.

"The thing is this, Marta," he continued, sitting himself down, taking his ease, while I remained standing. "I must confess that I was most taken aback to find Holmes on the train. You see, he and I had a distressing encounter in the past, which we will not speak of. But now I cannot help wondering if it just coincidence that brings us together again."

He paused, and regarded me, the question in his expression.

"I can assure you," I replied, "that Mr. Holmes was as surprised to see you, as you were him."

"Ah... Good. Very good. But then might I be so presumptuous as to inquire into the nature of your visit to Constantinople?" Seeing my frown, he added, "You see, dear lady, my mission there is of a wholly humanitarian nature. I should not like to think Mr. Holmes suspected me of any criminal intentions."

"As I have told you, Baron, Mr. Holmes's reason for travelling to Turkey has nothing whatsoever to do with you."

"Yes, but do you see..." Now he stood up again, too close to me for comfort. "Now he has seen me, he might be inclined to embarrass me by probing into my wholly innocent business."

"I doubt he will have the time."

"Is that so? Very good, very good." He stared deep into my eyes, then smiled again. "I wonder what your connection is to him. You are perhaps his special friend."

"I am his landlady," I replied.

"Oh really. How very interesting. How interesting that Mr. Sherlock Holmes should bring his landlady all the way across Europe with him, on this luxury train."

I sank down on to the seat to give myself time to think. What would get rid of the man?

"Mr. Holmes," I said at last, "has in the past served the Sultan in his usual discreet capacity, and was instrumental in avoiding a scandal that might have rocked the Ottoman Empire. Now the Sultan wishes to confer on him the Order of... well something or other. I cannot remember the name. Mr. Holmes kindly suggested that Dr. Watson and I accompany him for the ceremony."

It was the best thing I could think of under pressure, but it seemed to satisfy the Baron. He visibly relaxed.

"So your visit will not be a long one?"

"Oh no. A few days at the most. Of course, I hope to see something of the city while I am there. The famous bazaar, for instance."

"Excellent. Well, I hope you enjoy your stay, Marta… Mrs…er…?"

"Mrs. Hudson."

"A married lady, then."

"A widow."

"Ah…" I was appalled to find him sitting down again. He took my hand. His was indeed unpleasantly wet, as Madeleine had said, and as I had first noticed for myself. "I understand. I too am widowed and alone. My dear wife… a sad sad accident… We are fellow sufferers, Marta."

I extracted my hand from his, and repeated, pointedly, "Madame Muratova is in the next cabin, Baron. You were, I believe, looking for her."

"Yes…yes." Rather sadly, it seemed, he rose and opened the door. "Farewell, dear Marta," he said. "We may meet again. I hope so."

If the Baron had hoped to exert his alleged magnetic attraction on me, I am afraid that it failed miserably to have any effect. I was wood to his iron. I shut and locked the door behind him with a huge sigh, and only opened it later when I was sure it was Otto come to make up my bed. And if the Baron had indeed visited my neighbour after leaving me, they must have spoken in very soft voices indeed, for I could hear nothing at all of a conversation.

Later, I wondered if I should have alerted Mr. H to the Baron's visit. However, it could surely wait until the following morning. All the same, I was sufficiently troubled for the memory of it to disturb my rest, and it was many many hours before I fell asleep.

Chapter Eight

My head was throbbing from a night of broken rest when Otto roused me for my breakfast.

"We arrive at ten, madam," he said. "Will I call your maid to help you pack?"

I looked at my pocket watch, which read seven o'clock.

"That is still three hours away." I was annoyed. "I do not need so long to get ready."

"Apologies, madam, but I am afraid that we have lost another hour. It is already eight o'clock according to Turkish time."

On the train, I had little occasion to check my watch, since all was regulated by bells and announcements. Now I recalled how Paris time was one hour ahead of Greenwich mean time. It made sense, I supposed, that the further East one went, the earlier the sun rose, so to speak. Not that there was any sun. On lifting my blind, I saw the same leaden skies that had accompanied us most of the way across the continent.

"Very well, Otto," I replied, with a sigh. "It would be good of you to call Madeleine. Thank you…"

He bowed and left me. I adjusted my watch.

I felt I could still enjoy a leisurely breakfast, before the flurry of getting packed up, which really would not prove a flurry at all, since all the necessary items could be quickly stowed into my carpet bag: the trunk which held the bulk of my accoutrements having been left unopened in the baggage car. Once washed – and how I should love a bath: it was to be hoped I might enjoy one soon – I dressed myself in my travelling clothes, and then let Madeleine pack for me, since she seemed to think it was her place to do so. Of course, I might have performed the task in a slightly different manner and folded my robe and nightshift more carefully, but the girl was doing her best, and so I held my tongue.

Mr. H and Dr. Watson joined us as we pulled into Sirkeci railway station, built especially, as the doctor informed me, to receive the Orient Express and other trains coming from Europe. I was surprised at the splendour of the structure, having expected to find myself in a primitive country, lacking the comforts of civilised life.

When I expressed as much to the doctor, he replied, "But Mrs. Hudson, the Ottoman Empire has existed for many centuries, considerably longer than the British Empire. Whatever we think of its mode of governance, it has a rich and sophisticated culture."

Nevertheless, the signs were no longer in that alphabet with which I am familiar, but were instead embellished with strange swirls, loops and dots, the Arabic alphabet, I supposed. Goodness, I thought, it would not do to get lost in this country. One would never be able to get one's bearings.

As we waited among other passengers for an equipage to take us onwards, I spotted the Baron standing at a distance. He bowed to me with, it seemed to me, an ironic smile on his face. I proceeded then to inform my companions of the man's visit to me the previous evening.

"The Baron would have done better to ignore you," Mr. H said. "The more he protests his innocence the more I suspect him. As a result of what you have told me, am now quite convinced he is up to no good. Moreover, even though our mission here has nothing to do with him, we must make sure to try and keep an eye on his activities as well."

"I hope," the doctor added, as ever concerned for my welfare, "you did not feel threatened by the man, breaking in to your cabin as he did."

"No," I replied. "He suggested I might scream, but I considered that only as a last resort."

The doctor laughed, but Mr. H still looked grave.

"He is a very dangerous man," he said. "You did well, Mrs. Hudson, in fabricating a good reason for our presence here. You say you think he believed you."

"He seemed to relax. But what will happen when he discovers you are not, in fact, about to receive an honour from the Sultan?"

"I think we can overcome that difficulty," Mr. H replied, enigmatically.

Constantinople's newly built Pera Palace hotel, to which we, and apparently most of the other passengers on the Orient Express, were taken by carriage, could certainly vie with the Grand Hôtel du Louvre in terms of luxury. From the outside, indeed, it resembled many of those Parisian edifices I had come to know well. Inside, however, was something of a different story. Although it was clearly patterned after the best Western hotels – white and grey marble tiles on the floor of the entrance hall, soaring egg-yolk-hued marble pillars either side of a wide staircase whose red carpet led up to a mezzanine, chandeliers dripping electric light, and yes, even an electric lift, just like the one in the Grand Hôtel du Louvre – still, the ornamentation, the large brass vases, the very tables and chairs, spoke of the Orient, not to mention the occasional palm tree. Even the staff – all men – looked exotic in their gold-braided uniforms.

If I imagined I was to stay in this haven, even for one night, I was soon disabused of the notion. Mr. H and Dr. Watson – or Mr. Sherrinford and Dr. Sackler, as they were to be known here– were received as expected guests by a charming young man at reception, wearing the same strange headgear, a red cone with a black tassel, as that sported by some of the other staff (a *fez* as I later learned), He then turned to me, and addressed me in French.

"I am afraid I can find no mention of you, Madame Hudson," he said. Then, it seemed the penny dropped. "Unless you are the lady who has been invited to visit the harem of our beloved Sultan?"

I confirmed that I was indeed she, whereupon the receptionist gestured to a man standing a little apart, one I had taken to be the doorman, a tall and immensely fat negro in flowing fur-lined robes, and crowned with an extraordinary high white headdress, an inscrutable expression on his face. This apparition now approached me as if about to lift me up and carry me away bodily.

"Am I to go with this man?" I asked Mr. H apprehensively.

"It seems so," he replied. He too looked at something of a loss for once.

"I should rather not," I replied, my courage failing me, "unless you can accompany me."

"Ah, there is a letter for you, sir," the receptionist addressed Mr. H. He handed it over with something like awe, perhaps because of the distinctive crest imprinted on the envelope.

Mr. H stood to one side while perusing it, while Dr. Watson muttered to me that the black man who lingered a little way off, staring at us, was most certainly a eunuch from the palace. I tried to not stare back, following this intelligence. Madeleine was, I am afraid, less discreet, and I had to whisper a reproof to her. She blinked several times quickly, but desisted.

"Fear not, Mrs. Hudson," Mr. H said finally, folding the letter back in its envelope "I too have been summoned to the august presence, so we can travel together."

I was more than sorry to leave the luxurious hotel, where I was sure I would at last have access to a hot bath. However, there was work to be done. The eunuch seemed content that Mr. H and Madeleine should accompany me, but he looked askance at Dr. Watson.

"You had better stay here," Mr. H said to him. "Too many strangers make Abdul Hamid nervous."

I could see that Dr. Watson was rather put out, used, as he was, to partnering Mr. H in his investigations. However, we were in a strange country, dealing with a powerful ruler, whose whims must be obeyed.

As we left the Pera Palace, I noticed our fellow travellers staring at us, or rather, at our guide, whose shining black skin, long robe, headdress and immense girth made him stand out even in a crowd as motley as this. Among the gawkers, I caught sight of La Muratova and Katy, who waved at Madeleine. The Baron, however, was nowhere to be seen. I was relieved he was not to witness our departure in such a manner and with such a companion. It would most certainly have piqued his curiosity even more.

I almost expected to find a line of camels lined up to carry us, but nothing of the sort. A horse-drawn landau, just like those one might see in London, was to be our mode of transportation.

We travelled in silence. Mr. H is never much of a conversationalist at the best of times, and in any case our guide continued to gaze at us in a most disconcerting way. He had addressed not a word to us, but merely gestured where we were to go, so who even knew if he could understand English. Better not to discuss our business in front of him, just in case. Instead, holding hands with Madeleine, who for once was speechless, I entertained myself by looking out at this most exotic of cities, a strange mixture of the sophisticated and the primitive. Beautiful buildings of pale stone – palaces and mosques I supposed, with their towers, turrets and domes – soon gave way, as we mounted narrow streets, to rough dwellings and market stalls. Certainly, most of the people we passed – a swarthy race – looked very foreign to me, even though some of the men wore the Western dress of dark suits and shoes. However, the majority were clad in baggy trousers tightly gathered at the ankle, above leather boots, wide waistbands visible under the thick jackets they were wearing against the cold, turbans of cloth wound round their heads. The women, clad in black from head to foot, with only eyes visible, scurried among them for all the world like beetles.

Eventually we left the city behind, and started uphill along a wide highway. Wherever was the man taking us? I was more than ever grateful for Mr. H's presence. Soon enough, however, great walls loomed before us, and we reached a heavy wrought-iron door set in a stone arch. I could not help but be reminded of the entrance to Wormwood Scrubs, that prison so recently built in London to house malefactors. My spirits sank even lower.

However, once we had passed through the gate, opened at our summons, I was most pleasantly surprised, even though the palace was not at all as I had envisaged it would be. Indeed, one could hardly describe it as a palace at all. Instead of one imposing edifice, charming pavilions of white marble stood here and there among formal gardens that must look utterly enchanting in summer, and even now, under a light dusting of snow, seemed quite magical. Our landau took us by the side of a small lake, past the geometric intricacies of parterres, their low hedges set around fountains, past rose beds where some flowers were yet to be seen despite the wintry frosts. Men – servants perhaps, in long robes – hurried between the buildings. No women were visible.

We were driven to a pavilion surrounded by a walled garden. Two more black eunuchs were on guard at the gate and gave us unfriendly looks as we alighted from the landau. However, it was clear that we were expected. Our guide led us into summer again, through a conservatory filled with tropical blooms in vivid hues of orange, pink and purple, from which I was astonished to see tiny, brightly feathered birds fly up, disturbed by our passage. The air was heavy with moisture, and musky, not exactly unpleasant, but not fresh either. From here, Mr. H and I were gestured forward through a door leading to a reception room, while Madeleine was held back by the eunuch. She looked terrified, but I gave her a reassuring nod, though I was far from feeling reassured myself. Whatever had I let us in for, my little maid and myself?

Mr. H must have sensed my alarm for he muttered something to the man in a language which must be the Turkish he had been studying on the train. The other bowed assent.

"She is in no danger," Mr. H told me. "He understands that she is under my protection."

The room we entered was exquisitely furnished with thick patterned carpets, and a richly embroidered screen, featuring stylised tulips of blue and red. Ornamental cages containing twittering canaries hung from the walls. At the far end, I could see a small figure reclining on a sofa, two more black eunuchs beside him. He rose as we entered.

"Sherlock Bey," he said, speaking French in a deep and melodious voice. "You are most welcome."

"Votre Majesté!" Mr. H replied, bowing deeply and advancing to kiss the Sultan's outstretched hand.

I was aghast. Could this shrunken and emaciated little old man really be Abdul Hamid II, the great ruler of the Ottoman Empire? He was simply dressed in a kind of tunic, a plain black fez on his head. A huge hooked nose dominated his face, under hooded eyes, and set above a thick beard, surely too black to be natural. His grey skin looked to have been rouged over the cheeks. All in all, not an impressive presence, at all.

"Let me introduce Madame Martha Hudson," Mr. H continued. "This is the lady who will assist my investigations into your present problem."

Black eyes studied me critically from under those heavy lids, and I sank into a curtsey, wishing Mr. H had advised me how properly to behave in the presence of such royalty.

Abdul Hamid clicked his fingers and spoke rapidly to the eunuchs in the strange guttural language I had heard from Mr. H. The men bowed and departed.

"They will bring coffee and sherbet," he told us.

He gestured to us to take seats on a cushioned bench – an ottoman, no less! – beside a low circular table of great beauty. Coloured tiles were set in the centre of it, while the surround was of ebony inlaid with what looked to be iridescent mother of pearl and creamy ivory. So much luxury, almost too much.

As we waited, the Sultan fiddled restlessly with some black beads on a thin thread. They reminded me of the rosaries employed by Roman Catholics, and wondered if these too had a religious function. However, the Sultan did not look as if he was praying, just preoccupied. Later, I learnt that these *tesbih*, were also known as worry beads, and were widely used by fidgety men of all classes in Constantinople.

Although I found the prolonged silence awkward and oppressive, Abdul Hamid unwilling apparently to broach the subject of our visit until after the refreshments arrived, Mr. H seemed unconcerned. Meanwhile, I could hear women's voices and giggles from behind the embroidered screen, mixing with the twittering of the canaries. Were these the ladies of the harem? I could not ask, of course.

At last, the two eunuchs returned, one bearing a tray on which stood three tiny cups and a small, long-handled copper pot. He carefully poured out a thick dark liquid, and offered the tray to the Sultan, who took one of the cups. Then he presented the tray to Mr. H and finally to me, emphasising, I suppose, my low status as a mere woman. The other eunuch, a large napkin embroidered in gold hanging from his right arm, held another tray covered by a silk cloth, which, when removed, revealed three coloured glasses, containing some sort of juice. The Sultan pointed to one, which was set on the table before him, the other two in front of Mr. H and myself.

The coffee was very strong and bitter, and I was glad of the sweet rose-scented cordial, that accompanied it. I noticed too that the

Sultan waited for us to drink, before he did so himself. A charming courtesy, I thought. The Sultan then addressed himself again to the eunuchs, who bowed and withdrew. The whispering behind the screen stopped too.

Once the Sultan was sure we were completely alone, he started to speak in a heavily accented French. I had to concentrate hard to follow him. At least, he spoke slowly.

"As you know well, Sherlock Bey," he said, "I have many enemies. Many people who would like to see me dead. These people are ruthless. Now, I have reason to fear that they have infiltrated the palace, even into my harem. It was my refuge, Sherlock Bey. Now I do not feel safe even there among my women."

He paused.

"What exactly has happened to make you think this, Your Majesty?" Mr. H asked, putting down his coffee cup.

"These deaths. Sudden deaths among my favourites in the space of a few short weeks." His eyes flashed. "It is a warning to me, Sherlock Bey, that my enemies are closing in. Alas, there are few people I can trust. No one I trust completely."

The poor man, my heart went out to him. What a lonely existence he must lead. However, it seemed that his concern was less for the victims, than for himself.

"Might I ask," Mr. H was saying, "how did these women die?"

"Foolish accidents, it was claimed. One slipped in the bath and fatally banged her head. Another was bitten by a monkey and died of blood poisoning as a result. The third was strangled when her scarf caught in the wheels of the carriage that was taking her for a jaunt around the park. The fourth, my dearest Ayla, hardly more than a child, shot herself, it was said, while playing with a gun. The fifth fell from the roof of the harem." He shook his head. "My astrologer tells me a curse is at work but while I usually revere his words, this time I do not trust even him. This is no curse, Sherlock Bey, but the work of some of my numberless foes."

He flashed wild eyes at us, clutching at his robe, as if the flimsy stuff had the power to ward off any attack.

"It is," Mr. H said thoughtfully, "entirely possible, I suppose that these deaths were indeed unfortunate accidents."

Abdul Hamid reared up angrily.

"However," Mr. H forestalled his objections, "to have so many odd deaths so close together does indeed deserve an investigation, Your Majesty." He turned to me. "What do you think, Madame Hudson?"

The Sultan looked surprised that my opinion was sought.

"I agree, Your Majesty," I replied, shocked at what I had heard, and, like the Sultan, suspecting that these were unlikely accidents. "I shall be honoured to try and help you and Mr. Holmes get to the bottom of the mystery."

The Sultan nodded and almost smiled.

"Thank you, madame," he said. "You will take up residence immediately… I understand your maid is with you."

How did he know that? At least he called Madeleine a maid and not a slave.

"She is, Your Majesty," I replied.

"Your trunk and her bags have already been brought to the palace."

"You are most gracious. But," as I spoke, he looked up sharply again. Was I about to commit the unthinkable and contradict him? I merely asked, "is there anything else I need to know, Your Majesty? I am most ignorant of your customs here."

"My wife, Bedrifelek, will attend to you and will explain anything you wish to know. She and the others have been informed that you are one of those privileged English ladies who has a notion to explore harem life. Under no circumstances should you inform her or anyone else of your true reason for being here."

I nodded acquiescence, wondering, at the same time, if he mistrusted even his wives.

The Sultan turned back to Mr. H. "At the same time, I wish you, Sherlock Bey, to discover who outside the palace might be plotting against me in this heinous way. To avoid suspicion regarding your presence, and to avoid your true identities becoming known and therefore giving warning to the mangy dogs who are my enemies, I consider it more fitting that you and Doctor Watson should continue to reside at the Pera Palace Hotel. In any case, it will be much simpler for you to conduct your investigations from the heart of the city, rather than up here at Yildiz."

Mr. H inclined his head. "I understand, Your Majesty, but how will Madame Hudson and myself communicate at such a distance?"

"In a few days' time," the Sultan replied, "you will receive an invitation to attend a performance here in my theatre of *Medea* by that incomparable actress, Valentina Muratova. You will then have occasion to speak with madame, and learn what she has found out."

"Thank you, Your Majesty," Mr. H replied. "Yes, we had the pleasure of meeting La Muratova on the Orient Express."

"What a beauty! What talent!" The Sultan's eyes shone. For a moment, he was transformed. Then his expression darkened again.

"One more thing, Your Majesty," Mr. Holmes said. "You say that you have many enemies. But have you any suspicion at all which of them might be behind these deaths?"

"I suspect… well, Armenians, of course," Abdul Hamid replied. "For revenge." The London newspapers, as I recalled, had been full of reports of the recent terrible massacres here in Turkey of that unfortunate race. "Renegade Young Turks, too, have become a thorn in my side. You might well investigate them, to see if they are involved. And perhaps those treacherous separatists from the Balkan states of Macedonia, Bulgaria or Greece." His fingers nervily played with the loop of black beads.

Goodness, I thought. Mr. H will certainly have his work cut out. But the Sultan had not yet finished.

"Then," he continued, "there are those who consider that I usurped my wretched brother Murad, that he is the legitimate Sultan. A man turned imbecile through drink and debauchery."

"Where is Murad now?" Mr. H asked.

"Kept for his own safety in the Cheraghan palace below us here on the shores of the Bosphorus. While he remains alive, Sherlock Bey, I shall never be at peace."

He stared at my companion, as if willing him to rid him of this encumbrance. However, unlike those unknown assassins who had disposed of St. Thomas à Becket for King Henry, Mr. H just calmly asked, "Anyone else?"

The Sultan emitted a barking sound that I belatedly realised was a laugh. "If I started to enumerate them, Sherlock Bey, we should be here all night. However, I shall summon Bashir to take Madame… er… to her quarters in the harem." He sighed. "I pray the two of you will be able somehow to soothe the troubled heart of this poor monarch."

I am not sure how the Sultan managed to alert them, but suddenly the two huge eunuchs were standing behind us soft-footed in embroidered slippers. One, after Abdul Hamid murmured instructions, beckoned to me. However, Mr. H again addressed the Sultan.

"I should like, with your permission, Your Majesty, to exchange a few words of instruction with Madame Hudson before she leaves us."

Abdul Hamid waved a weary hand in acquiescence and took himself up off the couch. Mr. H bowed and I made another deep curtsey. The Sultan then disappeared behind the embroidered screen, accompanied by one of the eunuchs. The other stood waiting and watching, while Mr. H and I withdrew to a distant corner of the room, out of earshot.

"You will be all right, Mrs. Hudson," he said in hushed tones. I am not sure if it was a question or a statement. In any case, I could hardly change my mind now.

I nodded.

"Try to gain the confidence of the ladies, encourage them to talk without raising suspicion. You are able to do that, I suppose."

I nodded again, though rather insulted that he should doubt my discretion.

"Madeleine will be able to eavesdrop on the exchanges in Turkish, but for God's sake again tell her to be careful. I rather regret now that I did not find an older, more staid woman to be your companion."

"She will be perfect," I replied. "No one will suspect a child like that."

"I hope not." He paused and frowned. "The situation is far more serious that I had imagined. Those deaths… Be very careful, Mrs. Hudson. Dr. Watson and I need you." It was the nicest thing he had ever said to me. He even squeezed my hand.

"I hope I shall not disappoint," I replied.

We chatted a little longer, he warning me to mind what I ate, to allow others to try the food before taking any myself.

"You saw what the Sultan did, waiting for us to drink the coffee and not touching his sherbet drink."

"I thought he was being polite." The intelligence sunk in. "You mean he wanted to see if we dropped dead from poisoning, before tasting the drinks himself?"

"Precisely," was the dry reply.

It was hardly encouraging.

I left him then, following the eunuch behind that embroidered screen. I looked back at him one last time, and then I walked on, to enter at last the strange world of the harem.

Chapter Nine

And what a very strange world it turned out to be, beyond all my imaginings. At first, however, I was taken aback to find that the ladies lined up to meet me, curious-eyed, were clad not at all in the exotic robes depicted in the paintings I had seen. In one way, I was relieved to find they were clad in anything at all, since those same paintings usually showed them naked or dressed in the flimsiest, and most revealing of garments. But to find them in up-to-date Paris fashions, the very same styles that had been chosen for me by Madame Celestine in the Grands Magasins du Louvre, well, that was a huge surprise.

What hit me, too, was a wave of heavy perfume that almost took my breath away. It was something I should have to get used to, for as I was to discover, the residents of the harem were most partial to strong sweet scents.

The lady who stepped forward to greet me, introduced herself in French as Bedrifelek, and, even though Abdul Hamid had described her as his wife, she was not, as Dr. Watson had warned me, the only one. While I was staying in the harem, I got to know of at least eleven others (it was difficult to keep track of exactly how many there were), as well as numerous concubines. I could not imagine English wives putting up with that particular situation for a single moment.

Bedrifelek, sumptuously dressed in a gown of turquoise silk, with many (too many?) diamonds and sapphires adorning her neck, ears and wrists, was in her early forties, a pretty woman with pale skin, blonde hair and blue-grey eyes, not at all typical of the Turkish people I had seen heretofore.

"You must be tired after your long journey, madame," she said in French, beckoning to a rosy-cheeked young girl standing near. "Gulsima will take you to your room where your slave is already awaiting you."

"Thank you, Your Majesty," I replied. "You are most kind."

"You will certainly wish to take a bath before your midday meal."

Music to my ears, even though it sounded more like an order than a suggestion.

"That would be delightful."

Bedrifelek said something, presumably in Turkish, to the pretty young girl, who smiled at me and then led me through a veritable warren of passageways to what I supposed to be a guest room. Like the ladies' fashions, it was a disconcerting mixture of West and East, with thickly woven and patterned oriental rugs on the floor, elaborately gilded furniture, a crystal chandelier, a huge double bed under a canopy of exotic embroidery.

Madeleine turned as we entered. Never had she looked more relieved to see me. For a moment, I even thought she was about to rush over and hug me, but, with a glance at my companion, she desisted and merely curtsied.

"I am to have a bath," I said.

"Yes," Madeleine replied. "I have been made to have one already. They are very keen on cleanliness here."

"Well, of course, it is next to godliness, as they say," I replied. "So where is the bathroom?"

"Ah," Madeleine replied enigmatically. "Yes, the bathroom…"

Meanwhile, the girl, Gulsima, stood waiting, presumably to conduct me thither. It was a somewhat awkward moment. She did not seem to understand French, and Madeleine was not supposed to reveal her knowledge of Turkish. After we had stood looking at each other for a few moments, I made washing gestures with my hands. Gulsima nodded and beckoned to both of us to follow her, Madeline carrying the new kimono robe that Madame Celestine had selected for me.

A bathroom? What had I been expecting? Not this anyway. Apparently, I was not to lie soaking in a tub of hot, still water the way we are used to in England. At my disposal was a marble fountain – the only way I can describe it – rising from a shallow pool. Moreover, Madeleine, as my slave, was clearly expected to wash and even scrub me, while Gulsima stood by. Eventually, the latter understood that I should prefer to be left alone. The two girls then went out, while I availed of the delicious soaps and perfumed oils left for my use.

Eventually, much refreshed, I left the bathroom only to find Madeleine and her new friend sitting outside the door, giggling together. Lacking a common language, or so Gulsima believed at least, was apparently no barrier to communication between the two. They both jumped up on seeing me, and Gulsima led the way back to my room through that maze of passageways.

"You were lucky to have a private bathroom," Madeleine whispered. "I was put in with all the other slaves. And not a single one of them speaks French. I could hardly keep a straight face, listening to what they were saying about me, thinking I couldn't understand. Most were friendly enough, though, and kept touching my hair."

I suppose her mass of russet curls were a novelty to the girls.

"Did they say anything of interest?" I asked.

"Not really, though one who was less friendly than the others said she thought I might do for the astrologer. Then they all laughed. What did she mean by that, Madame?"

"It means that you must stay by my side as much as possible."

I was horrified, but tried not to show it. Madeleine was still a child. Could those girls think that some old man might take her for his pleasure? I would have to make sure everyone here knew she was under my care.

No sooner were we back in my room than a black eunuch with a silver tray appeared and set it on a small low table before me. There were salads, olives, cheeses and even tiny black beads of caviar, as well as a glass of that aromatic cordial of which I had already partaken. Gulsima smiled and nodded and said something, before leaving us. Madeleine translated it after she had gone to "May your taste turn to sugar," apparently a kind of Turkish equivalent of the French *bon appetit*, of which we, sadly, have no equivalent in English.

Why I was to take my meal alone in my room? Was it because I had arrived at a time after the others had eaten? Whatever the reason, already I would have to break one of the strictures given me by Mr. H: I should not be able to wait for others to try the food before me, unless of course I asked Madeleine to be my taster, something I was certainly not inclined to do. However, there was surely no cause for anyone to try to poison me, not just yet, anyway. I put it from my thoughts and decided to enjoy the meal.

Although there was no plate or glass for her, Madeleine shared my repast. But if I thought that this light luncheon was all I was to receive, I was soon disabused. In due course, the eunuch returned with another tray on which was piled a lamb stew, chunks of lamb on skewers, a huge heap of fluffy white rice, savoury pastries, a strange vegetable with a dark and silky skin, others, equally unfamiliar, in bright reds and yellows, all cooked in rich oil. Madeleine and I did our best, but more than we had eaten was left when the eunuch came to remove the tray. Even this was not the end of it. Now we were expected to consume pastries filled with nuts and oozing syrup, far too sweet for my taste, although Madeleine loved them. To end the meal, I was served another tiny cup of that incredibly strong black coffee prepared in front of me, the servant standing watching while I drank it and nodded my approval.

At last, this trial by eating ordeal was over, and Gulsima entered with a silver jug of water and a basin so that I could wash my hands. She was clearly most surprised when Madeleine, her hands sticky from the sweetmeats, availed of the chance to wash her hands too. Gulsima almost snatched the embroidered towel from her hands, and muttered something. I have to say that Madeleine's ability to keep a straight face to indicate she did not understand was most laudable.

"She disapproves of my eating with you," she said.

"Never mind her. She can assume it is one of our strange foreign habits," I replied.

Now Gulsima indicated that we should follow her, even though all I wanted to do was to lie down and rest. Madeleine helped me dress, for, of course, I could not go and meet the other ladies clad only in a kimono robe, elegant though it was. We picked out a grey watered silk as suitable attire, and then Gulsima took us through that warren of corridors again – would I ever be able to find my way by myself? Would I ever be allowed to? We finally reached a large salon lined on all sides with divans on which the palace ladies were reclining and, to my astonished eyes, smoking, but not cigarettes. They seemed to be sucking from narrow tubes, that were entwined round their bare forearms, and attached to strange contraptions set on the floor in front of them. These resembled rather beautiful lidded vases, their tall thin stems rising from round glass bases that contained water bubbling as the ladies inhaled. I was gestured to a divan and offered one of the contraptions myself. I shook my head.

The girl next to me laughed. Pretty, dark-haired, with fine features, and astonishingly green eyes, she had to be only a few years older than Madeleine, who had sat herself down on the floor at my feet as if she had been a slave all her life.

"Your face, madame!" my neighbour exclaimed in French. "I think you have never smoked a nargile before."

"I have never smoked anything," I replied.

"Then you should certainly start with this. You see, when the tobacco smoke passes through the water, it is cooled, so the effect does not sting. Please try it."

"Perhaps another time."

"As you wish."

She told me her name was Naime, and that she was the daughter of the Sultan.

"Forgive me, Princess," I said. "I did not know."

"No need for ceremony," she replied. "I am delighted to make the acquaintance of a European woman who can tell me all about her life."

"It isn't very interesting, I am afraid."

"To me, everything out there is interesting. Are you your husband's first consort?"

I explained that I was a widow, but that I had been dear Henry's only consort.

"Oh yes. I forgot. Christian men do not have more than one wife, do they? For us, that is very strange."

We continued to chat, even though Naime was smoking all the time, as were the others, with the result that the air in the room was pungent enough to make my eyes water. The Princess spoke an excellent French, which quite put mine to shame, and I soon discovered that, despite her enforced isolation in the palace harem, she was an educated person who knew something of the outside world, asking me about Queen Victoria, as if I knew that august personage personally. Of course, I was supposedly a woman of the upper class, but even had that been true, I doubted I would have had much intercourse with the British monarch.

When I asked Naime how she spent her time, she told me of her love of music.

"Like my father," she explained, "I have learnt to play the piano, although I prefer the works of M. Chopin to the Herr Offenbach that my father loves so much. I also try to paint." She gave me a shy look. "I can show you my pictures if you would be interested."

I replied that indeed I should be delighted. The talk then ranged to art in general. I told her that the reality of the harem, as I found it, differed very much from the depictions of it in the National Gallery in London.

She laughed merrily. "Of course, madame. Since those silly artists would never be permitted to visit us here, they work from their heated imaginations."

I went on to admit that I was rather disappointed to find the ladies in western dress, having expected something more traditional.

"Perhaps we should have put on the shalwar to gratify your expectations. Or even a veil, although we only wear those in the presence of men not of the family."

"But our dress must be so uncomfortable for you, the corsets and stays and so on. I find it so myself," I said. "In fact, my daughter Eleanor is part of the rational dress movement in England, the aim of which is to free women from the constrictions of tight-lacing and heavy undergarments."

Now Naime, who disagreed with me on the issue of dress – saying that even harem women must keep up with the times, though admitting she herself sometimes loosened her stays, especially after a big feast – had to hear all about Eleanor and my other daughter, Judith, who lives in Edinburgh. I was happy to describe the latter as a doctor's wife. However, I am afraid I balked at revealing Eleanor to be the wife of a humble grocer. Not out of snobbery, but because it might raise suspicions about my supposed elevated origins. Dear George Hazelgrove became, in my description, quite the man of business. I hated to tell fibs and changed the subject as quickly as I could.

All the time we were chatting, servants were going around the room with trays of sweetmeats and those same sherbet cordials that Naime informed me were made from the flowers grown in the palace gardens. I took a drink to cool myself, but refused the sweets. I was still full after that luncheon.

"What a shame, Madame Hudson," Naime said, "that you are visiting us in winter. You should be here in summer when the gardens are a delight to explore."

"They look beautiful even now," I replied.

"Well, another day I can at least take you to visit our menagerie. I hope the sight of wild animals will not terrify you too much."

I replied that, on the contrary, I should be delighted.

"I used to visit the zoo in the Regent's Park frequently when my girls were small," I told her. "It is near where I live."

"The Regent's Park!" she said. "How amazing that sounds. Does the Regent go there a lot?"

"Oh no," I replied. "He is long dead. Just the name remains."

"How sad."

I was not about to tell her that the same Regent was not a man to be admired, but added, "He lived a long enough life and became King George IV, uncle to Queen Victoria."

"Ah, I see. How very interesting it is talking to you, Madame Hudson. But now," she got up, "you must excuse me. I have to go and get changed for dinner."

"Dinner!" I exclaimed. "Oh, my goodness! I had such a big lunch. I am not sure I can manage to eat another thing."

She laughed. "I am afraid you must. There is to be a celebratory meal to welcome you as our honoured guest. And, of course, you absolutely have to meet the Valide Sultan."

I looked askance.

"Who?"

"The Queen Mother," Naime continued. "Although, you know, she is not my father's real mother, who died when he was only ten, after which Raime Perestu adopted him. Still, she is the most important person in the harem."

"Oh yes," I replied. "I understand. I have a gift for her."

It was a quantity of exquisite white and black Chantilly lace, which, I am afraid, was also paid for by the Sultan.

"She loves presents," Naime said. "And do not worry about eating up your dinner, madame. It is polite in Turkey to leave food, you know, to show that the host has provided more than enough to satisfy his guests. If you eat it all up, it looks like the host has been miserly."

"Goodness," I replied. "There is so much here to learn and understand."

Although I suddenly recalled an aunt of mine once chiding me for clearing my plate.

"You should always leave something for Mr. Manners, Martha," she had told me.

At eight years of age, I had wondered who this Mr. Manners might be, who ate the leavings of other people. I smiled at the memory. Still, I was worried that if I did not show appreciation here by eating a sufficient amount, it might also be taken as an insult.

Naime had gone, before I could ask her about it, and Madeleine and I sat looking at each other, at something of a loss as to what to do next, since no one else seemed inclined to talk to us, lowering their eyes shyly when I looked in their direction. I wanted to return to my room but was not sure I could even find my way back there. Once more, it was Gulsima who came to the rescue, popping up as if from nowhere.

The Queen Mother could not have been more gracious, holding out a heavily beringed little hand, and, I having been informed of the required etiquette, bowed and kissed it. Raime Perestu was a tiny woman approaching seventy, as I judged, who must have been very beautiful in her youth, and who yet retained something of her early bloom. Like Naime, she was pale skinned and light-haired, with blue eyes. Unlike the other ladies, she, at least, was clad in a gorgeous traditional dress, loose and richly embroidered, and, when I presented her with the gifts I had brought, she received them with all appearance of sincere delight. Because she was already wearing an exquisitely woven black lace mantilla, I suppose someone had decided I should give her something she would surely like. She welcomed me in low, musical tones, in the few words of French she knew, indicating that I should sit beside her. Next to her on the other side sat Bedrifelek, the other wives and daughters placed around the table presumably according to their rank, gloriously arrayed in their multicoloured silks, resembling, indeed, the birds of paradise in the conservatory. Naime was down and across from me, and gave me a big smile.

Now Sultan Abdul Hamid himself entered, the only man in this assembly of women. We stood and curtsied and he bowed in response and greeted his stepmother, who kissed his hand. I was not sure if I was to acknowledge that I had already met him, but this moment of possible embarrassment was averted when Bedrifelek turned to him and introduced me.

"You are most welcome, Madame Hudson," he said, and sat down in the vacant place. He even admired the lace gifts I had presented to his stepmother, as if he knew nothing about them.

Now servant girls came round with bowls of water and towels, so that we might wash and dry our hands before the meal, and then a huge retinue bearing laden trays came in and placed the contents in front of us,

It was all so tempting and aromatic that I quickly found my appetite returning, and was well able to partake of the dishes presented, even though I made sure to help myself to tiny portions. I covertly observed my neighbours to see how much they were taking and found that they ate as little as I did. Abdul Hamid, indeed, ate nothing at all from the trays, but was served a plain-looking dish of rice and eggs from a sealed container. I was supposing he must have a delicate stomach, until I remembered that Mr. H had told me that the Sultan lived in terror of being poisoned. No one around me showed any hesitation in eating, however, so I did the same. It was rather surprising to me that the Queen Mother ate with her fingers, but very delicately. The Sultan and the younger women, however, used silver cutlery, for the which I was most relieved.

It seemed polite to praise the food. I asked in particular about one of the dishes strange to me, at which the Sultan turned to a young black man standing at his shoulder, another eunuch. He must have been asked to explain. He told me that the little savoury pastries I was eating were called *piruhi*, soft cheese encased in paper thin dough and topped with toasted walnuts. They were quite delicious.

For all the lavishness of the meal, however, for all the courtesy of my hosts, it was a relief to me when it was finally over. There was so much ritual and ceremony involved, and, while I am sure that if I were to make an error in etiquette, they would have overlooked it as the shortcomings of an ignorant Western woman, still, I was on tenterhooks the whole time. Luckily, smiling and nodding seemed to go a long way to satisfy them.

I had not been in the harem for more than half a day and yet I was already feeling constrained and hemmed in. My room had only a small window, covered with some sort of mesh so that, while I could peer out on to a courtyard, outsiders could not see in. It only contributed to my sense of imprisonment. At least I had Madeleine to talk to, and she was full of stories, having dined with the slaves and concubines.

"I've changed my mind about them." she told me. "They aren't nice at all. For one thing, they hate Naime."

"Really?" I was surprised.

"They saw you talking to her and, madame, the things they said about her. All out of envy, I suppose, for didn't she seem very nice?"

"I hope they didn't realise you could understand them."

"Oh no, madame. I kept looking like this." She put on a wide-eyed innocent expression, which made me laugh.

"So what did they say?"

"Naime is her father's favourite, and the other sisters are jealous, so their slaves feel the same. They were horrid to Naime's slave too, who was eating with us. She got upset and went away before finishing her dinner... Then one of the slaves laughed nastily and said she'd ask Bashir to put her in a sack and throw her in the Bosphorus. Another added 'And her mistress, too.' Then they all looked at me, so I smiled stupidly, and the nasty one – well, they are all nasty, I suppose – said 'Her too!' 'That would be a crowded sack,' another one said. They thought that was hilarious."

I was most shocked. "You must be very careful, Madeleine."

"I reckon it was all just talk," she replied. "How else can they amuse themselves? They are so bored."

"Do not forget girls have died here in mysterious ways. It is not a safe place."

She had that stubborn look on her face that said, I should like to see someone try to get the better of me, so I decided not to argue further just now, especially since I was suddenly overcome with fatigue. Was it only last night that I had slept on the Orient Express?

Madeleine insisted on helping me undress – even though I am well able to manage by myself.

"It's what we slaves do," she said, fumbling with the ribbons on my stays.

After sending away a servant who called in with a tray of cakes, sweetmeats, fruits and glasses of sherbet – presumably in case we were overcome with hunger in the night – we retired, me into the splendid, if rather too soft bed that dominated the room and Madeleine into a small cot beside it. Perhaps it was the strong coffee

I had been prevailed on to drink after dinner, but, although I was very weary, it was a long time before sleep overcame me. I could not help dwelling on what Madeleine had told me, wondering if the deaths of the concubines I was to investigate were far from representing a threat to Abdul Hamid himself, being nothing more – though serious enough to those concerned – than the revenge of slighted girls on those seen as the Sultan's favourites.

Chapter Ten

No sooner had I finally fallen asleep than I was rudely reawakened by a loud wailing chant nearby. In a moment of confusion, I thought myself back on the Orient Express, with La Muratova performing her voice exercises in the next cabin. As I came to full consciousness, I could tell, of course, that it was no such thing. The sound was eerie and beautiful and unlike anything I had ever heard before. In fact, it was the Moslem priest, the imam, calling the faithful to prayer. Like Roman Catholic monks and nuns, Moslems are supposed to pray at regular times through the day, one of those times being dawn, around four in the morning.

All this I learned later from Naime, who proved only too delighted to explain her religion to me. That was after Gulsima had roused me with my breakfast, a thankfully relatively modest meal consisting of soft bread rolls with clotted cream, a salty white cheese, honey, fruit jams and olives, together with strong black tea. This time I did not share it with Madeleine. We had agreed, the night before, that she would spend as much time as possible with the slaves, to try to overhear more regarding the sorry fate of the five concubines.

Meanwhile, I bathed again, seeing that Gulsima expected it of me. In fact, as I was soon to discover, the ladies of the harem spent a large proportion of their time in the communal baths. It was a place where they could chat and relax, braiding each other's hair, massaging themselves with perfumed oils to keep their skin soft and supple (I had already noticed how beautiful it was). But that was later. This morning, when I returned to my room from my private bath, I found a strange female figure awaiting me, clad from head to toe in a black robe, the way I had seen the women dressed on the ride up to the palace the day before. I guessed it was Naime from her flashing green eyes, a supposition confirmed when she started to speak.

"I promised to take you to see the menagerie, Madame Hudson," she said. "I hope it will suit you to go now, for the animals are to be fed soon, and it is quite a sight."

I replied that I should be delighted, as indeed I was. It would be most welcome to breathe fresh air, even in wintry weather.

Naime admired the fur-lined brown cape and matching muff that Madame Celestine had forced upon me. At the time I had considered it quite foolish. Was I not heading to the warm South? What use would I have for furs there? Now, with that dusting of snow on the ground, I was most glad of it. Glad too, that I was not expected to cover myself completely, as my companion had done.

We were not to go alone, however, even within the palace precincts. A eunuch followed at a discreet distance. On the way, I rather bombarded Naime with questions. It was then she explained about the imam and the call to prayer.

"The Valide Sultan is very pious," she told me. "She spends much of her time praying." She paused. "If you wish to attend your Christian church at any time, madame, it can be arranged."

I thanked her, thinking, perhaps a little impiously, that it would be a good place to meet Mr. H without arousing suspicion.

As we walked through the palace grounds, Naime pointed out various interesting and beautiful buildings. I was most struck by a white and gold pavilion, a high and narrow tower rising beside it.

"That is where the imam calls us to prayer. You see, he is nearer heaven up there."

I thought of the poor fellow having to climb all those stairs in the cold and dark of winter, in the stifling heat of summer. Truly a holy man. I just wished he could make his call a little quieter.

Far off, across the gardens, I spotted another tall building.

"My father's porcelain factory," Naime said, in response to my query.

"Oh, how fascinating. Would it be possible for me to visit it some time?"

"I am sure that can be arranged."

We passed the theatre, where, in a few days, La Muratova would be performing "Medea."

"I am looking forward to it so much," Naime said. "I hear that she is quite wonderful. Another Sarah Bernhardt."

"I have heard the same thing," I replied, a little drily.

It was clear we were reaching the menagerie at last, from the rank smell, the roars and yelps and chattering of hungry animals. Now, as I had already informed Naime, I knew London Zoo well, my and the girls' favourite exhibit when they were small being the aquarium where, behind a great glass window, one might view all manner of marine life just as if one were under the water with them. Or the reptile house, with its snakes and sinister crocodiles. How my girls had shuddered at the sight of those teeth! Nevertheless, the collection of animals in the Sultan's menagerie was unlike anything I had ever seen before. The vast enclosure housed all manner of wild beasts, some I recognised, like the lions and tigers, giraffes, elephants, monkeys and apes, the zebras with their distinctive black and white stripes. Others were quite strange to me. Naime pointed to something large and horned that looked to be something out of prehistory, the name of which I had never heard before.

A veritable host of servants were preparing to feed the animals. Naime hurried forward to the tiger pen where a man was standing with a bucket of raw meat. To my amazement and horror, she took it from him, opened the cage door and climbed in. The great beast that had been reclining in a corner, uncurled itself and padded over to her. Naime set down the bucket and fed the tiger from one hand while stroking the beast's head with the other, murmuring to it in Turkish. I hardly dared breathe. The attendant beside me, however, seemed entirely unconcerned, as did the eunuch who had followed us in, and now stood waiting. Once the tiger had emptied the bucket, Naime gave it one last caress, and then came back out to us.

"You are quite mad," I said. "The creature could have killed you."

"Not at all," she replied, laughing. "Guzellik and I are old friends. I raised her from a cub and fed her milk from a bottle."

The attendant held out a basin of water and a towel, so that Naime could wash her hands. For my part, I felt quite weak. She was still laughing, as we continued our walk around the menagerie.

"The expression on your face, Madame Hudson! I am so glad you are not veiled, so I can see it."

She explained more about the collection, as we passed each enclosure.

"My father is like me," she said. "He loves animals. Most of the other women are, like you, terrified of them."

"I am not afraid of all of them," I replied. "Just those that might like to eat me for their dinner." I paused, wondering if I should raise the subject or not. I decided to risk it. "Although I understand that one of the girls here died after a monkey bit her."

Naime stared at me.

"Who told you that?"

"Well…" I could hardly reveal that the intelligence came from the Sultan.

"Ha! From your maid, I suppose. The slaves must have been chattering among themselves." I could tell she was suddenly angry. "The monkey had a sickness. Kumru was playing with it and it bit her finger. She got ill afterwards."

"And died."

"Yes."

"I am sorry to hear it," I said.

"It was God's will."

"I hope," I continued. "No one will get into trouble. Madeleine meant no harm telling me."

Naime made a dismissive gesture with her hand. "It is not worth troubling about. Kumru was a silly girl."

Given her reaction, to ask about the others would hardly be prudent. Indeed, I was rather surprised at the change in her mood and tried to distract her by asking about the zebra even though I knew quite well what it was,

"Is it a horse? I have never seen one with that colouring."

To my relief, she laughed again.

"A horse! Not at all, although the zebra must assuredly be part of the same family."

She then proceeded to tell me that the stripes on its fur were to confuse predators.

"Among high grasses," she said, "they cannot be seen so well... I suppose you have never been to Africa, Madame Hudson."

"Alas, no."

"I should love to go."

The poor girl. Did she ever even leave the palace? I thought it would not be rude to ask that at least.

"Oh, sometimes. We used to go down to the bazaar to shop. Although in the last year, since the Armenian troubles, my father has forbidden us, for our own safety."

And his, I reckoned.

The next two days passed in much the same way, bathing, eating and sitting around. It was incredibly tiresome, and I began to think that I was wasting both my time and the Sultan's money, since I seemed no nearer finding out more about those mysterious deaths. The palace ladies, apart from Naime, while undeniably polite to me, kept their distance, so there was little likelihood of any confidences. Indeed, from various remarks she made, I felt that Bedrifelek suspected I was not what I seemed. She quizzed me occasionally regarding the British aristocracy and their habits, in a manner that led me to think that my replies fell short. At least, Madeleine was able to make some progress. It turned out that most of the slaves and concubines could speak French after all, and one or two of them, including the nastiest of the lot, a certain Beylem, had suddenly decided to befriend her. My little maid was in high hopes that eventually they would open up to her, and that then I should at last have something to report.

It was not until the third day that, frustrated with doing nothing, I decided to take my knitting with me into the hall where the palace women liked to sit and smoke. Suddenly, I was surrounded by ladies wanting to know what I was doing. They marvelled at what was in fact rather plain work, although admittedly the jacket I was making for little Henry had a rather charming lacy edge to it.

Now they all wanted to learn how to knit. Puzzled eunuchs were ordered to go into town and try and purchase wool and needles. Seeing a chance to escape for a while, I suggested that I myself might accompany them. This was finally agreed to, the Sultan even permitting two of his wives to come with me, heavily veiled of course and travelling in a closed carriage.

The problem was that none of us had any idea where to find a shop that might sell what we needed. I suggested I might ask at the Pera Palace hotel (and incidentally leave a note there for Mr. H). Bashir, the eunuch charged with minding us, was doubtful, but, at the same time, was reluctant to go back to Yildiz empty-handed. In the end, the two wives were left in the carriage with the other eunuch, while Bashir came into the entrance hall with me.

To say that the charming boy at reception was confused by the request regarding knitting wool and needles, would be a gigantic understatement. He rolled his eyes and shook his head quite alarmingly, terrified, I think of the glowering negro, and it was a long time before he grasped what I was trying to ask him. Finally, I showed him the baby's jacket which I had had the foresight to bring with me. He again shook his head vigorously, disappointed that he could not be of help. However, a Greek lady happened to be standing nearby, and overheard what we were saying. She directed us to a stall in the bazaar whose Egyptian owner, she claimed, would be able to furnish us with the necessary items. Meanwhile, I quickly penned a note "to my friends" as I told Bashir. Since he had already seen me with Mr. H and Dr. Watson on that very first day, he gave me only a slightly suspicious look.

I was very discreet. I merely said in the note that I hoped to see them at church on the Sunday.

Without managing to catch sight of either my two gentlemen lodgers or any of my acquaintances from the train, I accompanied Bashir back to the carriage and we duly set off for the bazaar. Peeping out through a gap in the blinds, I could see that we were crossing a bridge over steely water. This had to be the Golden Horn, the river inlet dividing the old and newer parts of the city. The bridge was crowded with men fishing over the parapet, a quaint sight. We did not linger here, however, but were whisked along at a spanking pace, past a huge palace, and two imposing mosques set close together, to the Grand Bazaar itself. Naime had informed me that this vast establishment had been destroyed by an earthquake a few years earlier and only now was being rebuilt. Still, it looked lavish enough to me, a veritable temple to commerce, with arched arcades leading off in all directions and packed with all manner of little shops and stalls, aromatic with spices. A cacophony of voices bounced off the high walls, merchants calling out to passers-by to examine their wares. The two wives – please do not ask me their names: I had no idea who they were under those black veils – were clearly very excited to be out shopping. They lingered over stalls of gold bracelets and gem-encrusted rings, others of fine silks or sweetmeats, in particular that jelly-like confection we in England call Turkish Delight, but here endlessly varied in colour and shape. The merchant held out a tray of samples to us, and the wives selected some to taste which they discreetly slipped into their mouths under their veils. I did not think Abdul Hamid would be too pleased.

Bashir was as impatient as I to press on with the business in hand, but these were wives of the Sultan and could not be rushed. Impossible, too, to leave them be, unchaperoned. In the end, we managed to prise them away, their many purchases to be sent to the palace separately.

The Egyptian stall holder must have thought that truly Allah was smiling on him. We virtually cleared out his stock of wool and knitting needles, all held in dusty boxes at the rear of the shop, unwanted for many a long year, by the look of them. He could not stop bowing and smiling, and, as we departed, he bowed so deeply that his turban brushed the ground, his hands clasped in a gesture of respectful gratitude.

"Martha! Whatever are you doing here with these people?"

Good heavens! It was Eliza Dodds, accompanied by a tall, wide European man with a self-satisfied expression on his face, and an excessively thin woman, presumably his wife, together with a small peevish-looking child.

All four of them were regarding my companions with astonishment, the two black beetle-like women, the two huge eunuchs with their long robes, their tall headdresses, their gleaming black skin. I suppose, even here, in the heart of Constantinople, we must have made a strange sight.

"How lovely to see you, Eliza," I said. "Unfortunately, we are in a terrible hurry. Perhaps we can catch up another time."

With that abrupt riposte, I allowed myself to be swept away by a frowning Bashir, amused to imagine what Miss Dodds might be thinking: Had poor Martha Hudson fallen prey to those fearsome foreigners who abduct white women for their own nefarious purposes?

As we drove back through those massive gates into the precincts of the Yildiz palace, we passed a large man walking swiftly towards one of the pavilions. He was dressed in the flowing robes and turban of a Turk, and yet there was something about him that made me think that I had seen him before, though on that previous occasion appearing quite differently. But we moved on and when I alighted from the conveyance and turned to get a better look, he was no longer visible.

Chapter Eleven

Suddenly, I was the centre of attention, so many of the ladies wanting to learn how to twist the yarn into lacy shawls or elaborate garments for their children. However, I started them on scarves – not so interesting of course but easy to master – and most of them very soon lost interest. Finding they had to persevere, finding the jewels on their heavy rings so often got caught in the yarn, finding they dropped more stitches than they made, sent them into rages of impatience, and one or two of them even threw their efforts from them across the room, remaining in good humour towards me, at least. Nevertheless, a few of them, the more serious ladies, were determined to master the craft and we soon took over a corner of the hall, the only sound our needles clicking or my occasional advice. They even forgot to smoke.

Naime was not part of this knitting circle, though she sat by me, regarding us with indulgence, leaning back on the divan, sucking on her nargile.

Good as her word, she had brought some of her drawings and paintings down to show me. Many were meticulous renditions of flowers, quite well executed. I praised them, as I was surely expected to do.

"I had a tutor when I was young." she told me, as if she herself was now an old woman. "Mariam encouraged me." She rummaged among the sheets. "This is one of hers."

The watercolour depicted a richly coloured blue bird with a long thin beak, hovering beside a clump of orange flowers.

"A hummingbird," Naime said.

"It is quite exquisite," I said. "So where is Mariam now?"

Naime made a dismissive gesture.

"Gone," she said. "Long gone."

That was all. I knew by her manner not to enquire further, although my curiosity had been roused. Was Mariam alive or dead? And if the latter, did she die of old age, or was she taken somehow in the bloom of youth, like those other unfortunates?

This was Thursday. It passed in much the same rather dreary way as the others. Friday, however, was the holy day when the Sultan and his entourage went to the mosque, the day when he showed himself to his subjects in a lavish parade. As a woman and a Christian, I was not of course invited to join the palace ladies, but was permitted to view the retinue from a vantage point at the top of a flight of steps along the route, together with several other non-Moslem women, including one who introduced herself to me as Jeanne-Claude Cordelier, the wife of a French diplomat. She was most amused to learn that I had actually chosen to lock myself up in the harem.

"How can you stand it?" she asked. "Every time I go there, I cannot wait to leave. All that gossip and back-biting."

"I find it most fascinating," I replied. "And, of course, unlike those ladies, I can leave at any time."

I asked her how she spent her time, and was rather surprised to learn that she was a teacher.

"That is to say, the Sultan wishes for his children to learn to speak French, and has engaged me as their tutor."

"How many children has he?"

She laughed and waved her gloved hand in the air. "Twelve or thirteen, that I know of, but probably many more… Plus several grandchildren. I only teach the little ones, and some of the other girls, the slaves and concubines, you know."

I confessed to being confused still about the difference.

"Are they not all slaves?" I asked.

"Well, yes," she replied. "Even some of the wives were slaves once."

"Good heavens!"

"Yes, indeed. If a slave catches the Sultan's eye, she may rise to become a concubine or even a wife."

"Such a different culture from ours."

"Well, as to that," she replied, a faint smile softening the bitterness of her words, "is it not true that women, even in the supposedly highly civilised parts of Europe, are also slaves in one way or another, with only a few extraordinary exceptions?"

I nodded, even though privately I thought the two circumstances quite different. My daughter, Eleanor, is most active in the suffrage movement, working towards giving women the vote, the which would be a huge step forward in our emancipation. Just now, however, was not the time nor place, I felt, to enter into a discussion of the issue.

Jeanne-Claude, as she insisted I should call her, was a matronly woman of about my age, or a few years younger, in her middle forties perhaps, with a pale complexion and pale eyes, oddly combined with very black hair and eyebrows – dyed, I reckoned – that gave her a somewhat fierce look, immediately dispelled when she smiled.

"See," she said, pointing to an open landau, passing below us, "how the Sultan travels with one of his grandchildren."

"How sweet," I remarked.

She laughed again.

"Not really. It is because no assassin will risk killing a child."

"I see."

The Sultan's landau was followed by several closed coaches for the wives. What impressed much more, however, was the glittering retinue of infantry in blue uniforms and scarlet fezzes, more soldiers clad in what seemed more traditional dress, baggy scarlet trousers and black embroidered jackets ("Albanian zouaves," murmured Jeanne-Claude helpfully) beside the green and silver of the cavalry, mounted on fine Arab steeds. All of them armed to the teeth.

The surrounding hillside was alive with families waiting for a glimpse of their ruler. The landau passed us on and down a short distance to the mosque.

"The Sultan is clearly very pious, like his stepmother," I remarked.

"You think so? Because he goes regularly to the mosque?" my companion replied, softly, with a wry smile. "Not really. He pays much more attention to his astrologer. The *selamlik*... these Friday prayers... provide an opportunity for the Sultan to meet men who may be of use to him, to discuss Empire business. And, of course, to reassure the population that he is still alive and in good health."

"Is he? In good health, I mean? He looks ailing to me."

"Shh." Jeanne-Claude pressed a finger to her lips, a wicked look in her eyes. "Do not let anyone hear you say that, Martha. Of course, Abdul Hamid is in the best of health."

Oh dear. How careful one had to be all the time.

I was glad of my warm coat and fur hat, since the day was icy cold. Still, I shivered: someone treading on my grave?

"Let us go inside and have some coffee," Jeanne-Claude suggested.

I should certainly be glad of a hot drink, although the tiny cup doubtless on offer could hardly bear comparison, for me at least, to a rather larger restorative cup of tea. In addition, I had found that repeated indulgence in the beverage made my heart race unpleasantly. Nevertheless, when in Rome, and so on. At least, the drawing-room we entered was sufficiently warm for me to remove my coat.

"What is this place?" I asked my new friend, settling into a cushioned armchair.

"The barracks. We are privileged to be permitted to be here," she said. "It must be your influence, Martha."

I had not visited a barracks before, but I could never have imagined such a lavish setting for soldiers. I supposed the men who guarded the Sultan must be an elite corps.

We ordered our drinks from a young man in uniform, and talked inconsequentially at first. Jeanne-Claude was a cultured woman who was delighted to learn that I had spent time in Paris, which she missed, not, I was glad to hear, so much for its shops and restaurants, but for its museums and galleries, its theatres and concert halls. And yes, of course, she would be attending the performance of *Medea* in a few days' time. She had never managed to see Valentina Muratova act before, and now wondered how she would compare to the divine Bernhardt. On that score I could not venture an opinion, having never seen either on stage.

"Will the ladies of the harem be permitted to be present?" I asked, although I already knew the answer to be in the affirmative from Naime. However, I wanted to bring the conversation back to the reason for my sojourn in the palace.

"There is a special balcony for them," Jeanne-Claude replied. "For the wives, daughters and favoured concubines."

It was the opening I had been waiting for, and I raised, in as natural a way as I could, the subject of the recent spate of deaths.

"I was most alarmed to hear of it. So many young lives lost in such terrible ways."

"Yes," she agreed. "Shocking accidents." She paused. "I am rather surprised you are aware of it, Martha. These people tend to keep such matters hidden from us foreigners. I only know about it all because I was acquainted with the girls through my classes."

I used the same explanation as with Naime. "It was my maid, or slave (as I am informed she must be called) who overheard the gossip... You say 'accidents,'" I continued, taking the bull by the horns. "But can we be sure that is all they are?"

She stared at me.

"What do you mean? Why ever should you ask such a thing?" She looked about herself, but there was no one near to overhear our conversation.

"Such a series of unusual fatalities," I replied. "I cannot help but worry for myself and particularly for my little maid, Madeleine. I hope there are no homicidal maniacs running around the harem. We are so vulnerable there." Let her think me a gossipy fusspot, if only she could tell me something useful.

"I do not think you have any reason to be worried, unless..." She stopped, biting her lip.

"Unless what?"

"Nothing." She laughed. "It is all superstition anyway. The harem women love to see dark forces at work. They have upset you with their stories, Martha... Have you met the fortune teller yet?"

"No," I replied. She had shifted the conversation away from my initial question, and I did not feel, at that moment, that I could return to it. I was perturbed, all the same, by that "unless" of hers. Did Jeanne-Claude know or suspect more than she was telling me? Still, I could hardly blame her for her reticence. We had only just met and she knew next to nothing about me. In such an atmosphere of suspicion and dread, why should she trust me? I asked instead about the fortune teller.

"There are many, but in particular an old gypsy woman they like to invite to come and read their palms, or interpret their futures from the coffee grounds in their cups."

"I have heard of reading tea leaves, but reading coffee grounds is new to me."

Jeanne-Claude smiled and took my empty cup. She upended it, turned it back and then peered into it. A frown darkened her face.

"Aha," she said. "I see a man approaching. He is known to you, but you must beware of him. Keep away. Leave well alone." She gave me my cup back, still frowning deeply and shaking her head. Then burst out laughing at the sight of my face. "That's the sort of thing the old crone tells them."

I laughed too, and looked into my cup which seemed to me to show nothing more than a random scattering of grounds. At the same time, I could not help but wonder if Jeanne-Claude were giving me a warning. It seemed one was not supposed to ask too many questions around here. Not for the first time, I began to despair of ever fulfilling my assignment.

To tread on what I judged would be safer ground, I turned the conversation to Yildiz itself.

"Not what I was expecting at all," I said. "By no means my idea of a royal palace. More a city within a city. How many people live there, do you know?"

"Several thousand, I believe," Jeanne-Claude replied.

"So many!"

"Yes, indeed. Taking into account the ministers and their families, the soldiers, the servants and hangers-on, the wives and children, the concubines and slaves. They say there are three hundred musicians alone. A city within a city as you say."

"Yet so remote from the real one, Constantinople itself. From its people."

"Sultan Abdul Hamid is terrified of assassination." (I knew this already of course, but let her speak). "You saw how he takes his grandchild with him in the carriage for protection. Apart from the necessary Friday visits to the mosque, to show his citizens he is still alive and well, he seldom ventures out. The Sultan sees enemies everywhere, which is why he moved the entire court from Dolmabanche palace, vulnerably exposed on the Bosphorus, up to

Yildiz. They say the hill contains a maze of tunnels and secret passages, in case he ever needs to make a quick escape."

"The poor man. Imagine having to live like that all the time, in fear of his life!"

"Poor man! Do you not know that he snatched the throne from his older brother, Murad, the legitimate heir, who now rots in a gilded cell in Cheragan Palace at the foot of the hill? Abdul Hamid lives in dread that certain elements will try to reinstate his brother some day, although anyone who tried it in the past was brutally butchered." Jeanne-Claude had suddenly changed from a polite French lady into a veritable Fury, careless of her words. But as suddenly, she changed back, no doubt regretting that she had shown her hand so openly. "Of course, they say Murad is a gibbering idiot, an addict of hashish and alcohol. Still, this is the sort of ruler you are calling poor. Abdul Hamid does not deserve your pity, Martha."

She sipped at her sherbet drink. Since I said nothing, she added after a while. "Apologies for my outburst…" Then lowered her voice to a whisper. "You asked about the accidents and maybe you are right to question them. I should not be one bit surprised to learn that the Sultan himself is behind it all."

"The Sultan! Why ever would he do such a thing?"

"Who knows exactly? He is an explosive combination. A jealous and vengeful man." She shook her head. "I was especially fond of Ayla and find it difficult to believe the ridiculous tale that she accidentally shot herself while playing with a gun. Whose gun? How ever did she get hold of such a thing? In any case, it is not something she would ever have done."

"So what are you saying? Surely not that the Sultan had anything to do with her death."

She paused. Then looked up at me under those black brows. "It would not be the first time he has wreaked a fatal vengeance on one he thought had betrayed him… But Martha, say nothing of this to anyone. It is more than your life and mine are worth."

I promised easily. After all, I knew full well that Abdul Hamid was not behind the recent deaths, or why would he have employed Mr. H and myself to investigate? No, he regarded them with a superstitious horror. All the same, it was most interesting, I thought, that if blame were to be laid on anyone for the deaths, in Jeanne-Claude's opinion, it was Abdul Hamid himself who was responsible, even if he got his minions to do the actual deed. Perhaps this was a common suspicion, and, if so, were the poor girls simply pawns in a vicious game to discredit the Sultan? So many possibilities to consider. My head was reeling.

The young officer entered at that point to ask if we wished for more refreshment. We declined the offer, and shortly after went our separate ways, Jeanne-Claude admonishing me again to say nothing to anyone of our conversation and not to ask too many questions.

Chapter Twelve

On Saturday, Naime offered to show me round the porcelain factory, an offer I jumped at. Time was hanging heavy on my hands, frustrated as I was on all sides in any attempt to further my investigation. This outing would provide a pleasant break from that, and from the perfumed confinement of the harem.

Accompanied by the inevitable Bashir, we travelled not on foot but in a carriage, since the distance was farther than would be comfortable to walk in such inclement weather, it having snowed again overnight. The journey to the edge of the outer gardens took about ten minutes, towards a red brick building with the tall tower I had previously remarked from afar. Set with white stones and those colourful ceramic tiles the Turks seem to like so much, it looked nothing like a workaday factory to me, and more like a medieval castle with fanciful oriental embellishments. Yet this was assuredly the place, for the carriage stopped by its imposing entrance way, and Bashir helped Naime and myself alight.

The tower contained the administrative offices of the enterprise. We were met there by the manager, one Nazim Pasha, who welcomed us into his rather splendid office, a fine Persian carpet covering the floor, the walls holding shelves laden with, I presumed, examples of the products of the factory – vases, plates, bowls, trays – all extravagantly decorated in bright colours. It was also pleasantly warm within, thanks to a stove set in the middle of the room.

The manager was a fine figure of a Turkish man, middle-aged, wearing a fez and military uniform bedecked with medals, and sporting an impressive grey moustache that curled right up at the ends. He had been sitting at a desk covered with papers, but rose at our entry. He bowed to Naime and greeted me, then summoned the foreman, a Frenchman, a M. Tharet, to show us round.

I was, indeed, rather surprised to find so many Frenchmen employed in the factory, and questioned our guide about it. He explained that it was the French ambassador himself who had suggested that the Sultan set up a factory on the lines of the Sèvres porcelain factory.

"Nonsense," Naime interrupted. "My father had the idea all by himself."

The foreman bowed, a twinkle in his eye.

"As you will, Highness," he said. "All the same, you must agree that the expertise comes from France."

"That is true," she replied, "but soon enough our people will not only equal the productions of your Sèvres factory, but bypass them."

He nodded again, not about to contradict the daughter of the Sultan.

He had brought us into the workshop, a long narrow block filled with men busy at tables set with objects of the purest white porcelain, to be prepared for painting. Personally, I found these more beautiful than the finished pieces, which seemed rather overly flamboyant for my taste. However, I duly admired all I saw, for it was indeed amazingly skilful.

Particularly exquisite was the work of one M. Nicot, an artist just then employed in painting on to a rectangular plate a sunset landscape with a river and ruined castle. I could hardly imagine using the thing for its customary purpose. Indeed, I rather smiled to myself at the thought of serving my lodgers chops and gravy on such a fine dish.

113

"M. Nicot is most talented," Naime conceded, "but I think you will find that our own Halid Naci Bey is at least his equal."

She led me to another table where a man was painting a similar landscape on to another plate, a scene by a river with another ruined castle, though this time by moonlight.

"Delightful," I said.

"So which do you like the best?" Naime asked.

"I couldn't possibly say. They are both charming."

"But which would you choose for yourself?"

"Well," I replied diplomatically, "the moonlit scene is most atmospheric."

I think she was smiling with satisfaction under her veil.

M. Tharet led us to the far end of the room where a man was mixing something in a large vat.

"This is our mud-maker," the foreman explained.

Had I heard a-right?

"He makes mud?" I asked, peering into the vat. It indeed looked to be mud, or perhaps it more resembled the mixture I get when creaming butter, eggs and molasses to make a gingerbread cake.

My two companions laughed.

"This is the raw material," M. Tharet told me. "Clay, water and… well, the rest of it is a secret known only to the select few. The Chinese, who invented porcelain, guarded the same secret for centuries, you know."

"We only use Turkish clay here," Naime added.

"Yes," the foreman replied. "At first we imported clay from France, but soon found that there is perfectly good clay here too."

"Of course, there is."

M. Tharet then led us into the back room of the factory, where the pieces were fired. Two great kilns (French ones!) stood against the walls. It was unpleasantly hot here, reminding me of the oast houses of Kent, so recently visited by me, where kilns dry the hops ready for turning them into beer. The circumstances around that particular trip were so beset with bad memories that I tried to put them from me, and was glad that we did not linger in this place.[4]

On venturing back into the long workshop, we observed that new visitors had arrived at the far end. I was most surprised to see the Sultan himself, with a small entourage, including the manager, Nazim Pasha.

"Papa!" Naime called out.

I feared that His Highness would be displeased at the informality of his daughter. However, the Sultan turned at the voice with a warm smile.

"Is it Naime Hanim?" He called back, and I recalled that she was his favourite.

We hurried down to greet him.

He gave me a vague look.

"Ah yes. Madame... er... You are welcome. I trust you have enjoyed the tour of my factory."

"Exceedingly, Your Highness," I replied. "Such beautiful objects."

One of his companions, a large man in Turkish garb with a turban and long robe, was turned away from us, examining the porcelain pieces on the table beside him. At the sound of my voice, however, he turned abruptly. I started. For despite the foreign garb, despite the fact that his beard was shaven to the skin and all that remained was a blond moustache, I could not doubt but that before me stood the Baron Maupertuis. I suddenly realised that it must have been he I had previously half recognised in the palace grounds.

Before I could say a word, he gave a slight bow and said, "How pleasant to make your acquaintance, madame. I don't think we have met before."

What could I say? That we had, so very recently? Contradict him in front of the Sultan?

---

[4] See *Death in the Garden of England,* MX publications 2023.

The Baron took my hand before I could withdraw it, and raised it to his lips.

"Schmidt Pasha," he said.

"Martha Hudson," I replied, mystified both by his appearance and by his nom de plume.

"Marta! A lovely name." The Baron was still holding my hand, rather too tightly, and gazing into my eyes.

"Indeed," said the Sultan. "There is a fine opera of that name. I have tried to invite Adelina Patti here many times to sing the title role, but alas."

"It is an opera full of disguises, as I remember," I said, at last managing to pull my hand away.

"Yes. Everyone is in disguise." The Baron smiled broadly, revealing that gold canine of his. "For interesting reasons, I think."

The following silence was broken by the Sultan, who said something rapidly in Turkish to a fez-crowned young man standing beside him.

"You must allow me, madame, to present you with a souvenir of your visit."

He smiled broadly when the young man soon returned with two circular plates bearing, I rather regretted to see, not some charming landscape, but a likeness of the Sultan himself. He presented one to me and one to "Schmidt Pasha".

"You are too generous, Your Highness," I said, dropping into a curtsey.

"I shall treasure it forever," added the Baron.

"I trust," the Sultan continued, addressing me, "you are having a profitable stay, madame."

"It is all most enlightening," I replied.

"You do not feel," he gave a weak chuckle, "too constrained? It must be so different from your life in London."

"Thank you, Your Majesty, but I am enjoying the chance to relax. Your daughter is most attentive to my needs."

"Madame Hudson wishes to attend church tomorrow, Papa," Naime said. "I have told her that of course she may."

The Sultan nodded. "Of course."

Naime then asked if I had seen enough. Was I ready to return to the harem?

"Yes, indeed. It has been most instructive. M. Tharet is an excellent guide."

She turned to the Sultan.

"Dearest Papa," she said in cajoling tones. "I wonder might I stay with you here for a while. I love to watch the artists at work and I am sure Madame Hudson will not mind." She looked at me, and I smiled agreement. "Bashir can take you back, madame."

The eunuch had lurked all the time behind us, during our visit, like a dark shadow.

Now the Sultan looked thoughtful.

"Well," he said at last, "if Bashir can return straight away for you, I suppose that will be permissible."

"Oh Papa," she laughed, "as if I cannot make my own way through the gardens. It is not so very far. And I love walking in the snow."

He tightened his lips. "Bashir will return for you, Naime Hanim," adding something sternly to her in Turkish.

She bowed her head, and I left then, with the eunuch, my head buzzing with questions and notions. Whatever was the Baron up to? No good, I was sure. At least I should now have something solid to impart to Mr. H when next I met him.

Chapter Thirteen

The following day, being Sunday, I prepared to go to church, sanctioned by the Sultan. The trouble, as I soon discovered, was that none of the services were in English or even in French. And none were Protestant. I had a choice then, between Roman Catholic (in Latin), Greek Orthodox, Armenian or Bulgarian. I opted for the Greek church simply because it was the nearest. I was also conscious of the fact that, in my note to Mr. H, I had only mentioned "church," and not which one, which was most remiss of me. I could only hope that he would track me down.

Madeleine and I duly set off in a landau driven, for once, not by Bashir, but by another eunuch, equally big and black and scowling, down the hill from Yildiz to that part of the city known as Taksim, bumping over cobblestones and chilled by the continuing inclement weather, the snow having turned to that unpleasant rain that seems to seep into one's very bones. Some of the men in the streets, and there were only men, wore Western clothes but most were dressed in the Turkish style I had become accustomed to seeing. Many of them sat at tables under awnings in cafes, we travelling slowly enough for me to note that some were playing dominos or chess, or something I recognised, from its distinctive board, as backgammon. I decided to ask if such games were to be found in the harem, since it would be a good way to pass long hours there, and, at the same time, chat to the wives and concubines in a casual way, for up to now, apart from my little knitting group, most still kept their distance and regarded me with suspicion.

Madeleine had fared a little better, having befriended some of the slaves, including Gulsima and the previously hostile Beylem. However, she had managed no better than I to extract any useful information from any of them.

"They don't want to talk about it, madame," Madeleine informed me. "Or they make jokes," adding perceptively, "I think they are scared."

"Which suggests they don't believe the deaths are accidental."

"No..." Madeleine gave a little frown. "They talk a lot about the evil eye."

"The evil eye?"

"Yes. Beylem gave me this and told me to wear it at all times." She produced a glass bead hanging on a thin ribbon around her neck. Concentric ovals of dark blue, pale blue and white, with a dark blue spot in the centre, gave it the stylised appearance of an eye.

"Is that evil, then?" I was puzzled.

"No, not this. It is an eye for an eye, you see... To ward off the evil." She laughed. "Beylem said I should beware of you, because you have blue eyes, and could put a curse on me with a look."

"Good heavens!" I wondered if that was why the wives and concubines were so reluctant to talk to me.

"They don't mind me, because I have brown eyes," Madeleine continued.

"Mind you, most of the wives are blue-eyed, too," I said.

"That's because they aren't Turkish, they are Circassian, from the Caucasus. But their eyes are pale, while yours, madame, are darker and more vivid."

Good heavens. The girl already knew so much more than me.

By now, we had reached the church of Hagia Triada, which proved to be a huge domed construction of grey stone. The interior was so highly decorated that, even if Madeline and I did not understand a word of the service, at least there was plenty to look at. There had to be many Greeks living in the city because the place was already very full. I could see no sign of Mr. H or Dr. Watson, however, though it was early yet and I had been warned that the service might take some time. We found seats for ourselves at the back under a huge chandelier, where we could easily observe anyone else entering.

Eventually, men and boys in black robes filed in to the choir stalls, and three priests in richly ornamented vestments, white embroidered with gold, came out in front of the altar screen, swinging their censers. The air was soon pungent with incense. And then the chanting started. It was enough to cause shivers to run through me, the sound so ancient and primitive.

To say that what we experienced that morning was unlike any Christian service I have ever attended, would be quite the understatement. If I closed my eyes, I felt that I was being transported back to the days of the Byzantine empire. When I opened them, however, the architecture of this recently constructed building, though also echoing earlier days, returned me to the nineteenth century.

Not only was the service strange to me, it was very long. Madeleine fidgeted on the hard seat beside me, and after an hour, I decided that enough was enough. There was still no sign of Mr. H or Dr. Watson, and I feared they must be awaiting me in another church altogether. Or else that the hotel receptionist had failed to pass on my message.

We were not the only people leaving. In fact, the congregation was something of a moveable feast, people arriving and departing all the time, so there was no need to feel any more conspicuous than we already were in our Western dress, with my northern looks. Pale skin, deep blue eyes, and all!

Muttering excuses to the people sitting beside us, we extracted ourselves from the row of seats and started to make our way to the great doors by which we had entered. However, before we could reach them, I felt someone pull on my sleeve quite roughly, and when I turned, found myself, to my surprise and horror, staring into the unfriendly eyes of Baron Maupertuis – or should I say Schmidt Pasha, since he was still wearing Turkish garb.

He glanced at Madeleine.

"Go away, little girl," he hissed in English. "I need to speak to your mistress."

When she failed to respond, he snapped the same order in French. Madeleine, unimpressed, tossed her head and addressed me.

"Will I go, madame?"

"Not at all. This man has nothing to say to me that you cannot hear."

She folded her arms and gave him a challenging look.

"As you please," he said, "since your maid doesn't speak English, it is no matter anyway." He drew me into a side chapel, whether I wished to go there or not.

In truth, I was not at all averse to a conversation with the man. I might even learn something, and was hardly in any danger in such a hallowed and public place, with Madeleine standing by.

"I was most astonished to find you at Yildiz, madam," the Baron said, holding my arm in rather tighter a grip than was comfortable.

"No more than I was to see you, am I sure," I replied composedly.

He laughed and let go of my arm.

"I see you are not a woman to be intimidated," he replied. "Yes, I recall that much from the train. All the same, I am afraid you have lied to me. And not just to me, a mere underling, a worthless nobody, but to the Sultan of the Ottoman Empire."

"Oh dear. Have I? In what way, Baron?"

"As if you are unaware of the fact! All right, Mrs. Hudson, I shall indulge your feigned ignorance."

He smoothed his moustaches, tweaking the curled ends. "After your departure from the factory, I asked the Sultan who you were, and he informed me, in rather derogatory tones, I am afraid, that you were just another of those silly aristocratic European ladies who likes to dabble in the exotic orient and then go home with scandalous accounts to retell to your equally silly friends."

"How do you know that is not the truth?"

"Because you told me you were landlady to Sherlock Holmes. Hardly an aristocrat."

"But perhaps I was lying then."

He stared at me. Then laughed again.

"And what of your lies, Baron?" I asked. "Schmidt Pasha, indeed? Does the Sultan of the Ottoman Empire know that you are not what you claim to be? Does he know, for instance, that you have been in prison for perpetrating a massive fraud."

"How very spiteful of Holmes to tell you that! But you know, Mrs. Hudson, I am a changed man, here to make a fresh start. As I told you all on the train, I am come simply to pursue a humanitarian cause. It would be a terrible shame if I were to be frustrated in this by some meddling old woman."

"What did he say?" Madeleine asked, seeing my frown. I translated for her benefit.

"Monsieur!" This was Madeleine. "You are very rude. Madame is not old. She doesn't meddle."

I could not, of course, swear to the latter part of the statement but appreciated the first two.

For a moment, I saw rage bubble up inside the man, his fists clenched as if they would have liked nothing better than to knock the two of us senseless.

"Females should hold their tongues! Especially pert little skivvies," he hissed.

However, the moment passed as he regained control of himself, no doubt remembering where he was. I should not have liked, all the same, to be caught alone with him. But now he smiled so broadly that his gold canine glinted in the candlelight.

"I apologise, Mademoiselle. You are quite correct. Madame is not old. She doesn't meddle. Not at all. However, it seems to me it would be mutually beneficial if, under the unusual circumstances in which we find ourselves, each of us kept quiet about the true identity of the other."

I paused, as if thinking about it, and then nodded. Of course, what the Baron could not know was that the Sultan was fully aware of who I really was. I was not about to explain.

"I shall not betray you to the Sultan at this time," I said.

"Nor to Sherlock Holmes. Take an oath, if you please, madam."

I paused again before replying.

"Very well. I give my word I shall say nothing concerning you to either the Sultan, or to Mr. Holmes. On condition, of course, that you keep your part of the bargain."

"An excellent decision." He took my hand and shook it. I was glad to be wearing gloves.

As I turned to go, he blocked my way.

"Regarding what you are really up to, madam. Perhaps you will tell me, after all. Not now. Some other time. Our paths are sure to cross again soon enough at Yildiz."

"I assure you, Baron, I am simply fascinated, as the Sultan said, with the exotic east. If he mistook my credentials, then I am sorry for it, but it is hardly my fault."

"For now, I will accept your explanation. For now... However, there is one other thing."

I sighed. "What is it?"

"When I mentioned the name of Sherlock Holmes to the Sultan, saying that I too was a great admirer of the detective – how could I not be since he managed to foil my plans on one occasion? – and that I understood Holmes was to receive a medal of appreciation, the Sultan was most surprised. He said that Holmes had turned down the honour. Another lie, then, madam?"

"Not at all, Baron." Oh, how I needed to keep my wits about me with this man. "It was only on arrival here that he reconsidered, and decided it would be better to keep his connections to the Sultan out of the public eye."

"Yet he is still here."

I smiled. "He is most anxious, as I am, to see Valentina Muratova in the part of Medea. Something not to be missed on any account."

"And afterwards you will all return to London, I trust."

"You know as well as I do, Baron, that Mr. Holmes's plans are never written in stone. But I can assure you that our stay will not be prolonged further than necessary."

At last, some worshippers entering the chapel, I was able to sweep out, only to find that Madeleine was not with me. She ran out a few moments later and we rejoined the eunuch who was still impassively waiting with our carriage.

It was not until we had thrown ourselves back on to our seats and taken some deep breaths that we were able to look at each other and laugh with relief.

"Oh, madame," said Madeleine. "He is a very nasty man. He held me back and whispered such threats if we broke our word to him."

"I am not surprised. He is certainly plotting something, and is prepared to plough through anything or anyone that stands in his way."

"And yet," Madeleine continued, "you made a solemn promise not to tell Mr. Holmes."

She had understood that much.

"I did, Madeleine. But, you know, I made no such promise regarding Dr. Watson."

Chapter Fourteen

On our return to the harem, I received a most pleasant surprise. I had placed upright on a stand on a shelf in my room the plate presented to me by the Sultan, more out of a sense of duty than from the pleasure of regarding his face. In fact, I found the fierce image quite intimidating, and Madeleine liked it not at all.

"See how he stares back, no matter where you stand looking at him," she had remarked, on viewing it for the first time.

"That's the skill of the artist," I had replied, to which she just pulled a face, as if to say that the artist need not have bothered to be quite so skilful.

But now, we were both delighted to discover, set beside the Sultan and quite dwarfing it, the plate Naime had pointed out to me in the factory, the one depicting a moonlit landscape. Rectangular in shape, it was framed in gloriously worked gold ceramics.

"You could lose yourself in that scene, could you not, Madeleine," I remarked. "Imagine walking on that river bank, under those dark trees towards the old castle."

"That might be a bit scary," she replied. "I think I'd rather sit in that boat, looking at the distant mountains."

It was obviously a gift from Naime, and I was deeply touched, wondering, too, rather sadly, if regarding pictures like this was the nearest any of the harem ladies got to enjoying such a scene.

The immediate problem that faced me was how to communicate with Mr. H and Dr. Watson. However, that had to remain unresolved for now, since it was almost time for the midday meal, with all the rather tedious preparations that the ritual demanded, the washing and dressing, the combing and brushing, the choice of jewellery among the many pieces lent, or given to me by the Sultan, most of them far more ornate than I liked. I settled for a simple silver brooch, and, at last, was ready once again to face the Valide Sultan and the other ladies of the harem.

Over yet another excessively abundant luncheon, I was at least able to thank Naime for her gift.

"You liked it better than the plate painted by the Frenchman, didn't you?"

"I did," I concurred, as politeness demanded. "It is very beautiful. I was wondering," I continued, "if you ladies ever have a chance to visit such places."

"For our own safety, these days, my papa doesn't like us to leave the palace grounds," she replied, "but in the past, as the Valide Sultan has told us," smiling across at her step-grandmother at the head of the table, "there were picnics and boat trips on the Bosphorus. She has often described to us the painted and gilded *kayiks* – rowing boats, you know – where ladies could sit on brocaded cushions, admiring the landscape, listening to music, drinking sherbet and nibbling on lokum or baklava."

Naime had a faraway look in her eyes, as if trying to imagine such pleasures. "Grandmother tells us how they attached shoals of sparkling fish ornaments covered in jewels to the back of the boat, to fan out behind it as it moved forward. It must have been a wondrous sight. Of course," she went on. "in the summer, we can enjoy the delights of the lake here. You must come back then, Madame Hudson."

I replied, as politely, that I should love to, both of us no doubt realising how unlikely that would be. In any case, although I did not say as much, the lake was quite small and could hardly compare to the glories of the Bosphorus, tantalisingly visible in the distance from high points in the gardens, or from the palace's upper windows.

Naime proceeded to ask how I had got on at the Greek church. I described the service, she listening hungrily to my words. Then, considering I was not breaking any confidences, I added that I was surprised to meet there the man we had encountered on the previous day at the porcelain factory.

She pulled a face. "Schmidt Pasha," she said. "I did not like him. I hope he will not stay long."

"Why don't you like him?"

She looked wary then.

"I should not have said as much. I apologise," she replied.

"No matter, if that is how you feel. I have to say, I do not care for him either."

"Papa likes him a lot," she continued. "He is apparently a very famous scientist and inventor in his own country."

"Is that so?" Not as far as I knew.

"Yes, he has proposed some scheme or other to my father. Papa is very interested to learn more about it." She paused. "But I should not be mentioning it. It is supposed to be a secret."

God bless your indiscretion, my dear, I thought.

It now occurred to me that my meeting with the Baron was far from coincidental. He had of course overheard the Sultan giving me permission to go to church on the following day. It would have been straightforward then, for the man to find out where I was bound, or even to follow our carriage. The thought made me uneasy. Oh, Mr. H, where are you?

We were steadily making our way through the numerous courses on offer. I was particularly taken with a lamb stew containing almonds and dried fruits – apricots, figs and plums – and praised it.

"So good you like it, Martha Hamim," Bedrifelek called across the table. "It is called Mutancana, the favourite dish of Sultan Mehmed II."

"It is delicious," I replied. "The sauce is so unusually sweet."

"That is from our own honey," she said.

The Sultan's wife seldom addressed me, though I could not say that she was unfriendly. Just that most of the time she and the other wives were happy to leave me in the hands of Naime. Now Bedrifelek turned to the Valide Sultan, and must have told her how much the dish pleased me, for the old woman smiled back at me and nodded.

Now the chat among the wives, translated by Naime, turned to fortune telling. One of the wives, who was expecting a baby and who so far had only borne daughters, had been assured by a wise woman, as she announced proudly, that her next child would be a son. This news was greeted, I have to say, with less than the enthusiasm that might have been expected.

"Another candidate for heir," Naime whispered. "There is jealousy."

"Of course," said Bedrifelek, turning from the expectant wife with a sniff, "the wise woman is sometimes wrong."

"And more often right," retorted the other, looking smug.

The Valide Sultan then said something sharply to the two wives, who cast their eyes down, rebuked, and resumed eating.

"I have heard talk of an old gypsy woman who visits frequently," I said to Naime, "I should like to meet her. Perhaps she can tell my fortune."

Naime laughed.

"You are superstitious too, then, madame. I am sure one of her sort, if not the old woman herself, will be in the baths this afternoon, if it would please you to join us there."

I hesitated. Would I be expected to remove all my garments in front of the others? Modesty forbade it, surely. Yet unless I mingled more than ever with the women, I should never discover anything here, and time was passing. I agreed.

I had been pondering the possibility of using the same excuse as Lady Mary Wortley Montagu, whose letters as the wife of the ambassador to the Ottoman Empire, gifted to me by Dr. Watson, I had been reading with pleasure and interest. Visiting the harem, she was invited to join some ladies in the baths, but realised they would expect her to be as naked as themselves. Thinking quickly, she opened her blouse to show them her stays, which satisfied them that she had been locked into the garment by her husband, and thus lacked the power to free herself. I could hardly, as a widow, do the same, particularly since Gulsima knew well that I disrobed completely to bathe. My mind was relieved by Madeleine, who informed me that the bathhouse was as much a place to relax and exchange gossip as to wash, and that it would be acceptable for me to wear a shift.

"Although you know, madame," she continued, "it is most pleasant to be as nature intended."

"All well and good for you, who are young," I replied, a little shocked, "but I do not wish my old body to be scrutinised by strangers."

"Ha!" exclaimed my delightful slave, "but you are not old, madame."

Thus it was that, a little later, we made our way to the communal bathhouse. I am not sure what I was expecting, but not this. A vast hall of marble pillars, the floors and walls covered in patterned tiles, a skylight. Huge marble tubs with taps but no plugs. One had to wash, as I did in my private quarters, by pouring water over oneself and letting it run away.

Madeleine had explained this practice to me, as her own mother had explained it to her. Partly it stemmed from a horror of lying in dirty water. The chief reason, however, was that evil spirits they called *ifrits* and *djinns* were thought to dwell in still water. For the same reason, the ladies were forbidden to recite the Koran while bathing.

Apologies to readers who may be shocked at the following account, but necessity demands I be accurate in my description. My first impression, indeed, was not visual but sensual. A wall of wet heat, composed overpoweringly of heavy perfume and tobacco smoke, struck me the moment I entered, and soon my shift was clinging to me so that I might just as well be unclad. The indifference of the women – naked or nearly so, all shapes and sizes, and many of them revealed to be very large indeed, thanks no doubt to their consumption of sweetmeats between those heavy meals – soon overcame my shyness. Truth to tell, it was very comfortable to move around uncorseted.

I soon spotted Naime, like me in a shift, though while mine was white, hers was brightly patterned. She beckoned me over to a richly upholstered divan, surrounded by a crowd of semi-clad women, wives, princesses and concubines some of whom I recognised and acknowledged with a bow of the head.

"You wanted to consult a fortune teller," Naime said. "Here is Didem. She has the gift."

If I was expecting some old crone, I was soon disabused. Didem was young, beautiful in a wild way, black hair tumbling over shoulders covered with a heavily embroidered yet somewhat soiled jacket, slender brown wrists jingling with bangles, bare brown feet, with rings on dirty toes, emerging from those garments that in England we call bloomers. She was clearly overdressed for the overheated place we were in and yet not a bead of sweat showed on her face.

She studied me silently, licking thick red lips, while Naime spoke rapidly to her in what I supposed was Turkish. Madeleine standing by would surely be able to translate later. Then Naime called over the slave girl whose sole task was to serve coffee to the bathers.

She prepared some for me and Naime, according to the usual way, heating a small pot until the liquid bubbled up, and then carefully pouring it into each cup in turn, so as to create a froth on top. Of course, I already knew what would happen when I had drunk it up. However, the ritual was slightly more elaborate than that conducted by Jeanne-Claude. Naime showed me what to do next.

"When you have finished your coffee, place a saucer over the cup like this and swirl it round to settle the grounds." I copied what she was doing. "Then flip the whole lot over."

The other women smiled and nodded at me as I attempted the same, successfully enough.

"Take this coin," Naime said, producing one, "and put it on top of the saucer. It will remove the bad powers."

I saw that the coin was gold and did what I was told.

"You go first," I said to Naime, who nodded and passed her cup to the gypsy, whereupon the coin disappeared into the latter's belt.

Didem then studied the cup for some considerable time. Her predictions were, disappointingly, predictable. To sum up, love was on the horizon, although the girl must be patient.

Patient, I thought. What else could she be here where she had no control over her own fate? However, Naime seemed happy and the others smiled and laughed. No sign here of the hatred of the favourite that Madeleine had reported. Perhaps they all hid it well, or perhaps they looked forward to the day when she would marry and they would be rid of her.

Now it was my turn. Didem took my cup and peered into it. Finally, she raised black eyes to mine and started to mutter. Naime looked confused, and seemed to ask the gypsy something. Didem, still staring at me steadily, replied, whereupon the princess spoke sharply to her, the gypsy just shrugging her shoulders and placing the gold coin I had given her, unwanted, on to the divan.

Despite the heat of the place, I felt a sudden chill. I had embarked on this encounter light-heartedly, without any belief in the practice, imagining the gypsy must be a charlatan. But what if she genuinely possessed powers? My true position in the harem was supposed to be a secret, but could this woman expose it?

"She sees danger." At last Naime spoke. "Where there was light there will be darkness. She says you must leave at once for your own sake."

The other women were no longer smiling, but were staring at me, shrinking from me.

Making an excuse, which was in fact nothing but the truth, I pleaded that I found the heat unbearably oppressive, and returned with Madeleine to my room.

Once there, in privacy, she told me what had actually been said.

"Naime told the woman that you are an esteemed visitor, interested in Turkish customs, although you do not speak the language. The gypsy then asked if you were the Englishwoman, although I am surprised," she added, "that the gypsy had ever heard of England."

"Yes, that's strange." I thought for a moment. "Did she say 'the' Englishwoman, or 'an' Englishwoman?"

"Does it make a difference?"

"Probably not."

Madeleine screwed up her face quite comically in an effort to remember. "You see, Madame, Turkish is different. It doesn't have 'the' at all… But I felt that was the sense of it. That she meant 'the Englishwoman who is visiting.' But maybe not…"

"Never mind. It is probably unimportant."

"Anyway, Naime didn't translate for you everything the gypsy said." Madeleine paused.

"What else then?"

"She said you are not what you seem… That you have the evil eye."

Oh dear. I was hoping that the visit to the bathhouse would break down barriers between the women of the harem and myself. Instead, it had erected them higher than ever. No one would want to speak to me now. Mr. H would not be pleased. Even more to the point, nor would the highly superstitious Sultan Abdul Hamid.

Chapter Fifteen

I had hardly had time to dress myself when Naime rushed in.

"I am so sorry, Martha," she said. "That gypsy is a bad woman."

"Because she says I have the evil eye?"

"How do you know that…?" Naime was astounded.

Another blunder. After a pause, my resourceful little maid stepped forward.

"The slaves have been teaching me some words in Turkish, Your Majesty," she said. "I recognised it when the gypsy said *nazar*."

"I see." Naime remarked. "Your accent is excellent, Madeleine."

"Thank you. My teachers are very good."

"Anyway," Naime continued, "I told the others that it was not true. That you are who you say you are and that you are a good woman. That is right, isn't it?"

I hated to lie to her.

"Do you doubt me, Naime?"

"No, but…"

"But the others will. Isn't that so?"

She lowered her head.

"If I tell you something," I said, "will you solemnly promise to keep it to yourself for now."

She looked up at me.

"What is it?"

"Madame!" Madeleine's tone held a warning. I decided to ignore it.

"Let us sit down," I said.

I took Naime by the hand and led her to the couch. Then, keeping hold of her hand, I explained that her father had engaged Mr. Sherlock Holmes and myself to investigate the mysterious deaths in the harem.

"It seems the dead girls were all favourites of his. Your father, as I understand it, is very afraid of plots against himself, and feels this might be part of such a one."

Naime stared at me.

"Is this true?"

"I should not be telling you. Your father would not be pleased. But I do not want to lie to you."

"You have been spying on us!"

"Very unsuccessfully, I am afraid. I have discovered nothing. Now, thanks to this Didem, it seems I shall fail completely in my task. I might as well leave immediately."

Naime looked thoughtful.

"No," she said at last. "I was very sorry when dear Ayla died in such a horrid way. If my father has engaged you to discover if there is anything amiss, I will help you. In any case, I am better placed to ask questions."

"Thank you for your trust in me," I said, and we embraced warmly. "However, you must know there could be danger here. I should never forgive myself if harm were to come to you."

"Some of them hate me already, because my father favours me," she replied. "So, Madame Hudson, I am always careful."

Good heavens! Imagine having to live in such a way, in such an enclosed space!

We parted then, and I completed my toilette in preparation for the evening meal. I must confess, I looked forward to this with some trepidation, wondering how I would be received. My fears, indeed, were partly realised since I was greeted with downcast eyes. Even the Valide Sultan, who must have been informed of the gypsy's words, turned her head from me. Only Naime behaved in her usual friendly way.

The food was as lavish as ever, but I could hardly eat a thing, let alone savour it. I soon excused myself from the table, pleading a headache. I am sure they were all delighted to see the back of me. Instead of sitting in my room, however, I donned my fur-lined coat and fur hat, and took myself for a walk in the gardens. It would help me to think.

The eunuch at the gates of the harem could hardly prevent me, a guest, leaving the place, although I could see that he was most uncomfortable at having to make way for an unaccompanied woman. I made sure my step was confident and purposeful as I walked away, his eyes no doubt boring into my back.

The gardens were very dark with only a few lamps to guide me, and I began to wonder if I was being foolish. However, my eyes soon accustomed themselves to the blackness, which after all was not complete. A sliver of moon and a sprinkling of stars provided enough illumination for me to discern paths glistening with frost. I wandered without any clear aim and soon found myself crossing one of the many little bridges over the waterways that led to the lake. I decided that the view of this broad expanse of water would calm my spirit further, so I made my way towards where I thought it lay. I must have gone astray, however, for ahead of me loomed one of the many pavilions dotted around the grounds. Skirting it, I found myself in a woodland, the eerie shadows of the bare branches dancing around me, and the sudden screech of a nearby owl making me jump. Now, while I am not usually superstitious, I could not but think in dread of the evil spirits who, the Turks believe, dwell near water.

This would never do, and I tried to retrace my steps. However, it quickly came to me that I was lost. I had no idea in which direction lay the harem and there was no one to ask. Even the moon had disappeared behind a cloud. Moreover, I was getting colder with every step.

Perhaps before now I had not fully comprehended the extent of the palace grounds. Nothing looked familiar. The pavilion I came upon was not the same one as before. The bridge I crossed was not the one leading back to the harem. I found a bench and sat upon it to try to recover my sense of proportion.

There was, I reasoned, no call to panic. Vast though it was, there were limits: Yildiz was circumscribed by a wall. And Madeleine, on finding me missing from my room, my coat gone, would be sure to raise the alarm, wouldn't she? The eunuch at the door would reveal that I had gone out and not returned, wouldn't he? If I failed to find my way back before that, of course.

It would not do to sit still. The frost was biting into my face, my fingers, my toes. I had to decide which way to go, in the hope that it would lead me somewhere familiar. I stood up.

Suddenly, I became aware of murmuring voices. I was saved! I moved towards the sound, and soon discerned two people standing beneath a tree ahead of me.

Was it something about them that caused me to hesitate? They were so absorbed in each other that they had not heard me approach. Nor were they likely to see me, standing motionless as I was among the shadows of the wood. A passionate embrace and then the girl slipped out of her lover's arms.

"Gulsima!" the man called after her.

She ran back, and embraced him again. Then ran off for good, while he hurried in a different direction. Gulsima! I had not recognised her in the dark. How she had managed to escape from the harem I had no idea, but, assuming she was returning thither, I followed her path. There was no sign of her on the way, but with great relief I saw the walls of the building that was indisputably my goal looming ahead of me. After all, I had not wandered so very far: it had just seemed so in the thick dark. Nodding nonchalantly to the eunuch, I passed into the walled garden and then into the harem itself, most relieved. Perhaps Gulsima, I mused, had bribed the eunuch to enable her to go out and in.

Madeleine, curled up on my bed – snoozing, the minx – had not even noticed my absence. So much for her raising the alarm!

"I assumed you were lingering over dinner, madame," she said, sitting up. "My goodness," she added, "your nose has gone all red."

"It's the cold," I replied sharply, thinking, fond as I was of her, the girl took altogether far too many liberties.

I did not inform her that I had got lost in the park, nor that I had seen Gulsima there. Instead, I told her how distantly I had been treated by the other women at dinner.

"They are afraid of you now," she commented. "You with your evil eye."

"Thank you for that, Madeleine," I said. "You may make me a cup of tea for me to drink in bed, if you would kindly agree to climb off it."

"Yes, madame."

The following afternoon would see the long-awaited performance of *Medea*. More importantly, I would at last have an opportunity to speak with Mr. H and the doctor. Not that I had very much to tell them, apart from the unexpected and provoking appearance of Baron Maupertuis at the palace in the guise of Schmidt Pasha, an intelligence I hoped might compensate to some extent for my lack of progress in the other matter.

I decided to keep to my room for the rest of the day, continuing to plead a headache, an excuse I was sure the wives and daughters would gladly accept. My only companion, apart from Madeleine, was Lady Mary Wortley Montagu, whose letters diverted me pleasantly enough. I had long ago finished with *Jude the Obscure*, with some relief, let it be said, since it is a dismal tale that lowers the spirits mightily. Lady Mary was proving far more cheerful, as well as enlightening. Her insights into the life of the harem, relatively unchanged over nearly two centuries, I could recognise from my own experiences. What fascinated me, in addition, was her description of witnessing inoculations against smallpox, the horrid disease which had killed her own brother and afflicted her in her youth, destroying her complexion. She even arranged for her children to be "engrafted," as she called it. In this instance, at least, the Turks had shown themselves to be well in advance of the British.

The performance of the play was due to take place in the afternoon, to be followed by a banquet presided over by the Sultan for esteemed visitors, myself and presumably Mr. H and Dr. Watson included among the number. After we had partaken of a light lunch, delivered to my room by a eunuch attendant, Madeleine helped me dress for the occasion in one of the finest outfits chosen by Madame Celestine, a dark green dress of silk satin, embroidered with tiny pearls. If it was understated by Ottoman standards, to my mind it was all the more elegant for it.

"Madame, you look lovely," Madeleine remarked, adjusting the collar and setting a choker of larger pearls around my neck.

Out of respect for the practices of my hosts, who had something against women uncovering their hair in public, I allowed mine to be encased in a green and blue silk turban, a large emerald pin holding it in place. My reflection in the mirror showed me someone I hardly recognised, although the effect pleased me mightily. I looked quite the aristocrat I was pretending to be.

Madeleine then helped me into my coat for the short journey to the theatre, a building adjacent to the harem, whither I was conducted by Bashir. While I could not say the eunuch was friendly, at least we were getting used to one another and he had stopped glaring at me.

I had never yet entered the theatre, was prepared to be impressed and was not disappointed. The lobby was richly decorated in the oriental style, and already packed with a colourful crowd of visitors. It was warm, and I was happy to have my coat taken to the cloakroom. I then looked about myself for my two gentlemen, but instead my eyes alighted upon another familiar figure, Eliza Dodds, accompanied by a boy of about nine, the same I had seen with her in the Grand Bazaar. I suppose that I must have been starving for the company of Europeans, for I found that I was actually glad to see her.

Eliza blinked at me for moment, as if trying to place me. Then, "Martha!" she exclaimed. "Good heavens, it is you?"

I laughed. "Do I look very different?"

"Well…" She regarded me up and down. "I had not realised you were become so grand." Turning to the child, she continued, "Edward, this is my friend… Say hello to Mrs…. er…"

"Hudson," I said. "Hello, Edward."

The boy looked at me scornfully, uttering not a word.

"He's very shy, bless his little heart," Eliza explained.

In view of the scowl on Edward's face, I doubted it. Just rude and spoiled.

"Mama and Papa are here too." Eliza looked about herself vaguely. "Somewhere… It's all so exciting, isn't it? Do you think we shall see the Sultan?"

"Most certainly."

"Good heavens!" she replied with a giggle. "Whatever would my friends in Norwood think! Eliza Dodds hobnobbing with the Sultan of the Ottomans!" Then her puddingy face fell. "But Martha, I am almost fearful. He is very bloodthirsty, you know. And quite mad. What if he decides to murder us all, like he did all those Armenians?"

"Hush," I said. How foolishly indiscreet she was. In front of the child as well.

"But of course, you know him intimately," she continued.
"No," I replied. "Not at all."
"Oh, Lady Barnard said…"
"How is Cecelia?" I asked, anxious to change the subject.
A flush rose to Eliza's already ruddy complexion.
"She is very well," she replied in tones turned suddenly icy.
"Not here tonight?"
"No."
It was very definite.
"So Edward." I turned to the child. "Are you looking forward to the play?"
"No," he replied. Equally definite.
"Now, Edward," Eliza cajoled. "Of course, you are." She laughed, a little hysterically. "Mama and Papa thought it would be educational for him to come."
"Mm," I smiled back. I could not help wondering, nevertheless, how a play about a woman who slaughters her children could possibly be good for a young boy. I wondered too, where exactly Mama and Papa were at that moment, but, since Eliza did not seem to know, it would have been pointless to ask.
"Martha." Eliza leaned forward confidingly. "It would be most agreeable to meet you somewhere in town, if you have time. I should love a chat with you."
There was something so pleading, so desperate in her expression that I felt I could not refuse.
"I am not sure how much longer I will be staying on," I replied, "but I will certainly try. Give me your address."
"Oh, can we not arrange something now. I am free every afternoon for an hour or two while Edward has his music or French lessons."
I had so little knowledge of the city outside the walls of Yildiz, that I could not at once think of a place to meet.

"The Pera Palace," I said at last, the obvious choice. Since Mr. H and Dr. Watson were still staying in that hotel, I might kill two birds with one stone, as that unpleasant saying goes, by fixing to meet Eliza there.

"Tomorrow?" she asked. "At two of the clock?"

"Er... Yes. I'll try."

At that propitious moment, I espied the welcome heads of Dr. Watson and Mr. H looming above the crowds.

"Excuse me, Eliza. There are my friends," I said. "Good bye, Edward."

"Tomorrow," she whispered.

I nodded. The child picked at his nose, grimaced and said nothing.

I was not worried about Eliza, since I had already learnt how she quickly she panicked with little cause. Nonetheless, to escape from the cloying atmosphere of the harem even for an hour or two was an appealing prospect, especially now that I was being ostracised there. Without an idea, just then, how I could arrange to leave the palace precincts, I made my way through the throng to my gentlemen.

"Where were you on Sunday?" were Mr. H's first abrupt words. No how are you? Or you are looking well, or any such pleasantry. "Dr. Watson and I waited through the longest and dreariest service one could imagine, all in vain."

I explained that, among the many places of worship in Constantinople, I had decided that the Greek Orthodox church, being the nearest, would be the most likely for a visitor to the palace to attend.

"We, however," Mr. H replied sternly, "judged that you would attend the Roman Catholic church, as being the more familiar."

"I apologise," I said.

"Never mind, Mrs. Hudson," the doctor commented with a wink. "At least Holmes was able to practice his Latin."

"Forgo the foolish remarks, Watson, if you please." Mr. H said. "Time is short. Come over here, away from curious ears." He led me to an alcove behind a pillar. "So what have you learnt, Mrs Hudson?"

"Precious little, I am afraid."

I recounted as much as I had heard and suspected regarding the mysterious deaths of the harem girls, adding that no one seemed willing to discuss them. I also informed him of yesterday's encounter with the gypsy woman.

"Now that the ladies think I have the evil eye, no one will speak to me at all, except for the Princess Naime."

Mr. H threw up his hands in exasperation.

"How very unwise of you, Mrs. Hudson," he said, "to lay yourself open to such superstitious nonsense. Dr. Watson led me, wrongly it seems, to believe that you were a woman of some perspicacity and discretion."

"It was thoughtless, I know that now," I replied, ashamed, "and yet I reckoned that it would have the opposite effect and warm the ladies to me more."

"Which it might well have done," Dr. Watson broke in. "How could Mrs. Hudson know in advance how hostile this gypsy would be?" The dear doctor. Ever on my side.

Mr. H was frowning deeply, so I quickly changed the subject.

"I have something to impart to Dr. Watson," I told them, "which I had to swear on oath not to tell to you, Mr. Holmes."

"You intrigue me greatly, Mrs. Hudson," the detective replied, somewhat sardonically. "I shall take myself out of earshot."

I then informed the doctor of the Baron's unexpected manifestation at Yildiz, in the guise of a pasha.

"He forced me to swear to say nothing to the Sultan or to Mr. Holmes about him. However, he did not include yourself in that prescription."

Dr. Watson laughed. "How very Jesuitical you are become, Mrs Hudson! Now I suppose there is nothing to prevent me imparting the same to Holmes."

The which he proceeded to do immediately. Mr. H immediately perked up.

"Schmidt Pasha, you say! How absurd! And what in heaven's name is the man up to? No good, anyway, you can be sure of that if it is such a secret."

"Apparently, the Baron has presented himself to Abdul Hamid as a scientist and inventor," I said.

"Has he indeed!"

"Yes. Princess Naime told me that he and her father are working on something together. He has become quite a favourite."

"Then he will almost certainly be here tonight."

"Especially," Dr. Watson added, "given his friendship with La Muratova."

"Indeed," replied Mr. H, drily. "They certainly appeared to have an understanding."

The attendants were now ringing bells that signalled to the audience to take their seats, so we joined the queue ascending the magnificent marble staircase to the boxes. On the way, I spotted another familiar face, that of the Frenchwoman, Jeanne-Claude Cordelier, on the arm of a distinguished grey-haired gentleman I supposed to be her husband, the diplomat. She nodded and smiled a greeting, the which I returned, although we were too distant from one another to exchange any words.

It was odd, I suddenly realised, that, although Jeanne-Claude presumably visited the harem on frequent occasions for the French lessons she gave, I had never seen her there. I supposed there must be a special schoolroom for teaching, and dismissed the thought.

Once ensconced in a comfortable armchair in our box, I had leisure to look around me. By London standards, the theatre was small enough, allowing for a hundred or so audience members in the stalls, the space surrounded by elevated boxes, supported on pale columns. Below the stage was a pit for the orchestra, where musicians were already tuning up.

The overall effect was light and airy, the pale walls painted in stripes of cream, green and gold, colours repeated in the plaster work of the frieze that ran around the base of the boxes, while the high domed ceiling featured gold stars on a blue background, charmingly emulating the night sky. I expressed surprise that, although the auditorium was indeed striking and beautiful, one would not know one was in Turkey, since it more resembled theatres found in London or Paris.

"That is hardly surprising," Dr. Watson replied, "since, Mrs. Hudson, I understand that the architect is Italian, as, indeed, is the theatre director."

That information might not have surprised the doctor, but it did me, at least until I remembered how much, according to Naime, her father admired European culture.

The royal box, facing the stage, was still empty. Across from us were the boxes reserved for the ladies of the harem, clustering there clad in the black robes that covered everything except their eyes. They had to be uncomfortably hot, I thought, since I, even in my light dress, was finding the theatre stuffy.

While we waited for the Sultan to arrive, I tried to make conversation.

"What have you gentlemen been doing all this time? Have you made any discoveries among the Sultan's enemies?"

"Very few pertinent ones, is that not right, Holmes?" Dr. Watson replied. "Despite you having managed to infiltrate several opposition groups in your various disguises."

"It is most frustrating, not to say exhausting," Mr. H agreed. "There are enemies and plots a-plenty, of course, as the Sultan intimated, and I am writing up a detailed dossier of these for him. However, none can be linked so far to the palace deaths. This convinces me, more than ever, that the answer lies at Yildiz. We must continue to rely on you, Mrs. Hudson," He sat back, with something of a sigh, clearly exasperated not to be able to take over the investigation himself. Well, I was doing my best, under difficult circumstances.

"And you, Doctor," I asked, "how have you passed the time?"

"To tell the truth, I have rather been kicking my heels," he replied, "although, as well as the usual sights, I have managed to visit a couple of hospitals. What interests me is the degree to which doctors here rely on herbal remedies. Much more than we do. In addition, they provide free healthcare to the poor and indigent."

"Most laudable," I said, somewhat taken aback. If only such were the practice in London, where the poor suffered so dreadfully from curable diseases.

I told the doctor, then, what I had just read about the smallpox inoculations promoted by Lady Mary Wortley Montagu, as practised in Turkey before ever they reached our shores. It seemed, I said, that the Ottoman empire was more progressive than the British in this regard.

"Indeed," he agreed, "although, you know, Mrs. Hudson, it was an Englishman, Mr. Edward Jenner who refined the treatment, making it safer by using a cowpox strain instead of the smallpox one. Still, we may thank both the Turks and Lady Mary for her pioneering work," He glanced at his friend and lowered his voice to a whisper. "As for Holmes, he has found a case to distract him, unrelated to our investigation, which is just as well from both our points of view, since otherwise the stalemate regarding the harem deaths would have made him quite unbearable."

"I heard that, Watson," Mr. H remarked. He has, as I have often noticed, a preternaturally acute ear. "It is a small thing, Mrs. Hudson, a trifling case of a missing heirloom. Quite frankly, I should not bother with it at all if I were home in Baker Street, but, given your lack of progress in the matter which has brought us to this benighted place, it has provided me with a welcome diversion."

"There is the Baron!" I exclaimed, ignoring the slight, and indicating the Sultan's box, which at last was starting to fill up.

"Where?" Mr. H peered across. "I don't see him."

"In the turban and robe. He has shaved off his beard."

"Good Lord!" exclaimed Dr. Watson. "I should not have known him. Well spotted, Mrs. Hudson."

The final arrival was Sultan Abdul Hamid himself, greeted by cheers and applause from the audience, all rising to their feet as engineered by the palace guards, who were positioned fully armed, at key places in the auditorium, as if to say: Woe betide anyone not showing sufficient enthusiasm! I recalled Eliza's fears, and tried to spot her in the seats below, without success. Probable it was that she, Papa, Mama and Edward were in another box.

At that moment, the lights went down, the orchestra struck up the overture, the curtain rose on a scene evoking most effectively a palace in Ancient Greece, and the performance started. It was, of course, in French, in verse moreover, and Dr. Watson spent the first act fidgeting mightily beside me. Valentina Muratova as Medea, strikingly clad in a clinging garment of such a dark red that it appeared black, with a jewelled breastplate and a headdress composed of feathers and leaves, declaimed extravagantly, at other times entering into passionate embraces with her youthful lover, a muscular and swarthy Jason rather shorter than herself. She wept copiously when he finally headed off to find the Golden Fleece.

I was glad that I had a passing acquaintance with the original myth, for otherwise I should have been all at sea. The language of the play was far removed from the colloquial French to which I was accustomed. Nevertheless, I whispered the plot to the poor confused doctor, receiving dark looks from Mr. H for my trouble. But really, I kept my voice very low.

In the next scene, Medea, learning of Jason's intention to marry a new bride, plots revenge. Her rage, as presented by La Muratova, needed no translation. In fact, it was perhaps a little too extravagant. The curtain fell at last to ominous chords from the orchestra and much acclaim from the audience.

During the interval, we left our box to walk about, stretch our legs and look at other people. Attendants were handing out glasses of sherbet, as well as the inevitable bowls of sweetmeats. I took a drink but refused the other.

"Good evening, Baron."

I had not noticed our proximity to the man, which had no doubt been engineered by Mr. H. At his greeting, the Baron spun round, or rather Schmidt Pasha did, looking for all the world like a denizen of these parts, despite his blond moustache.

"Well, well, well, so you are still here, Holmes."

Mr. H made a curt nod.

"Of course, Baron. We absolutely had to stay on to see La Muratova as Medea."

"How very clever of you to penetrate my disguise. Although, after all, you are a detective..." The Baron glanced at me. "Unless, of course, a little bird told you." He smiled wolfishly. "I trust, Marta, you have abided by the other clauses of our agreement."

Meaning, presumably, that I was to reveal nothing of his criminal past to the Sultan. I nodded, and he turned back to Mr. H.

"I hope I can trust you too, Holmes, to refrain from discussing my misspent youth with anyone. As I have already told you, I am a reformed character now, and thus surely entitled to a second chance."

Despite his apparent bonhomie, the Baron's eyes hardened as he gazed at my companion.

"If you have truly reformed, then I congratulate you," Mr. H replied in measured tones. "Far be it from me to blacken your name without due cause. However," and he smiled back at the man, "if I find any evidence at all that you have reverted to your old ways, I shall of course not hesitate to bring this to the attention of the relevant persons."

"You need have no fear on that account, my friend."

Mr. H nodded, though frowning his doubts.

"Still waiting for the Sultan to present you with your medal, Holmes?" the other continued. "Or no, I forgot. You have refused it. May I inquire why you would insult your host by such a rejection?"

"It is no insult. The Sultan agreed with me that it is better that my services to the Empire should remain secret."

"Perhaps you are still in his service, then, my friend." The Baron's watchful expression belied his pleasant address.

"And you, Baron. Are you in the Sultan's service? Now that you have gone native," he added.

"Gone native, is it!" the man laughed. "Well, you know, gentlemen, I can highly recommend this costume, for comfort as much as elegance." He gave a little twirl. "You should try it, Holmes, if you have not already, of course. I know only too well to my cost of your own love for disguises. Ha ha!" He tweaked his moustache. "But no more of that... However, I see by your face, that you still suspect that I am up to no good. To have no faith in the redemptory possibilities of human nature, that is truly sad, my friend. As I informed you before, my presence here is entirely philanthropic. The Sultan, recognising my noble intentions, has been gracious enough to invite me to stay in the palace. An honour I notice he has not vouchsafed to you, gentlemen, although your landlady, here, seems to have met with more success." He turned again to me. "Let me, first of all, compliment you on your beauty and stylishness, tonight, Marta. Quite the English rose, is she not, gentlemen." He kissed his fingers. "Although I have to admit, I am rather surprised. I should have thought they would have chased you out of the harem by now." He raised his eyes to the boxes containing the Sultan's ladies. "Or perhaps they have."

"Now why ever should you think that, Baron?" I replied.

"Oh... I believe a little bird mentioned something of the sort. Something about an evil eye. Ha ha! These people are so superstitious."

I smiled at him. "Another little bird! Goodness! So many of them twittering away these days... But I wonder, was it, by any chance, a little gypsy bird of your acquaintance, Baron?"

"Ha ha ha! No, Marta. I know of no such person."

Despite his denial, I was suddenly certain that he had somehow inveigled the fortune teller into maligning me, though why he should do this was a mystery. Whatever his true purposes were inside the palace, the Baron must have seen me as a threat to them.

"No matter," I replied, "since, as you can see, I am still here. And, by the way, we are not so well-acquainted that you may address me by my Christian name. I am Mrs. Hudson to you. Please remember that if we ever happen to meet in the future."

I turned my back on him and walked away, the doctor and Mr. H coming after me.

"Splendid, Mrs. Hudson," the doctor said. "Wasn't she splendid, Holmes?"

"She was."

I was astonished. A compliment from Mr. H.

"However," he went on, "we must somehow undo the harm of the gypsy's words. The Sultan wishes for an interview with me after the play. I shall explain your problem to him, Mrs. Hudson, although he may not be too pleased to hear how little progress has been made in your investigation."

"Thank you," I replied. "Although, you know, I am inclined to suspect there is nothing to discover, that the accidents to the girls may be no more than that. That the Sultan is worrying unnecessarily."

"Hm," Mr. H replied. "It is true that Abdul Hamid reckons himself beset by enemies on all sides, real or imaginary... Well, we shall see. In any case, I should like you, as an insider, Mrs. Hudson, to keep a close eye on the Baron's activities. If he is indeed become a philanthropist, I'll eat my hat, and Watson's too."

The bells announcing the second half of the performance having rung, we made our way back to our box and settled down to watch the seemingly inexorable course towards the play's tragic end, when I started to notice something amiss. The fire seemed to have gone out of La Muratova, and she was speaking her lines mechanically. It was most puzzling. Suddenly, the diva tore off her headdress, and stepped to the front of the stage.

"No, no, no, it is impossible," she declaimed. "That I, Valentina Muratova, who have performed Medea all over the world, should be forced to give way to this. I refuse to continue. It is a travesty." She made a histrionic gesture towards the royal box. "Sultan, they have rewritten the play and made me change the lines. Suddenly the ending is to be happy. Ha!" She strode back and forth. "How ridiculous! Medea who is driven in a fury of revenge to murder Jason's new wife, to stab her own children to death, suddenly they want her to change her mind, so that everyone can live happily ever after. No, no, no, no, it cannot be! I will not do it!" And she marched off the stage.

Everyone sat frozen. Furtive eyes were turned to the box where sat the hunched figure of Abdul Hamid. After a moment, he stood up and left his box.

"What a scandal!" muttered Dr. Watson. "What now, I wonder? Will we still have the celebratory banquet?"

It seemed not. The audience, shocked, was being directed to leave, and shuffled out in silence. No doubt they would all have plenty to say on the subject later.

"Will the Sultan still want your interview?" Dr. Watson wondered.

"Let us wait and see," Mr. H replied. "Meanwhile, Mrs. Hudson, I suggest you return to your room. And be careful. You have made an enemy of the Baron, and he is a dangerous man."

So much for his initial assurances that my role would be without peril to myself. However, I was not dismayed, reckoning I was a match for any Schmidt Pasha.

"I will hope to see you tomorrow at the hotel, gentlemen," I said, gathering myself together, explaining how Eliza Dodds had entreated me to meet her there.

"Very well," Mr. H replied. "With any luck I will have good news for you then."

I found Bashir waiting by a carriage to take me back to the harem, although I could easily have made the short journey myself on foot. No sooner had I climbed in, than I was climbing out again. Once back in my room, I was soon joined by Madeleine, who was most surprised to see me back so early, and was eager to hear what had transpired.

"The girls are full of rumours," she said. "They say the Russian woman stormed off in the middle of the play."

"Yes. She objected to the rewritten happy ending."

"My goodness. The Sultan will probably chop off her head for that." There was a distinctly and reprehensibly gloating tone to her voice.

"I don't think even Abdul Hamid would resort to such extreme measures, Madeleine."

"Oh, the girls tell me he has done much worse than that."

"I don't doubt it, but surely not to a visiting celebrity."

She looked apologetic. "Of course, I don't really want Valentina to have her head chopped off or any such horrid thing. I was only thinking that then, you know, poor Katy can go and live with her beloved papa."

"Yes, one cannot help but feel sorry for that poor mite."

Madeleine helped me disrobe. Gorgeous though the dress was, it was so tightly corseted – and I am afraid the constant heavy meals were adding to my natural embonpoint – that it was a great relief to put on something looser.

"By the way, madame," Madeleine was carrying the dress to hang it up. "Gulsima has disappeared."

I stopped in my tracks.

"What did you say?"

"She's gone. Without a trace."

I sat down on the bed, my thoughts spinning.

"She had a beau, you know," Madeleine continued. "The girls are saying they ran away together."

"When was this supposed to have happened?"

"No one has seen her since last night."

But last night the couple had parted company, the girl returning to the harem. Had she risked going out again? I informed Madeleine what I knew of this.

"That's a mystery," she said. "Perhaps you can find out what's happened, madame."

"I?"

"Aren't you a detective?"

I shook my head. "I have never felt less like one," I replied.

Chapter Sixteen

I had more pressing concerns than the disappearance of a slave girl. The next morning, Naime came to me in haste while I was still eating my breakfast. She was wearing the *charsaf* that covered her entirely.

"Madame Hudson, you are required to accompany me immediately."

"Where to?"

"Just come, please."

It sounded ominous but I could hardly refuse. Had the Baron managed to persuade the Sultan to send me packing? Certain it was that Abdul Hamid would not be in a good mood after the debacle at the theatre on the previous night. Without even finishing my tea, I gathered myself together and hurried with Naime and the inevitable eunuch out of the harem and across to another pavilion, where we made our way along narrow passageways, arriving at last at a small, gloomy cell where an emaciated man was seated cross-legged on a carpet, eyes closed, in a posture of meditation. A long grey beard straggled down over his dark robe. He was wearing the green turban of a holy man.

"Abul Huda, this is Madame Hudson."

The man opened startlingly pale eyes, but spoke not a word nor made any gesture, his face expressionless. I have to say the circumstances did nothing to reassure me. Who was this person and why was I here?

"Abul Huda is the Chief Astrologer," whispered Naime to me.

The man beckoned to me to approach, his delicate fingers tipped with long nails. Someone who did no physical work, then. I knelt in front of him, he gazing into my eyes for a considerable time. I gazed back, wondering if I should speak or not. What does one say to a chief astrologer? In the end, I kept silent. At last, he addressed Naime in their own incomprehensible language. She smiled, and drew me away, out of the dark and prison-like room. All very mysterious.

"The best news," she said, as we made our way back. "Abul Huda has confirmed that the gypsy was mistaken or lying. You are a good woman. You do not possess the evil eye."

As if I ever thought that I did, but it was a relief to have it confirmed by such a peerless authority. Now, surely, the ladies of the harem would no longer turn from me. Mr. H must have managed to speak to the Sultan last evening, after all.

I informed Naime, then, that I wished to leave Yildiz briefly to go to the Pera Palace hotel to meet an Englishwoman who was in distress.

"I hope that will be possible," I said.

"Of course!" she laughed. "You are not a prisoner here, Madame Hudson. I shall arrange a carriage, and, while you are away, I will inform the others of the astrologer's ruling… Ha!" she continued, "I should not like to be that gypsy girl, if she ever dares venture back into the harem."

"Whatever do you mean?"

"Oh… Nothing."

"Do you mean she will come to harm?"

"Will she have her eyes scratched out? Of course not."

Did I believe her? I decided to broach the issue in another way.

"You do not like Schmidt Pasha, do you, Naime?"

She looked askance. "No. I detest him. Why?"

"From something he said to me at the theatre yesterday, I strongly suspect he was behind the girl's pronouncement. To discredit me, you know."

"I see." She frowned. "But why should he wish to do that?"

"A good question, Naime, and one we need urgently to answer."

What a change from the subdued life of Yildiz was to be found at the Pera Palace Hotel. When I arrived, it was quite buzzing with people, women chatting unconstrainedly with men and not a black-robed figure scurrying among them. Of course, most of them were Europeans, landed from the most recent Orient Express, excited to find themselves in such exotic surroundings.

I soon spotted Eliza Dodds, sitting uneasily in the entrance hall, and looking, in her plain grey garb, quite out of place amid all these butterflies. She jumped up at the sight of me.

"Oh, Martha," she cried, "I am so very glad to see you. I was wondering if you would be able to come."

"I promised that I would."

"You said that you would try. I suppose," she gazed at me fixedly, the second person to have done so that day, "you are having an exciting time at the palace."

"Well…"

"Whatever happened at the theatre last evening, Martha?" she babbled on. "Not speaking French, I could make neither head nor tail of it. Was it so very scandalous? Lady Barnard seemed to think so."

"Lady Barnard?"

"My employer."

"Ah!"

I explained how Valentina Muratova had suddenly refused to act the revised script that had been forced upon her.

Eliza Dodds looked puzzled.

"But aren't happy endings so much better than unhappy ones?"

I smiled. "In life, certainly. But that is not how the play was written. It explores themes of passion, jealousy and revenge..."

Oh dear. I could see I was confusing this poor spinster even more.

"I must say," she asserted firmly, "that, when I read a story, I like it to end well. People getting married and so on. Typical of that dreadful woman to stir things up. Remember how badly she behaved on the train, Martha."

"Yes," I said, trying to hide my impatience, "but I am sure you didn't ask me here to talk of Valentina. What is the urgent matter you wanted to discuss, Eliza?"

She looked about herself uncertainly.

"I do not want to say anything here, with all these people about... We must find somewhere else to talk."

Although no one was paying us the slightest attention, I decided to indulge her, and approached an attendant, asking in French if he could suggest somewhere quiet. He nodded politely, and led us to a salon area with comfortable armchairs. Two seats by a low table served our purpose admirably for, although there were other people present, no one was close to us, and no one was talking loudly. Most of the others present were gentlemen with their heads buried in newspapers.

"You are so lucky to be able to speak French, Martha," Eliza remarked. "I am afraid I have no language other than English."

"It is never too late to learn," I replied, smiling.

She frowned, and I wondered if I had insulted her by suggesting she was getting old. More likely, her frown was due to her preoccupation with her own concerns. Once we had settled and ordered teas to be brought, I asked how she was finding the family she worked for, guessing this was part of what was troubling her.

"The child is a monster," she replied. "He derives his greatest pleasure in life in playing vicious tricks, particularly on me. Lord and Lady Barnard are not much better. They treat me like the lowest servant, while the servants themselves are all natives, and stand-offish, and do not speak English."

"That sounds most unpleasant."

"Yes, but you know, I am well-fed and well-housed with a nice little room of my own. And I am paid much more than I could earn in Norwood, with nothing to spend it on. I will save as much as I can before returning home."

"So what is troubling you?"

"It is Cecelia," she said. "You asked about her yesterday and I could not speak in such a crowd... Particularly with the boy all ears beside me." She rubbed her hands together nervously. "She has gone, Martha."

Another disappearing female!

"Gone back to England?"

"If only. No, Martha. She has entered the household of a... a Turkish man."

Miss Dodds's eyes welled up. "I will never see her again. She is lost to me. Lost to all that we British respect and hold dear."

"I don't quite understand, Eliza. Has she married this person?"

"Oh, how should I know what they do in this god-forsaken country? She spoke of marriage. That is to say, she told me that the man had proposed marriage. But there was no church service. Nothing of the sort. She just packed up and went off with him."

So much for happy endings, I thought.

"Worst of all," Eliza continued, her disconcerting stare fixed on me, "she has become a Mussulman!"

She sat back, as if expecting me to be as shocked and horrified as she was.

"Is that so bad?"

"How can you ask, Martha!"

"Islam is a great religion, you know. I have been learning something of it."

It was true. Naime had been pleased to instruct me in the teachings of the Koran, and, while I could not always agree with the way the holy book was interpreted by the clerics, I suppose the same could be said of the way our Christian Bible is used to the advantage of the priesthood, particularly against women. At its heart, the Koran seemed to me worthy of the greatest respect.

"I hope you are not planning to turn away from the one true God, yourself, Martha! These Mussulmen are barbarians who carry off women with pale skin, fair hair and light eyes. Lady Barnard told me all about it. I pray to heaven every night that I myself will be spared their advances."

She pursed her lips, a stubborn look on her plain face, as if challenging any man to try to take such liberties with her.

"What about your parents? Do they know what has happened?" I asked.

"*My* parents?"

"Well, yours and Cecelia's."

"Ahh." She fidgeted in her chair, took up her cup and without drinking any of it, set it down again. "You see, Martha, Cecelia isn't exactly my sister."

Mr. H on target as usual.

"Oh?"

"No, Cecelia is an orphan I took into my care. I suppose it would be truer to say she is my ward. Not officially or legally, of course."

Rather old to be a ward, I thought.

"In fact," she continued, looking down, as if shame-faced, "I regard her, Martha, as the child I never had. Of course, as an unmarried woman, it would far too scandalous if I tried to pass her off as my daughter, and so it was just easier to travel as sisters…"

My heart went out to the poor lonely woman. I murmured commiserations, while admitting to a secret satisfaction that in fact Mr. H had been quite wrong about the nature of the relationship.

"Oh, Martha." She grabbed my arm. 'Cecelia is such an innocent." Now the tears were pouring down her cheeks. "Whatever can I do?"

"She is old enough to make her own decisions, I suppose," I replied.

"Old enough in years but not in wisdom… If I tell you she is a little simple, would you believe me?"

I nodded. Cecelia, on the few occasions I had met her, had not struck me as brimming with intelligence.

"I am sorry for you, Eliza," I said finally. "But I cannot see that you can do anything about it. Cecelia has made her decision."

"Yes, but I thought perhaps Mr. Holmes…"

"What?"

"Your friend…" She smiled now, knowingly. "I am afraid his big secret is out. Lady Barnard was full of the news. Sherlock Holmes and Dr. Watson here in Constantinople! You should have given me a hint, Martha. I thought that you and he… well… never mind what I thought."

She actually winked at me.

I sighed. It was inevitable, I supposed, that my gentlemen's true identities would come out, especially given Mr. H's most distinctive appearance, and the Baron blasting out his name whenever they met. It was unfortunate, all the same.

"I am sure, Martha," Eliza was saying, "that Mr. Holmes can get dearest Cecelia back for me."

"What?"

"Isn't that what he does?"

She looked so abject, so needy, I could not help but pity the woman. "I will mention your situation to him, Eliza, but…"

"Oh, thank you so much," She leaned over and rather awkwardly embraced me. The unmistakeable odour of moth balls rose from her garments. "You know, Martha," she continued. "I always thought Cecelia was like me. Not interested in harking to the seductive words of men. Instead of which she runs off with the first creature to pay her a compliment."

God forgive me, but I could not help but wonder, regarding Eliza's homely form, her ruddy complexion, her frizz of gingery hair, how many seductive words she had ever heard. However, I nodded sympathetically, not knowing what else to say.

After a prolonged silence, during which she stared hopelessly at me, I rose to my feet.

"Ah well," I said, "I had better go in search of my friends."

"Of course. I shall wait here to learn what they say."

"Oh no," I replied a little too quickly, for her eyes narrowed. "Mr. Holmes is a very busy man, Eliza. And he works slowly and painstakingly. We will be in touch."

I tried to leave, but she held me back with a grip so tight it left marks on my wrist for some time afterwards.

"But you don't know where to find me, or where to find Cecelia," she said.

"Silly me," I replied. "Write the details down for me, if you please."

She had already done so. I took the proffered paper and placed it in my reticule.

"You are my one and only hope," she declared, as I walked away.

Oh dear. Whatever would Mr. H say?

I returned to the hotel entrance hall to find some sort of a row in progress. At the centre was none other than Valentina Muratova, surrounded by her trunks and suitcases. She was shouting at the receptionist, while he lifted his shoulders and opened his hands wide in the universal gesture of helplessness.

"My dear lady," he protested. "It is not my fault. There is nothing I can do about it."

The altercation had attracted the crowd, among them, Dr. Watson.

"What has happened?" I asked him

"I am not sure. Something to do with her hotel bill, I think."

If the lady's performance on stage on the previous evening had been histrionic, it was nothing compared to the one we now witnessed. She swept about the hall, waving her arms in the air, the pink ostrich feathers on her enormous hat fluttering in sympathy. In loud tones she denounced the receptionist (a fool), the hotel manager, who by now had joined him (an idiot), the Pera Palace hotel (a dump), the director of the theatre (another idiot), the tinpot country she found herself in... Suddenly she caught sight of my companion.

"Monsieur Jean," she cried, and, much to his horror, rushed to his side. "Save me! Explain to these fools that their Sultan engaged me to perform for him, and furthermore engaged to pay all my expenses. *All* my expenses! These fools refuse to understand."

Reluctantly, Dr. Watson let himself be dragged to the reception desk. I followed.

The manager started to speak and wave his hands around.

"I don't understand," Dr. Watson said helplessly. "I don't know French."

Valentina looked about herself with wild eyes. She spotted me.

"You!" she said, grabbing the same poor wrist that just recently had fallen victim to Eliza's crushing grip. "You... I forget your name... but you can speak to them."

I repeated in temperate tones what the actress had just said.

"I regret, madame," the manager said, "that we have received clear instructions from the Sultan's Vizir, that the Sultan will not be paying one piastre of Madame Muratova's bill. She must pay it herself."

163

The lady herself intervened at this point. "Pay the bill! I can't pay the bill. Look," she said placing the offending document in front of me, "look how much…"

I observed that, apart from the basic cost of room and board, many extras were listed, from coiffeuses and manicurists, to an extraordinary number of bottles of champagne, truffles, foie gras, caviar from Beluga. The resulting sum almost caused my eyes to pop out of their sockets.

"Dear me," was all I could utter.

"Yes, it is absurd, is it not?" She seized the bill from me and ripped it into tiny pieces, throwing them up in the air so that they fell like the flakes of snow that were even now covering the city outside the hotel. "This is what I think of it."

"But surely your fee for the performance will cover everything," I said weakly.

"Ha! Ha!" she shouted. "Yes, you would imagine so, would you not. But this philistine of a Sultan refuses me my promised fee because I did not act as he wished. I refused to utter the inane words put into the mouth of the great Medea by some sycophantic word pedlar… No, no, no. I am an actress. I do not make compromises even for kings." She rose up, hand pressed to her bosom, to her no doubt fast-beating heart. "I, Valentina Muratova, at whose feet the crowned heads of Europe have bent in submission and worship, I have never been more insulted in my life. I spit upon the name of this Sultan Abdul Hamid the Second…"And she actually spat on the floor.

There was a sudden shocked silence. She had gone too far. Much too far. I felt someone drawing me away. It was Mr. H.

"We must not be associated with her," he whispered.

But, as we shrank back through the crowd, I spotted a huddled little figure, seated on a chair in the corner, shivering with fear. It was Katy, the daughter. I could not abandon her and broke free from Mr. H to comfort her.

She sobbed on my breast.

"Why is she always like this?" she muttered. "I hate her. I hate her so very much."

"Hush, child," I said, and stroked her hair, not knowing what else to do, thinking at the same time that, in her shoes, I would likely hate my mother, too.

"Well, well." It was Mr. H who spoke, shaking his head. "Look who has just arrived. The original bad penny."

I raised my eyes to see whom it was he meant. An all too familiar figure was making his way through the crowd: the Baron Maupertuis, dressed on this occasion in the European manner, a fur coat glinting with snow carelessly draped over an elegantly cut suit, a gleaming top hat on his head, an ebony cane in his grey-gloved hand.

La Muratova gave a great screech and fell into his arms.

"Now, now, Valentina! Whatever's the matter? Tell me, my darling girl."

She needed no further encouragement, pouring out her woes once more at length.

"Some mistake clearly," the Baron remarked finally. He drew out a wallet from his inside jacket pocket, and from it extracted a wad of notes.

"I am sure this will cover everything," he said, tossing the money down on the desk. The manager, judging the amount from the heap, nodded to the wide-eyed receptionist.

Then, tipping his top hat, the Baron escorted La Muratova out of the hotel to a waiting carriage.

"You had better go with them," I said to Katy.

"Can't I stay with you and Madeleine?" she begged.

"No, my dear. I am afraid not. But perhaps you can return to your papa when you get back to France."

I took the girl by the hand and led her outside, hoping that her mother had not forgot about her daughter in the heat of the argument, and was not about to leave without her. The irritable way in which she now told "Yekaterina" to hurry and get in, did not inspire confidence.

"To the train station," the Baron instructed the driver. "Fear not, Madam Hudson," he called to me. "I am not abandoning you, just making sure this lady leaves safely." He kissed his gloved fingers in my direction as they drove away.

"Good heavens!" I exclaimed. "What an unseemly spectacle."

"The two of them deserve each other," Dr. Watson remarked.

"Come," said Mr. H. "We must talk."

Re-entering the hotel, we made our way to the very same quiet salon where I had so recently met with Eliza Dodds. Luckily, she had already left, but still I explained her problem. Mr. H frowned.

"Did you really believe I might waste my precious time engineering the return of the woman's friend?" he asked.

"Not at all," I replied. "But I had to promise that I would ask you."

"Well, you have done so. Let that be an end to it."

For him, maybe. I should still have the unpleasant task of informing Eliza that Mr. H could not, or would not, do anything for her.

He then asked if I had further plans regarding the investigation, and if I was still being shunned by the ladies of the harem.

"You have solved that problem for me," I said, "I must thank you for intervening with the Sultan on my behalf."

Mr. H looked surprised. "In what regard!?"

I explained about my meeting that morning with the Chief Astrologer.

"It is not me you have to thank," he replied. "I did nothing. The Sultan was so discommoded by what happened at the theatre that he refused to see anyone last evening."

"Oh…" In that case I could only think that it was Naime herself who had ensured the restoration of my good reputation. Bless the girl.

I then explained about Gulsima, how the sweet little slave had gone missing, and, that though the general opinion was she had fled with her lover, I had the deepest misgivings about it.

"When they parted in the garden, I certainly did not get the impression that they were planning to meet again that night. Most strangely, it was as if she disappeared before she reached the sanctuary of the harem. I fear something bad has happened to her, as it did to the other girls."

"Interesting," Mr. H remarked thoughtfully. "Well, perhaps this will give us something to tell the Sultan at last. Press on, Mrs. Hudson. The lack of progress is most frustrating."

I promised to do my best.

"In the meantime," Mr. H continued with a sigh, "I suppose I must try and discover what has happened to Lady Barnard's missing heirloom."

"Lady Barnard," I exclaimed.

"What is it, Mrs. Hudson?"

"Well, just that she is the employer of Eliza Dodds," I said. "Eliza is governess to her son. What a coincidence!"

"Hmm," said Mr. H.

"Holmes doesn't care for coincidences," Dr. Watson remarked with a smile. "Though sometimes, of course, that is all that they are."

Chapter Seventeen

On my return to the harem, I found Madeleine in my room, trying to look busy, folding garments that had already been folded neatly before I left, and dusting already pristine surfaces. From a tell-tale dip in the bed, however, I could not but suspect she had been lying there a moment before I entered. No harm. I supposed it was difficult for the girl to find things to do.

"Any news of Gulsima?" I asked.

"Oh no, Madame. She must be far away by now with her beau. The others are so envious."

"Tell me, Madeleine, what did she take with her?"

The girl looked at me, puzzled.

"I don't know. Her things, I suppose."

"Could you find out for me?"

"Now, madame?"

"If you please."

She nodded and headed off. While I waited for her to return, I laid myself down on the ruffled coverlet to try to clear my head. So many odd things were suddenly happening. Were they all connected in some obscure way? Impossible to know as yet, but, like Mr. H, I was not fond of coincidences.

Madeleine soon returned, a grim expression on her face.

"Madame, she has left everything behind, her favourite dress, even her amulets."

That was exactly what I did not wish to hear.

"Will the others speak to me, do you think?" I asked. "Now that I am no longer cursed with an evil eye."

"I am not sure, Madame. You can try."

We proceeded forthwith to the bathhouse where the girls were assembled as usual when not busy about their duties, drinking sherbets and eating sweetmeats, chatting, plaiting each other's hair or anointing themselves with unguents. What an utterly boring and futile existence, I thought, not for the first time.

In my haste, I had not bothered to disrobe, and so found the damp heat almost overpowering. The girls viewed me with suspicion when I entered, although not with the overt hostility of heretofore. Word had spread that I was no longer someone to be feared. And when I informed them that I was worried about the fate of Gulsima, given that she had apparently left without her most treasured possessions, they even quite warmed to me. Why, after all, should a foreign visitor, a dignitary as they thought me, care about a mere slave girl?

I explained how, on the night Gulsima disappeared, I had taken a walk in the garden and had happened to see her with a man, her sweetheart. How, when they separated, she had run back towards the harem, and he had gone in another direction. It had not seemed to me, I said, repeating what I had told Mr. H, that, from the nature of their farewells, they had immediate plans to elope.

"However," I continued, "when I reached the harem door, there was no sign of her."

The girls inexplicably started to laugh and giggle among themselves.

"Of course not," the one Madeleine had told me was called Beylem finally spoke up. She was a rather fierce looking young miss with pointy features in a pale face framed with dark hair. "We don't come and go through the main gates unless we have permission, Madame. The eunuchs wouldn't let us."

"I see," I said. "So how did Gulsima manage it?"

They chatted then in what I supposed to be Turkish, until Madeleine gave an imperceptible shake of her head, as if to indicate that she was not able to understand, either. I knew that many of the girls were Circassian, and sometimes spoke their own language among themselves. Presumably this was what they were now using.

"Madame," Beylem addressed me finally in French, "we should like to trust you."

"You can, of course."

"Do you think something bad has happened to Gulsima?"

"Well, I hope not, though I understand that bad things have happened to a number of you already."

"Madame Hudson is here to find out why," Madeleine put in, rather to my dismay, since we had been sworn to secrecy. I suppose she reckoned if I had already confided in Naime, the rest of them might as well know what I was about. "You see," she continued, "she is a friend of the famous detective, Sherlock Holmes, and is helping him investigate the deaths here."

Now I was far from thinking that the name of my lodger would mean anything to these Circassian slave girls, but, as had happened several times before, in places far distant from this, it was as if Madeleine had spoken a magic password. They all smiled broadly, and some even seized my hands or touched my hair and dress.

"Sherlock Holmes!" one exclaimed. "We love him."

"He is here? Where?" another said, looking around as if to spot him lurking behind a pillar.

"Not here exactly, silly," Madeline said, laughing. "In town. Detecting!"

"We were so happy to discover he had not perished at the big waterfall," Beylem put in.

I must have looked astonished, for she went on to explain that his exploits had long been favourite reading matter in the harem. Sultan Abdul Hamid, had ordered that the accounts of his adventures, written up by Dr. Watson, be translated into Turkish.

Once the Sultan had done with them, he graciously permitted them to be read aloud to his ladies – wives, daughters, concubines and slaves – who enjoyed them mightily.

"Is Sherlock Holmes also looking to find out what has happened to Gulsima?" she asked

"He is occupied with other matters," I replied. "It is I who wish to find out what has happened to her and to be sure she is safe."

Beylem then took my hand with a conspiratorial air, and led me to a distant couch, looking around to make sure we could not be overheard. As cover, she proceeded to loosen my hair and comb it. I was taken aback but she had a gentle touch and it was far from unpleasant.

"There are secret underground passages all over the Palace grounds, Madame," she said in a low voice. "One even comes out here in the harem, although we are not supposed to know about it. I think it was built in case we needed to escape in a hurry. You see, Madame, the Sultan has many enemies who might wish us harm."

I recalled how Jeanne-Claude Cordelier had informed me of the same thing. "And that is how Gulsima came and went? Through a tunnel?" I asked.

"Yes, it is."

"Can you show me?"

She paused, considering my request. Then nodded.

"Yes, but not now. There are too many watching us." She indicated a eunuch, standing by the door, glaring at us suspiciously. "Tonight, late. I will come to your room. Tell no one. Not even your friend, the Princess Naime."

The final words were spoken bitterly. I nodded, although I was dismayed. Surely Naime could be trusted.

Beylem pressed my hand. "We were so happy to think that Gulsima had left with her sweetheart. But now…"

"Maybe I am wrong, my dear."

"No, Madame. She would not have gone anywhere without her amulets. To protect her against harm, you understand. Something terrible must surely have happened to her."

I could hardly wait for dinner to be over, even though the wives and even the Valide Sultan, were again casting gracious eyes upon me.

"I reckon I have you to thank for this," I whispered to Naime, who smiled back.

"Not at all, Madame. I simply passed the information to my father. He was most displeased. That gypsy had better not show her face here again."

"Did you mention anything about Schmidt Pasha?"

"No. I did not dare. That man is still very much the favourite and, after all, you had no proof he was involved,"

"That is true. Even though I am sure he was."

"You know, Madame Hudson," she continued. "He and my father are hatching some sort of a scheme together."

"So you said before. Have you learnt anything further?"

Naime shook her head.

"No more than I already told you. But Papa seems very taken with it, whatever it is."

"Well, please be so good as to let me know if you hear any more."

She promised to do so, then invited me to join her in the smoking salon after the meal. Pleading tiredness, I excused myself. I was sorry to deceive her, but had promised Beylem, who presumably had her reasons.

It was very late indeed when the girl finally tapped on my door. Indeed, I was starting to wonder if she were coming at all. Beylem was carrying a tray with a carafe of water and a bowl of nuts, in case, as she said, anyone should ask why she was wandering the passageways at that hour. She also carried a headscarf, similar to the one she was wearing, for me to put on as a rudimentary disguise, although I doubted that anyone would take me for a slave girl even in the half-light. Personally, I thought it would be better if I went as myself, since I was sure I could brazen it out if challenged, but Beylem insisted. She was also unwilling for Madeleine, eager to be part of the adventure, to accompany us.

"Better she should stay here. We don't want to be too many in the tunnel. And if anyone comes looking for you, Madame, she can make an excuse and say that you are sleeping."

I did not care for this plan at all. Far too many lies and deceptions. However, Beylem was stubborn on the point and I had to agree.

We set off cautiously, she slightly ahead of me, so that, again if accosted, we could disclaim any suggestion that we were together. Luck was on our side. We encountered no one, and, in our slippers, moved silently and quickly, soon reaching a section of the harem I had not visited before, the kitchens. Beylem entered first to see if the coast was clear, and then beckoned for me to join her.

Under other circumstances, I should have loved to spend time exploring this fascinating space where all our wonderful meals were prepared. However, I had not time to waste just now and hurried after my guide to a great stove set beside a tiled wall. To my amazement, Beylem squeezed herself behind it. There was only just enough room for me, rather larger than the slender girl, to follow. Almost immediately in front of us, I saw a steep flight of stone steps leading down into impenetrable blackness, and, to tell the truth, I had misgivings. Was I being led into a trap? I had trusted the girl, but perhaps unwisely. This was the person, after all, whose jealousies, I had once suspected, might have driven her to dispose of favoured rivals. And no one knew where I was.

Before my second thoughts caused me to go back, Beylem struck a match and lit a lamp placed just inside the entrance. She smiled reassuringly at me.

"This way," she whispered, proceeding downwards. "Take care, because the steps are uneven."

She was not wrong and I descended slowly, not much helped by the flickering lamp that was casting eerie shadows on the rough walls of the tunnel. Indeed, the effect was quite unnerving, as if we were being accompanied down by those same evil spirits the girls talked about so much. Things improved slightly when we reached the bottom of the steps and the passage flattened out. All the same, it was very narrow and I had to fight off the impression that the walls were closing in on us.

From time to time, we passed dark caverns, the entrance or exits of other tunnels. However, we kept straight on and, in truth, it was not long, to my great relief, before we reached another, shorter flight of steps that led up into the palace gardens. We emerged from an alcove behind a pillar outside one of the pavilions, which one it was I could not tell in the darkness.

"Nothing!" Beylem whispered. "No sign that Gulsima came this way. Shall we return, Madame?"

I nodded. What else could we do?

Beylem turned and I followed her reluctantly back into the tunnel. A wild goose chase, as they say. But, as the lamp flickered in her hand, something caught my eye at the foot of the stairs, some sort of a filthy rag. I caught hold of Beylem's sleeve and pointed at it. Picking the thing up, I found that the patterned fabric was stiff, and stained black.

"Is that blood!" I exclaimed.

Beylem was staring at it in horror.

"That's Gulsima's scarf."

"You are sure?"

"It is her new scarf, Madame. She was so pleased with it and showed it to all of us."

I took the lamp from the girl's trembling hand and cast its light over the whole area. By the look of it, dirt had haphazardly been kicked over the flagstones, but dark patches revealed a place where more blood had been spilt.

"Did she trip and fall down the steps, do you think, Madame?" We both knew this could not be the case. Where was her body? If injured, moreover, she could surely still have dragged herself back to the harem.

"I am afraid the poor girl was attacked here," I said.

"So where is she?" Panic sounded in Beylem's voice. "Where is Gulsima?"

That, I could not answer.

We made our way back very slowly, examining every inch of the tunnel for more evidence. Not far from the bloody scene, Beylem's sharp eyes spotted one of those charms in the form of an eye that had been given to Madeleine and that can be seen everywhere in Constantinople. Maybe it also belonged to the hapless girl, in which case it had not brought her any good luck. But it could also have been lost by anyone else using the tunnel. I took it with me anyway, along with the scarf.

Once safely back in the harem, Beylem showed me the way to my room, for I doubt I could have found it by myself. I invited her in. She was reluctant but agreed for a minute. Of course, Madeleine was awake and itching to hear all about our expedition.

"What will you do, Madame?" she asked, when I had told of our grisly discovery.

"I shall inform the Sultan."

"But Madame," Beylem broke in, "you will have to tell him you went into the tunnel. He will ask how you knew about it, and if you say that I showed it to you, I will be in great trouble."

"Hmm," I said. "What do you suggest, then, Beylem?"

"I don't know. I wish… I wish we had never gone looking. Then we could all still believe that Gulsima had got away with her sweetheart."

Yes indeed, false hopes are always more comforting than harsh truths. However, the fact remained that a sweet girl had been attacked and most probably killed.

"But why would anyone want to harm her for falling in love?"

Beylem looked surprised at my question.

"She never said exactly who was her lover," she replied, "but we thought it must be one of the princes. She didn't deny it, anyway. The punishment, if she was discovered, would be… as we have seen. It has happened before."

She fell silent.

"What do you mean?"

She bit her lip. "I cannot say any more."

"And what punishment for him? The lover?"

She shrugged. "They banished him. I suppose the same would happen if they discovered who Gulsima's lover was. That was why she never said. To protect him."

All the same, I could not let it rest. I would confront the Sultan, show him the evidence. Perhaps it was all part of the plot against him.

"Don't worry," I told Beylem. "I won't mention your name."

"They can easily find it out," she said in dismay. "Then I will be beaten or worse."

"I'll say it was me," Madeleine burst in. "Tell me where the secret passage starts. I'll say I found it and that madame and I explored it together. They can't punish me, can they? I'm not one of the Sultan's slaves."

"That sounds like a good idea, Madeleine," I said, and checked with Beylem, who nodded uncertainly.

The black eyes of Abdul Hamid II were boring into mine.

Once he realised that I had nothing to tell him about the accidents to his concubines, his reception of me, as arranged with some difficulty by a curious Naime on the morning after the adventure in the tunnel, was become far from friendly.

He heard, with displeasure, and even some incredulity, the news that I and my attendant had penetrated the secret tunnel from the harem. When I laid the blood-stained scarf in front of him and informed him that it belonged to the missing slave girl, he could hardly have been less concerned.

I found this attitude most bewildering.

"Perhaps, Your Highness," I said, "the same person who attacked Gulsima is responsible for the spate of deaths of the other girls."

"About which you have discovered precisely nothing, madame. It seems to me that your presence here is serving no good purpose, despite the prior assurances of Mr. Sherlock Holmes that you were the very person, with his assistance, to solve the mystery."

I bowed my head in acknowledgement of my failure so far.

"All the same, Your Highness," I replied. "Surely it is at least worth pursuing the possibility that they are all linked."

He gazed over my head for some long while, until I started to wonder if he had gone into a trance. Finally, he said, "The fate of the wretched slave girl, Gulsima, who betrayed my trust, has nothing whatsoever to do with those other cases. That is my final word on the matter." His restless hands played with his black beads. "I shall allow you three more days to find out who is behind the deaths of my other women," he continued, "after which, if you still fail to succeed, you can return to wherever it is you came from."

Cast out, like Valentina Muratova! I hoped that I would not be expected to pay my expenses in the way that she did, for I had no money and should be obliged to walk back to London.

"And take this disgusting rag away with you," He tossed the bloody scarf to the floor, so that I had to bend down to pick it up. "No more wanderings, by you or your slave, madame, into places where you have no business to go."

Had the Sultan no notion of how it was to conduct an investigation? With so many constraints, one could hardly hope to succeed, although I did not, of course, argue the point.

"Furthermore," he continued, "forget about those tunnels, madame. They will soon have outlived their usefulness anyway, and will be blocked up."

I must have looked inquiringly at him, for his face had twisted into a cunning smirk.

"Yes, soon I expect to amaze the world with my new impregnable security measures."

How interesting! No doubt this was the scheme being cooked up by the Baron. I would have to tell Mr. H about this as soon as possible.

Abdul Hamid waved a dismissive hand at me. I bowed my humble way out, seething all the same at his indifference to the apparently grim fate of one of his slave girls. Or might it be even more sinister than that? Had the Sultan discovered Gulsima's affair, and ordered her to be punished as had, apparently, happened before? The thought made me shiver. The sooner I could quit this place, the better.

Chapter Eighteen

Mr. H was examining Gulsima's scarf with a forensic interest. "Undoubtedly blood," he said. "Eh, Watson."

"Undoubtedly."

After my interview with the Sultan, I had realised no time was to be lost and informed Naime that I must go forthwith to the Pera Palace hotel.

"Again!" she exclaimed.

"I am afraid so."

Naime had been curious to learn the matter of my discussion with her father, and was most put out that I declined to share it. However, I was determined not to put Beylem in danger, and, given Naime's sharp intelligence, the Princess was bound to realise how unlikely it was that Madeleine had "found" the secret passage by accident. She would conclude, therefore, that one of the slave girls must either have shown it to her or led us there herself. Since Naime was devoted to her father, she was also sure to relay her suspicions to him, and I feared the vindictiveness I had observed in him might lead him to wreak indiscriminate cruel punishments. Thus, it had been a slightly sulky Princess, who arranged for the carriage to take me once more bumping over the cobblestones to the heart of Constantinople.

"Well, now," Mr. H said, after I had related the Sultan's reaction to him, "I am afraid your suspicions, Mrs. Hudson, are not misplaced. The Sultan takes betrayal very seriously. It is quite likely the girl is at the bottom of the Bosphorus by now. It would by no means be the first time."

I regarded the detective with horror.

"Drowned! On orders of the Sultan!"

"It is a traditional way of dealing with supposed miscreants here. Put them in a sack and throw them into the water."

So the dreadful rumours were true!

"Pity the poor boatmen," Dr. Watson interjected, "who find the bodies when they rise to the surface."

The image was almost too much for me.

"So you are telling me, Mr. Holmes," I said, "that we have come all this way across Europe to give assistance to a barbaric monster."

At that moment, like La Muratova before me, I was inclined to tell Abdul Hamid to go to hell, whither he was no doubt bound in any case.

"You have to understand something, Mrs. Hudson," Mr. H continued, in irritatingly patronising tones. "We find ourselves in a place where our British ideals of civilised behaviour are not practiced. Although, on occasion, we ourselves can be as brutal and barbaric as any Turk. Is that not so, Watson?"

"Certainly," the good doctor replied. "What I have witnessed in the colonies would make your hair quite stand on end, Mrs. Hudson. I realised then that we British have little justification for asserting a moral superiority."

"All the same..." I started to say.

"The Ottoman code, as practiced for centuries, is well known." Mr. H interrupted me. "Your slave girl would been fully aware of what she was risking by breaking the rules."

"So you agree with the Sultan that her case is unrelated to that of the others?"

"I am inclined to think so, yes."

"And that it is not worth pursuing?"

He gave a rueful nod. "Her fate, I imagine, has already been sealed. Better let well alone."

"Unbelievable," I snapped. "Ottoman code..." (I am afraid I nearly said "be damned!") 'Ottoman code or not, I need to find out what happened to the poor girl."

"I would most strongly counsel against it, especially since the Sultan has given us a very short time to produce results in the other deaths. In fact, Mrs. Hudson, I must insist that you concern yourself solely with the task for which we are being paid."

Was that all it was to him? I had never considered Mr. H to be mercenary, even though I understood that he was richly rewarded by some of his wealthier clients. Was a young woman's life of no worth because it was not relevant to "the task for which we were being paid"?

I glanced at Dr. Watson, who looked down. Ashamed I supposed. I hoped so.

"On a different subject," Mr. H remarked, running long fingers through his hair, "it may interest you, since it concerns an acquaintance of yours, to learn that I have solved the mystery of the missing heirloom, and have returned it to Lady Barnard."

I could not express an enthusiasm which I did not feel, and said nothing.

"It was, in fact, that same acquaintance who proved to be the thief."

"What!" Now I was truly astonished. "Eliza Dodds a thief? I cannot believe it."

"Ah, the way you ladies stick together!" Mr. H smiled indulgently. "But you have met the woman on only on a few occasions, is that not so? How well can you claim actually to know her, Mrs. Hudson? Moreover, how well do you know the facts, to be able to pronounce so strongly a not guilty verdict?"

"Well enough," I replied.

"Come, come!" He smiled some more. "In the end it proved rather irritatingly trivial and straightforward, and hardly worth my involvement. But for the fact that Lady Barnard mistrusts the Turkish police... Well, I do not blame her for that, eh Watson?" He made a steeple of his fingers, a characteristic gesture of his. "The fob watch," he continued, "– a timepiece of no great worth but pretty enough and of sentimental value to Lady Barnard, since it had belonged to her mother – was soon discovered by me concealed in your friend's reticule. She must have hastily placed it there after I ordered a search of all the rooms."

"Did she admit to the theft?"

"No. In fact, she expressed great surprise when the watch tumbled out of her bag. I was impressed with her acting. But you see, Mrs. Hudson, it was all very much in keeping with the woman's state of mind. I have often observed similar phenomena. In the present case, having recently been abandoned, by one she considered her closest friend..."

"Her daughter actually," I said.

"What?"

"Eliza regards Cecelia as her own daughter."

He gave a dismissive wave of the hand. "That just strengthens my case all the more. This pathetic and lonely middle-aged spinster found herself attracted to shiny trinkets. She simply could not resist temptation."

The smug expression on his face made my blood boil.

"Balderdash!" I exclaimed, smashing my hand down on the table.

The two gentlemen jumped.

I was too polite to say exactly what I thought, that Mr. H's experience of women was, to my certain knowledge, extremely limited. Suddenly I found myself championing someone for whom I did not greatly care. However, I was convinced that Eliza would not have taken some bauble not belonging to her. Aloud, I reiterated my belief in her innocence, describing her as a diligent worker, of sound Christian principles, a woman who was saving as much as possible before returning home. She would hardly jeopardize this for the sake of a worthless watch.

"If I were you, and if I were investigating this *trivial* case," I said, "though admittedly one that could ruin a woman's reputation and her chances of making an honest living for herself in the future – so not trivial to her at all – I should look no further than her unpleasant and over-indulged charge, Edward, a lad fond of cruel practical jokes and by no means enamoured of the stern hand of a governess. How easy for him to slip the watch into her reticule, in order to blacken her name and relieve him of her unwelcome attentions."

Mr. H stared at me, while Dr. Watson burst out laughing.

"There you are, Holmes. I told you the woman was a marvel, but you wouldn't believe me. She has solved the case for you without even being on the spot."

To my utter astonishment, Mr. H started to laugh as well.

"Mrs. Hudson," said he, actually shaking my hand, "if I ever wished to hire an assistant – apart from Watson here, of course – I should certainly consider you for the post. Not," he added hastily, "that I have any intention of so doing any time soon. But your deeper acquaintance with the parties involved has at least provided a convincing further direction for my investigation. I shall interview the little brat immediately, although I am not so sure that Lady Barnard will appreciate hearing accusations levelled against her son."

"Perhaps you can frighten him enough, so that he stops persecuting poor Eliza," I said.

"If you are correct and he is the guilty party, be assured that I shall most certainly put the fear of God and all the angels into him."

It was time to leave if I had any chance of progressing our investigation. I bade farewell to the gentlemen and made my way down to the hotel lobby. Before I could quit the place, however, I found myself accosted.

"Madame Hudson! Martha!" It was Jeanne-Claude. "How lovely to meet up with you again," she said. "I was hoping I would have the opportunity. In fact, I should be most honoured if you would join me for luncheon. My carriage is outside and our home not far distant."

I had to refuse, charming though the prospect was.

"I am afraid I have a prior appointment," I replied. "Perhaps another time."

"At the very least, will you not take a cup of coffee with me here?"

I supposed that a half-hour delay would not signify, and happily acceded to her suggestion. We made our way to the hotel's splendid patisserie, a fantasy in pink, walls, furnishings, marble floor, all of a roseate hue. Above us hung chandeliers dripping crystal, and high windows on three sides had views to the wintry city without. Over tiny cups of Turkish coffee and cakes soaked in syrup, we chatted amicably.

"I am rather surprised that you are still at the palace, Martha," Jeanne-Claude said, raising her tiny cup to her lips and regarding me over the top of it. "I should have thought you would be wearied of harem life by now."

Delightful though I found the woman's company, I did not feel it appropriate to confide my true mission to her. Instead, I replied, "It is very restful. In recent times, you see, my life has been quite hectic."

"Oh, that sounds exciting. Do please explain."

Without going into detail, I described my adventures in Ireland[5], Paris and Kent.

---

[5] *Mrs. Hudson goes to Ireland*, MX publishing, 2020

"Good heavens!" she exclaimed. "It seems that death, murder even, follows you around, Martha." She chuckled. "Perhaps it is true, after all, that you have the evil eye."

I looked at her sharply. How could she know about that? She noticed my expression, and explained, "Word gets around. The girls love nothing better than a good gossip."

"Of course," I replied. "You spend time with them teaching French. I am surprised that I have never seen you in the harem?"

"I come and go very discreetly," she replied. "And the schoolroom is somewhat separate from the rest of the building."

"Next time, you must visit me."

"Certainly. If you are still there."

Talk then turned to the fiasco that was *Medea*.

"The Sultan cannot abide tragic endings," Jeanne-Claude said. "He always insists that plays or operas be changed so that the ending be happy. Most trying for all concerned, with the results that are often absurd."

Laughing, she described some of the rewritten performances she had seen, *La Traviata*, for instance, where Violetta is cured of her tuberculosis and reunited with Alfredo, *Madame Butterfly* where Lieutenant Pinkerton recognises Butterfly as his first wife, without abandoning his second.

"I do not believe you," I said.

"It is true," Jeanne-Claude replied. "But only in Turkey!"

"Someone should have explained all that to Valentina Muratova before she travelled here."

"I am sure they did. However, she seems to be the sort of person who never listens to what people tell her."

I could not quarrel with that assessment, it being exactly how the diva had appeared to me. I went on to describe the scene in the hotel foyer. Muratova's fury at not having been paid for her performance, compounded by the fact of her being expected to foot her hotel bill as well.

"She was in high dudgeon, I can tell you."

"So how ever did she wriggle out of that one?" Jeanne-Claude asked. "I cannot imagine that she paid for it herself."

I recalled the Baron, top-hatted, pleased with himself, throwing a heap of banknotes on to the reception desk.

"No. Someone paid it for her."

"Lucky woman."

"In fact," I added, "you may know the man. The Baron Maupertuis."

Her pale eyes flickered under those heavy black eyebrows, but she shook her head.

"I do not think so."

"Here he sometimes goes by the name of Schmidt Pasha."

She laughed. "Well, I should certainly remember that. In fact, you are right. I think I have seen him, a European dressed as a Turk." I nodded. "How very generous of him."

"Yes, I wondered at it myself. He may be a reformed rogue who claims to have turned over a new leaf, but such philanthropy towards a silly woman seems excessive."

"A reformed rogue? You intrigue me. Nevertheless, I expect someone as beautiful as Valentina Muratova," Jeanne-Claude said, "will often find gentlemen willing to help them out of difficulties."

Even so, I thought, the Baron did not seem to me to be a man who would part with his money lightly.

I did not realise how much time had passed before we finally went our separate ways, it being so very pleasant to converse with someone cultured and intelligent, who shared my values. It was only when I was half-way back to Yildiz that I realised I had failed to mention to Mr. H the other intelligence from the Sultan, that he was arranging some extraordinary new security measures for himself, no doubt aided by his new confidant, the "scientist and inventor" Schmidt Pasha.

Chapter Nineteen

"Oh, madame," exclaimed Madeleine on my return. "You have missed such excitement."

"What is it?"

"Of course, I wasn't permitted to be present, but I heard all about it. The girls were buzzing like bees around a hive."

"Madeleine, I have no idea what you are talking about. Please explain. What is it?"

She helped me off with my coat.

"It was that horrible man."

"The Sultan?"

"No, no. Not him." She hung the coat up and started brushing it to remove the dust of the journey. "The man who was in the church."

"The Baron? What has he done now?"

"He gave a demonstration of plans for the security of the palace. The girls said it was like magic."

Yes, indeed, it was as I had suspected. But what a wonder the man was, to have been able to deposit Valentina at the railways station and then return to Yildiz in time to present his proposal, presumably once more in person of Schmidt Pasha. What a pity that I had delayed so long at the hotel and missed the fun. I determined to search out Naime at once and hear more about it.

I had also missed lunch, which was no harm, especially since I was still full of the cakes that Jeanne-Claude had pressed upon me.

Assuming Naime would have adjourned to the salon for a post-prandial smoke, I made my way thither. On entering, I spotted her at once with some of her sisters, reclining on a couch, nargiles on the floor beside them. She beckoned to me to join them. They were all puffing away, and once again I had politely to decline indulging in that particular practice.

The talk, happily for me, was all of the Baron' plans. Not that any of them seemed able to describe with any clarity exactly what he intended. Some sort of a huge magnetic field was the consensus, but when I asked how it would work, they smiled and shrugged their shoulders. All they could tell me was that trusted members of the household would be required to wear a device when entering and leaving the palace.

"Schmidt Pasha said that for the ladies it would be designed to look like a brooch or pendant, for the men, like a medal," said one.

"I hope it is pretty," said another. "I shall not like to wear it if it is ugly."

"And did he show how his plan would work?" I asked.

"Yes, he did," the first girl said. "Schmidt Pasha set up a small version of it in the hall we were in to demonstrate. A guard, wearing the medal, had to cross the room, through the magnetic beam, which he did without any trouble. Another guard was then required to cross without the medal. He received a severe jolt of electricity, which sent him crashing to the ground. It was most amusing."

Not for the guard in question, I thought.

"Schmidt Pasha said that the force of the electricity could be increased even to kill any intruder," another remarked with a shiver.

"Our father is very excited," Naime said. "He reckons it will provide absolute security against his enemies."

I could not see how.

"What if," I asked, "the enemy has already gained entry to the palace precincts?"

It seemed a network of these magnetic forces would criss-cross the whole of Yildiz. Abdul Hamid himself would be surrounded by them. A spider in the middle of an immense web, as it seemed to me.

"But if the enemy somehow gets possession of one of these protective devices? What then?" I continued.

The girls shook their heads.

"Not possible," one replied. "They would only be given to those whose loyalty was unquestioned."

"And, of course, everyone here is entirely loyal to the Sultan," said another.

I pretended to join them in their euphoria, but inwardly was full of reservations. The whole business smelt as bad as a fish market on a hot day. Three thousand people all absolutely loyal to the Sultan! I was certain Abdul Hamid did not believe that himself. More pertinently, never mind his supposed conversion to philanthropism, how could the Baron ever be trusted, in view of his past history? I would have to try to find out more about this amazing invention and apprise Mr. H of it as soon as possible.

Naime was more perceptive than I thought, and guessed that I was not convinced.

"I know you dislike Schmidt Pasha as much as I do, but you should have been there, Madame Hudson. Then you would not have doubted. What delayed you? Where were you for so long?"

I explained how I had met Jeanne-Claude at the Pera Palace and that we had taken coffee together.

"Jeanne-Claude?"

"She teaches here."

"Yes, you know, Naime," one of the others remarked. "The Belgian woman. Madame Cordelier,"

"No, not Belgian," I replied. "She is French."

The girl shook her head. "Her husband is French, but she is from a town in Belgium. She told us about it."

That was a surprise. Why had she not said as much to me? All her talk of Paris and how much she missed it, had implied that she was a native of the place. It was no matter, I supposed, and yet it disturbed me just a little.

Anxious to try and progress my mission, I indicated to Naime that I should like a private word with her soon. She agreed to attend me in my room a little later, whereupon I departed, relieved to be quit of the smoky atmosphere of the salon.

It was with some impatience that I awaited her arrival. Of course, I was her inferior and could hardly expect favours. All the same, it was a full ninety minutes by my fob watch before she bothered to put in an appearance. What could have delayed her, I wondered, other than gossip and her pipe?

Of course, I did not show my annoyance. I simply explained the ultimatum given me by her father – that I had just three days to complete my mission – as well as his insistence that Gulsima's disappearance had nothing to do with what had happened to the other girls.

"Well," she said, "I can certainly put in a good word for you with my father. It might help extend your stay."

I thanked her.

"No promises. If my father has made up his mind you are to go, then that will be the final word on the subject. As to your second point, my father is correct. I am sorry to say it, but Gulsima broke the rules, and, if she was punished, it was no more than she deserved."

"So you think she is drowned in the Bosphorus for the crime of falling in love."

"Madame Hudson. She is a slave. She is not permitted to have secret meetings with men. In any case, girls like Gulsima know well that they are not to leave the harem, unless authorised to do so."

"And what of her lover?"

Naime looked puzzled. "What of him?"

190

"Does he escape unpunished?"

"When we know who he is, if we discover it, he will probably be sent into exile."

Just as Madeleine had reported, and not quite the same fate as his poor beloved, then.

"You know," Naime added, "if the man wished to marry her, he could have sent in a petition, which would have been considered. The fact that the business was so underhand leads me to suspect…" She paused.

"What do you suspect?"

"Just that the man wasn't in a position to marry her, for whatever reason."

"A match of which the Sultan would certainly have disapproved?"

She bent her head in acquiescence.

I could not help but think of Gulsima, recalling her lovely smiling face, her gentle manner. And then as I had seen her in the garden. How tenderly the couple had embraced. How they had parted and how she had run back to be embraced again. A moment of happiness before utter disaster. It was all very sad. Abdul Hamid's desire for happy endings clearly did not extend to the real life around him.

I had to move on, however, and asked Naime if she had discovered anything further about the deaths of the other girls. She shook her head.

"I am sorry, no."

That was disappointing. In view of her indifference to the fate of Gulsima, however, I could not help but wonder how much effort she had put into investigating. I would be better off quizzing the slaves more rigorously, if they would talk to me.

There was one more request I had of the Princess before we parted.

"You have explained to me," I said, recalling a conversation in the salon soon after my arrival, "why Turkish women cover themselves so completely, that it is partly from modesty and faith, and partly for their own safety."

Naime smiled. "I know you European women find it very strange. But for us it is normal. Why do you ask again now?"

"I was thinking that I should like to borrow one, to understand the effect of it. And also," I gave what I hoped was a convincing reason with a chuckle, "because it looks to be so very cosy and warm in your cold weather."

My real intention was something quite different: the fact that the garment offered almost total anonymity to the wearer. With such a disguise I could move about unnoticed.

Naime gave me a searching look. She was not naïve, after all. Still, she nodded and promised to lend me one of hers.

"Your slave can come with me now to fetch it," she said.

I bade her farewell for the time being, summoning Madeleine to accompany her to collect the *charsaf*. My maid beamed, delighted to have something to do at last: so often I brushed aside her offers of help, preferring to look after myself.

I was left alone at last to ponder further on the intelligence regarding the Baron's proposed for new security measures. Now, I am no scientist but have spent a goodly number of years in close proximity to one, and wondered what Mr. H would make of the plans for a protective magnetic field around the Sultan and his entourage. Not much, I reckoned. Perhaps even more to the point, I have on occasion attended the Egyptian Hall in London to view the magic shows of Maskelyne and Cooke, masters of illusion, and have witnessed how they reproduced the seemingly supernatural effects of many a charlatan claiming spiritual or psychic powers. I wished again that I had been present to view the demonstration, which sounded to me similarly dubious. There was no doubt in my mind that the Baron was seeking to perpetrate a fraud on the Sultan, a bold undertaking indeed, but presumably one that had the potential to reward him with untold wealth. I could hardly request permission again to return to the Pera Palace hotel, and yet I was sure that it was imperative to inform Mr. H of the news at the earliest opportunity. What was to be done?

I was beginning to feel the walls of the harem pressing in on me to an almost unbearable extent, and, after Madeleine returned with the heavy black garment that was Naime's *charsaf*, I decided to go for a walk in the gardens to clear my head.

"May I come with you, madame?" Madeleine asked.

The poor girl. She was even more confined than I was. I should perhaps have preferred to go alone to try to unravel the tangle of my thoughts, but I agreed.

"Will you wear that, madame?" she asked, pointing to the *charsaf*.

"Not right now." That was for another time. Instead, we donned our warmest regular clothes, for it would be very cold outside.

For a mad moment, I even considered using the tunnel to leave the harem, thereby avoiding the unfriendly stares of the eunuchs on duty. However, the Sultan had expressly forbidden me from going near the tunnel again, and, if we were to be discovered down there, it would assuredly have been the proverbial straw that broke the camel's back. No chance of remaining in the harem any longer, then. We left instead conventionally, through the front gate. To my surprise, Bashir was standing there chatting to one of the others and gave me an almost civil nod, his eyes lingering longer and critically on Madeleine, whose only concession to local custom was a scarf around her head, her face remaining unveiled. However, she was known to be my slave, so it was up to me to decide how she presented herself.

The snow had stopped falling, but had covered the garden in an enchanting icing, as if transforming it into a huge Christmas cake.

We trudged along pristine paths, violating their purity with our footprints.

"It would be so easy," Madeleine remarked, "for anyone following us to see where we went."

If only, I thought, it had been possible to examine the snowy ground around the exit of the tunnel after Gulsima went missing. Tracks might have shown if she had been dragged away.

By daylight, it was simplicity itself to find our way to the lake. We paused on one of the bridges to regard the vista, the which proved utterly charming, a little island set in the middle of gently lapping water, a pretty pavilion rising up on the far side of the lake. Several white ducks swam towards us and I wondered if they were used to being fed, so tame they seemed. Perhaps the girls, when allowed out, made pets of them.

"It's so peaceful, Madame," Madeleine remarked.

"Well, it seems that way at least," I replied, thinking of the violence regularly perpetrated behind these elegant walls.

Suddenly, the silence was broken by loud roars and yelps. We looked at each other and laughed.

"It must be feeding time at the menagerie," I said.

"Oh, how I should like to see that," Madeleine exclaimed.

"Of course," I recalled, "you didn't accompany Naime and me when we went before. Perhaps we can visit it again together."

"Right now this minute?"

"Well…"

Madeleine smiled excitedly. "Do they have lions and tigers?"

"Indeed, they do. Lots of other creatures, too. Elephants, monkeys, giraffes, zebras… Something prehistoric-looking with a horn."

"A rhinoceros?"

I looked at her in surprise. "Yes, I think that is what it was called. How did you know?"

"The nuns took us once to see the animals in the Paris zoo. I particularly liked the rhinoceros. So strange and fierce. I even drew a picture of him. Soeur Patrice said it was very good."

Her eyes sparkled at the memory.

It was quite a walk to the menagerie, given the weather conditions that forced us to plod through thick snow, but the girl was so keen to see it, that I felt I could not demur, even though I knew I should really be about my mission. At that moment, in any case, my sentiments regarding Sultan Abdul Hamid were considerably less than charitable. In fact, I could quite happily have wished him and his suspicious mind to go to blazes, were it not that the fate of vulnerable young girls was involved. Unless the mystery was solved, there could be more deaths.

In the distance, the tower of the porcelain factory came visible. I pointed it out to Madeleine, but she showed little interest: it was only the animals that she wished to see. I hoped she would not be disappointed and that we would be admitted to the place, without Naime or another of the ladies as chaperones.

There was no problem at all. The zookeeper remembered me, and smiled and nodded as we entered. A pleasant half hour was spent then with Madeleine rushing eagerly from cage to cage. She laughed merrily at the antics of the monkeys. I was glad to see them well-confined and wondered which one had bitten the poor slave, or if it had been destroyed.

"See," she said, pointing to another cage. "There's the rhinoceros. How miserable he looks."

It was true. In the cold and snowy setting, the strange creature looked most unhappy, shuffling around in dirty straw.

"I suppose he is used to warmer weather," I said.

We lingered by the elephants for a while before moving on to the tiger's pen.

Madeleine stared for a long time at Guzellik, just then eating lunch, a bloody sight, for she was busy tearing some poor goat apart. I hope it was already dead when given to her, but could not be sure, and could hardly ask.

"How fierce he looks," she said.

"It's a she," I replied, and informed her how Naime had fearlessly entered the cage, to feed the beast from her own hand. I shuddered a little at the memory. "She reared her from a cub, you see, and the creature knows and trusts her."

Madeleine made big eyes at me.

"Nothing would ever make me go in there."

"Nor me," I replied.

At last, she had seen enough, so, thanking the zookeeper who bowed again and smiled, we started trudging back towards the harem.

"Will we be staying here much longer?" Madeleine asked a little plaintively. I supposed she was as homesick as I was.

"I hope not." I laughed. "I think we are nearly ready to leave, aren't we Madeleine?"

"Yes, but I shall miss you, madame."

I put my arm around her and squeezed her shoulder.

"I shall miss you too, Madeleine. But you can always come and visit me."

"That would be lovely." She looked sad, as if thinking how unlikely such a trip would be for her.

"I am sure we can arrange it," I said. "But just now, I don't know about you, I'm freezing. Shall we get back to somewhere warm?"

She nodded and we took a slightly different path, as pristine as the other, the harem building eventually looming within our sights.

We had almost reached it, when another figure caught my eye, hurrying through the snow, a woman in European clothes. I was pleased to recognise Jeanne-Claude Cordelier, and an idea suddenly came to me. I called out to her, unnecessarily as it happened, since she had already paused at the sight of us.

"Jeanne-Claude!" I said, "We meet again."

"Always a delight, Martha," she replied.

"I wonder," I continued, "if I might ask a big favour of you."

"Yes, if I can," she replied, smiling.

"I should like to send an urgent letter to someone staying at the Pera Palace hotel. Could you deliver it for me?"

"But, of course. Unless you wish to accompany me back down to the city now, Martha. My carriage is at your disposal."

I considered the offer for a moment. However, I had already made the trip down earlier in the day, and it would assuredly be thought very strange if I rushed off again so soon. Besides, it was quite likely that Mr. H and Dr. Watson would not be at the hotel when I arrived. Much better to send a note. I thanked Jeanne-Claude, but declined her kind offer, and she willingly accompanied me back to the harem.

"You have been teaching a class?" I asked, as we made our way to my room.

"Yes, yes. A class." She laughed. "Alas, my students are not always enthusiastic to learn."

"The girls seem to speak French very well. Better than I do."

"Not at all," she smiled. "Your French is excellent, Martha. As for my pupils, some of them, it is true, are quite fluent. It is the little princes who cause me the most heart-ache. I cannot be too strict with them, you see..." She stroked Madeleine's red curls, now released from the confines of the headscarf. "Your pretty maid speaks French beautifully," she continued.

"That is because I am French, Madame," the girl replied a little pertly. "From Paris."

"Oh..." She laughed. "Pardon me, I thought... no matter... Paris, a wonderful city!"

"I understand you yourself are originally from Belgium, Jeanne-Claude," I said.

"Someone must have been talking about me," she chuckled. "No secrets in the harem! Yes, indeed, I was born there, but studied in

Paris. That is where I met my husband. Luckily, for otherwise I should have had to return to the smokestacks of Charleroi."

While I hunted out paper, fountain pen, ink and an envelope, she wandered about my room, admiring its appurtenances, particularly the painted plate.

"From the porcelain factory here?" She picked it up to examine it closely. "I must get something like it. So very pretty."

She chatted to Madeleine in rapid French, while I penned the message to Mr. H, explaining what I had learnt of the Baron's scheme. "I am sure," I concluded, "that you will be as sceptical as I am about this. I fear that the man plans a massive fraud against the Sultan."

I sealed the letter and addressed it to Mr. Sherrinford at the Pera Palace hotel.

On viewing the inscription, Jeanne-Claude raised her black eyebrows just a little, and an amused smile played on her lips. Oh dear, was Mr. H's incognito so universally discovered. However, she said nothing regarding the matter, and placed the envelope in her reticule.

"It will be safe with me, Martha," she said.

I attended her to the door that led into the walled garden around the harem. We embraced and, as she walked away, I noticed how her boots were leaving imprints in the snow. It suddenly struck me as a little queer that, since presumably she had visited the harem earlier to teach her class, her footprints should surely have been visible. However, the snow, as I clearly remembered, had been unmarked when we left. All I could see now were my own and Madeleine's prints leaving and coming back, just the once, and Jeanne-Claude's arriving. Well, presumably she must have come and gone the earlier time by a different route, or taught the little princes elsewhere in the palace estate.

Chapter Twenty

I felt it was incumbent on me to apprise Beylem and the other girls of the indifference of the Sultan to Gulsima's fate, even though it would hardly come as a surprise. I would not mention Naime's equally unconcerned reaction, since they disliked her enough already.

Assuming they would be in the bathhouse at this hour, cleansing themselves before dinner, I duly made my way there with Madeleine, this time wearing my shift, modestly covered with a robe. As ever, the initial blast of humidity in the place took my breath away. Through swirls of the perfumed mist, I soon espied the slave girls huddled together, and made my way over to them. Strangely enough, they proved loth to discuss their friend at all, and I surmised they had decided the subject was too dangerous, given the many listening ears.

They were only slightly less reluctant to discuss the deaths of the other girls.

"Horrible accidents," was the consensus.

I asked if there were any common elements, a question which puzzled them.

"How could there be?" Beylem replied.

"I don't know," I said, "but it would assist my search greatly if we could find some sort of a pattern. Perhaps if you describe to me the circumstances of each incident, I can try to discern something common to them." They frowned and looked doubtfully at each other. "It would be most useful to Mr. Sherlock Holmes," I added, "and, since the Sultan himself has authorised the investigation, you need not fear you will get into any trouble by telling me."

Whether it was mention of their hero, Mr. H, or of the Sultan's approval, the girls relaxed. In fact, suddenly they could not have been more helpful. When I said that I wished I had brought pen and paper with me, one of the girls rushed off instantly to procure the same.

The first girl to die, Esma, they told me, fell in the bath, fatally banging her head.

"How terrible! Was it here? Were you all with her?"

"Oh no, madame," Beylem replied. "She was alone."

"Alone in the baths!"

"It was one of the private baths. One like yours, madame."

"Whose, then?"

"No one's. Just an empty guest room."

"Why was she there?"

They shook their heads. "No one knew."

"Perhaps she wanted some quiet time to herself," I said, at which they looked at me astonished. The notion of craving solitude was quite alien to them.

"Her head was most dreadfully injured, madame," another girl put in. "Quite broken."

"Did you see her then?"

The girl, Zehra, nodded.

"I was the one who found her, madame. It was horrible. She was just lying there in a pool of her own blood." She shuddered. "I had gone there to make sure it was clean for a new guest."

I pictured the bathroom I sometimes used, unable to imagine how such a fall could achieve that degree of damage. Of course, the oils with which the girls liked to anoint their skin would make the marble surfaces slippery. Even so, Esma must have fallen very awkwardly, to crush her skull badly enough to cause her death. If indeed, that was the true explanation.

"How was she dressed?" I asked.

Zehra raised her eyes to mine.

"She was bathing, madame. She wore no clothes."

"But, Zehra," I continued, "she couldn't have been lying in the bath itself. Otherwise the fountain of water would have washed all that blood away."

"You are right, madame. She was lying by the door."

"Did you have to push the door hard to get in? I am sorry to have to ask," I added, seeing that she was becoming distressed, "but I wish to have the clearest picture."

"No," she replied in a small voice. "I did not have to push the door."

The reason for my question, in case my readers have not deduced it yet for themselves, is that if poor Esma's body were blocking the entrance, it would have strengthened the case for an accident. But since it was not, then someone else might have been present.

"What about the girl who died after being bitten by a monkey? Was that in the menagerie?"

"No, in the salon," Beylem replied. "Someone had brought along their pet, and Kumru was playing with it. It did not seem that her wound was serious, but that night she developed a fever, which got worse and worse until she died of it."

"The poor monkey was destroyed." We all looked at the girl who said this, a plump and rosy-cheeked girl called Cemile. The poor monkey, indeed!

"Well," she added a little apologetically. "It wasn't really the monkey's fault, you know. It was the fault of the person who let it loose among us."

True enough, I supposed. "And who was that?" I asked, but no one seemed to know.

Hanife had fallen from the roof of the harem, though what she was doing up there – it was forbidden to go there alone – was a mystery.

"There's a lovely view of the Bosphorus from there," one said. "You can watch the ships going up and down and imagine you are on one of them."

You can imagine you are escaping, I thought.

"They said she must have got dizzy when she went too near the edge."

"How high is the barrier?"

A low enough wall, it seemed, though hardly dangerously so.

I duly noted down the fact.

As for little Ayla, aged only thirteen, the girl particularly favoured by both the Sultan and Naime, my interlocutors had no idea how she had got hold of a gun.

"Did it belong to one of the guards?" I asked.

"Oh no, madame," Beylem said. "It was a pretty little thing, such as a lady might use."

I seized on that point. A gun belonging to a lady.

"It looked like a toy," Cemele added, "which must have been why Ayla was playing with it, not realising it was loaded with bullets."

In my youth, growing up in the countryside, my brothers had taught me how to use a gun. One could not make it work just by pulling the trigger. The safety catch would have had to be released first. I supposed a child might do that, but not so easily.

"Who here would have such a thing?"

The girls looked at each other.

"The wives of the Sultan," one said. "Maybe. Others too, but not us, madame."

Of course not. Guns in the hands of slaves would hardly ensure a peaceful night's sleep for Sultan Abdul Hamid.

"Or visitors," another added.

"Do you have a gun, madame?" Beylem asked.

"Me?" I laughed. "Good heavens, no. I would have no use for such a thing."

Ironic words, in retrospect.

"And wasn't there," I continued, "a poor girl who was strangled by her own scarf?"

"Usul. But that was quite definitely an accident, madame. The carriage was travelling fast and the driver didn't realise what had happened until he stopped."

"The scarf had unravelled and somehow got caught in a wheel."

"Her head nearly snapped right off, madame."

I did not care at all for the relish with which the girls recounted the more gory details of the deaths, the bizarre circumstances of which I could understand would unnerve an already fearful ruler.

"Is it true that the victims were all favourites of the Sultan?" I asked.

There was an awkward pause.

"Sultan Abdul Hamid," Beylem said at last, "loves us all."

"Yes, though some more than the rest," Cemile added. The others looked at her. "What?" she snapped. "Madame asked so I must tell her the truth. Yes, he particularly liked those girls."

The elaborate evening meal, with all its pomp and etiquette, its never-ending parade of rich dishes, its inconsequential conversation, had become something of a trial for me, but one that had to be endured all the same. To my left sat the first consort of the Sultan, Bedrifelek, with whom I had hardly conversed since I arrived. Although always polite, she still seemed suspicious of me – I think she guessed I was not the aristocrat I claimed to be. Our chat now was utterly banal, she asking if a certain dish were to my taste, and I dutifully replying that indeed it was most delicious. Or whether, since I was wearing a ruby necklace – not mine, of course, but she did not know that – did I not prefer rubies to all other gems, diamonds, sapphires, emeralds and so on. I replied that, in fact, I was rather partial to amethysts.

"Ah yes," she replied, with a touch of malice, "as a protection against drunkenness, perhaps. Well, you will not need that here, Madame Hudson, for, as you have seen, we do not imbibe intoxicating liqueurs the way you do in Europe."

I laughed. "I did not know that amethysts had such an interesting power… But, actually, Your Highness, I love the stone because the ring my late husband, Henry, gave me on our engagement was a beautiful deep purple amethyst set in gold. Whenever I wear it – as indeed I am doing now," showing it to her, "I remember him and our blissfully happy times together."

It was all true, but at the same time I was quite willing to be a little malicious, myself. Gossip, relayed via Madeleine, was that relations between the Sultan and his First Consort were cold.

Abdul Hamid himself sat, as he sometimes did, at the head of the table, hunched over his own meagre plate of rice, and looked at me not once, until Naime whispered something in his ear. Whereupon he glanced my way and seemed to nod, though without changing his expression. The Valide Sultan, seated beside him, also turned her face towards me, and even gave a little smile. This was encouraging, in one way, at least. However much I wanted to go home, I needed to get to the bottom of the Yildiz mysteries, not just for the sake of the Sultan, but in order not to let Mr. H down. I also wanted to discover exactly what Baron Maupertuis was up to, and, if possible, thwart his machinations. And then, of course, there was the fate of Gulsima to consider, though that was perhaps the least likely to have a happy outcome.

A servant was coming round at that moment with a jug of ice cold spring water, and I readily accepted a refill in my crystal goblet, to clear my palate and sharpen my thoughts.

At last, the meal was over and I was able to join Naime in the smoking salon to learn my fate.

"My father says that you can stay longer," she told me, smiling. "Of course, I respected your confidence, and did not reveal that I knew anything about your mission. Instead, I told him how you have been teaching me English, so now you had better give me a class or two, not to show me up as a liar."

"I should be delighted," I replied, "especially since you have been so kind to me."

"The other news that will interest you," she continued, "is that my father intends for Schmidt Pasha to give another demonstration of his magnetic field tomorrow for those who missed out the first time. He wishes to show off the scheme before some foreign dignitaries." She laughed. "Apparently, the man was not one bit pleased, but what can he do. He must obey the Sultan, who is giving him the money to develop the project."

"How much money?" I asked.

"I don't know exactly. Very much, I think."

I could well imagine the Baron's dismay, assuming, as I must, that his project had no substance. The more people who witnessed the thing, the more likely the deception would be uncovered, with incalculable consequences for himself. The scoundrel was playing a very dangerous game.

"That is excellent news," I said. "I shall be most fascinated to see how the magnetic field works, though I doubt I shall understand much."

"Like the rest of us," Naime replied.

"I wonder," I added, "if word might be sent to Mr. Holmes and Dr. Watson, who are residing at the Pera Palace hotel under the names Mr Sherrinford and Dr. Sackler. I know that they would love to be present. As Mr. Holmes himself is something of a scientist, it would mean more to him than to the rest of us."

"What a splendid idea!" Naime clapped her hands. "I am sure my father would be delighted for such eminent visitors to attend. I shall send them an invitation this very moment."

Of course, by now Mr. H would have received my letter regarding the matter. In light of that, he would assuredly welcome Naime's invitation most eagerly.

She beckoned to a slave, who went off, soon returning with all items necessary for the penning of a missive.

"Will the gentlemen understand French?" she asked me.

"Mr. Holmes most certainly will," I replied.

"Good, for he would hardly understand Turkish, and I know no English. Not yet, anyway, madame."

Don't be too sure about Mr. H and Turkish, I thought, wondering how far he had got with learning the language since he started studying the grammar on the train. Quite possibly, knowing him, he was already fluent enough to converse in the exotic tongue.

I went to bed in a slightly more sanguine state of mind. Even if I failed to uncover the mysteries behind the deaths of the slave girls, by exposing the charlatan attempting to defraud him of millions, Abdul Hamid was sure to be immensely grateful. I could hardly wait for the morrow.

Chapter Twenty-one

Where were they?

It was the following afternoon and a select audience, mostly of Europeans, was seated in a circle in one of the splendid halls of the palace. Schmidt Pasha's demonstration of the powers of his magnetic field was about to start, and yet there was still no sign of Mr. H or Dr. Watson. Whatever could have happened to them?

I kept looking around to see if they would enter at the last minute, and, in doing so, recognised a few faces among the other invitees. There sat Lady Barnard and her husband, along with the execrable Edward. Presumably they thought it would be educational for him to witness the wonders of science. No Eliza Dodds, however, and I wondered if she had been dismissed, despite her innocence regarding the theft of that wretched timepiece. I hoped not, and resolved to find out as soon as my other commitments permitted.

Armed guards lined the walls – even here in the heart of his palace, presumably among friends, the Sultan was terrified for his safety. On entering, he took a seat well apart from the rest of us, and surrounded himself with some of the ladies of the harem, head to toe in black. Once all were settled, he signalled to Schmidt Pasha, who had been waiting, somewhat uneasily I thought, an intriguing-looking boxed contraption alongside him, to start his demonstration.

Much as I disliked the man, I had to admit he made a splendid sight – much more splendid than the Sultan, in fact – in his rich Turkish robes, his scarlet fur-lined kaftan embroidered in gold, a red fez with a black silk tassel perched on his head. This outlandish outfit, however, suggested more strongly than ever to me, that we were to witness an entertainment, rather than a scientific presentation.

Behind him, hanging on a screen, was a huge map which I soon recognised as being of the Yildiz palace and grounds. It was surrounded by and criss-crossed with many thin markings, all emanating from and ending in towers along the perimeter walls. Schmidt Pasha explained, holding a thin cane as a pointer, that these indicated the projected lines of magnetic force.

"Each one," he said, "will have built into it a control mechanism to strengthen or weaken the power of the field. Thus, if enemies try to rush the palace, they can be mown down in seconds."

I glanced across at the Sultan. He was nodding and smiling, while some of the ladies beside him clapped their hands.

The actual demonstration was much as I had suspected it would be: skilfully and slickly done to convince the credulous. For me, however, who, as I have remarked before, have attended a goodly number of magic shows, it was nothing more or less than another of those. Following his sketchy explanation of the science, Schmidt Pasha turned to the box, which he said was a miniature version of the ones ultimately to be constructed. He might well have exclaimed, "Abracadabra!" when he pressed a button on the top of it, and a narrow beam shot out across the room, to gasps from the audience.

"For the purposes of the demonstration, the beam is blue," he explained. "However, in practice it will be quite invisible."

The Emperor's new clothes, I thought, recalling a fairy tale much favoured by my grandchildren.

Schmidt Pasha now signalled to a guard who stepped forward.

"As you can see," he announced, "this man is wearing a protective amulet."

The guard pointed to a large medallion hanging around his neck.

Schmidt Pasha waved him forward, and, sure enough, the man crossed easily through the supposed magnetic beam.

Now it was the turn of the poor unfortunate without the shield – and how reluctant he looked in advance of his ordeal, even though, as Schmidt Pasha explained to us in advance, the strength of the beam in this instance was mild. Even so, it sent the man writhing to the ground in apparent agony. Now, whether he was privy to the trick or the unknowing victim of it, I could not tell, and could not guess how the effect was achieved if this were so. But a trick it most certainly was. Oh, why were Mr. H and Dr. Watson not present? My lodger would surely have seen through the subterfuge. Schmidt Pasha switched off the beam and the guard, still staggering, shuffled off.

The whole audience jumped to their feet and applauded vigorously, while Schmidt Pasha made a deep bow, the tips of his blond moustache twitching as if he were about to burst out laughing. Only I remained seated, my hands in my lap, not able to feign enthusiasm even though I felt most conspicuous as the only witness unimpressed and unconvinced.

Was it my imagination or, at a particular moment, did the miscreant glance my way with a triumphant smirk? Had he somehow engineered the absence of my gentlemen? Well, I resolved to get word to them as soon as possible, despite his best efforts.

Not immediately, however, for the guests were to be treated to a reception, with coffee, sherbet and the inevitable sweets. As the Sultan and the harem ladies had done, I tried to slip away discreetly, but was thwarted by Lady Barnard, who blocked my way.

"Edward tells me you are a friend of his governess," she said. The same child stood beside her, a sneer on his face.

I had noticed before, in the Grand Bazaar, how painfully thin this woman was, with almost as many lines of discontent etched on her powdered face as the lines of magnetic force on the Baron's map of the Yildiz estate. These made her look older than she presumably was, to have a child of Edward's age. Her manner was unpleasing, and the expression on her face, as she addressed me, suggested there was a bad smell around.

"Not exactly a friend," I replied. "I met Miss Dodds and her...er... sister on the Orient Express on the way here, and have encountered her a few times since. At the performance of *Medea* for instance."

"Ah yes, what a fiasco that was!" Lady Barnard's eyebrows almost disappeared into her chignon. "Imagine the arrogance of that Valentina woman, a mere actress!"

"Well, I can understand that an artiste..."

"Nonsense. She was paid to come here and perform, and that is what she should have done... I cannot abide people who get above themselves." She pulled a face, looking me up and down at the same time, as if I too were one such (the which, of course, I was). Then she sniffed. Definitely a bad smell. "I didn't think much of the piece anyway," she continued. "Far too Greek. And quite unsuitable for dear Edward."

The boy was staring fixedly at me, his teeth – too big for his face as usual for children of his age – bared in a grimace. I kept my reticule tightly closed, in case he felt inclined to drop something into it.

Since I did not wish to discuss Euripides, nor yet the newer French version of the ancient myth, with this ignorant woman, I changed the subject.

"How is Miss Dodds?" I asked.

Lady Barnard's face clouded. She glanced at her son.

"There was some unpleasantness, but luckily it has been cleared up. However, I do not think Constantinople suits a woman of Eliza's background. She is from Croydon, I believe."

"Norwood."

Lady Barnard stared at me, her eyes the stony blue of lapis lazuli. If anyone had the evil eye, that person surely stood before me.

"Croydon, Norwood, Timbuctoo... whatever does it matter? The fact is that Eliza does not fit into Constantinople society, and anyway, Edward does not like her."

I regarded the boy, still smirking. Woe betide his next governess, I thought.

"As for her sister, it is an absolute scandal," Lady Barnard continued. "Becoming the common law wife of some native, indeed… No, I am sorry but we cannot associate ourselves with such people, and the sooner Eliza goes home, the better. It is just a pity that we wasted good money on her fare here. And, indeed, on that of her disgraceful sister."

I trusted they would waste some more good money on poor Eliza's return fare, and not make her pay for it herself, as the Sultan had done to La Muratova. It was most unlikely, in Eliza's case, that a benefactor like the Baron would step forward to assist her.

"I should like to pay her a visit, all the same," I said, thinking to commiserate on her loss of a situation, or congratulate her escaping from such an unpleasant one.

"Of course, the woman is no longer resident at our villa. That would be most inappropriate. She is staying in our rooms in the city for now until she leaves."

Poor Eliza, to be discarded in such a way. I requested Lady Barnard to give me the full address, which she did, though with an ill-concealed ill grace.

Meanwhile, I noticed that Lord Barnard was deep in conversation with Schmidt Pasha.

"Were you impressed with the demonstration, Your Ladyship?" I asked.

At last, she expressed a degree of animation.

"Indeed, we were. In fact, my husband is of the opinion that we should install the same system to protect our own villa."

So the Sultan was not to be the Baron's only prey. In fact, a whole queue of credulous gentlemen was waiting to shake his hand and talk to him.

"I cannot help but feel exposed in this country," Lady Barnard continued, "with so many unsavoury types around. Especially since I mislaid my gun."

"You mislaid your gun!" I exclaimed.

She turned disdainful eyes upon me.

"That is what I just said."

"I apologise, Your Ladyship, but you see I heard recently of small, bejewelled gun..." I hesitated. I did not wish to reveal that the same gun had killed a child.

"Yes? Where? Speak up!"

"Here in the palace. In the harem."

She shook her head. "It could not possibly be mine. I am happy to say that I have never ever ventured into that particular den of vice."

Clearly not, if she thought of it in that way. But even though she was never in the harem, as she claimed, someone else might have taken it there.

"Where is it now anyway, this gun you mention?" she asked.

I shook my head. "I don't know."

"Tssk!"

Clearly, I was proving most unsatisfactory.

At that moment, I happened to glance at Edward. There was something horribly gleeful in the expression on his face, and I wondered could the disappearing gun have something to do with him. I clutched my reticule closer to my side.

Just then, Lord Barnard returned to his wife, rubbing chubby pink hands together.

"Fellow said he can do it. Not cheap, o'course, but one has to be prepared to pay for quality service, what! Can't rely on getting much of that in this benighted country."

"It would prove a great relief to me, Monty," Lady Barnard said. "I would be able to sleep peacefully in my bed at last."

"Thought the fellow was a native," Lord Barnard said, utterly ignoring my presence. "In that get-up, don'cha know. But he's one of us, Lettie. At least, a Christian, not a d...d Musselman... German or something of the sort."

"Dutch, I believe," I said.

Lord Barnard at last deigned to include me, briefly, in his field of vision.

"Much the same thing... Anyway, Lettie, he said he'll call on us tomorrow. Give the place a lookin' over to see if it's suitable for his thingamajig."

"Did you mention the dogs, Monty?" Lady Barnard asked. "I should not at all care for dear Odin or Thor to get hit by some deadly ray."

I edged away before I could hear his reply and, if they even noticed, they did not try to stop me. What bad manners, I thought: not even asking me my name. No wonder Edward was the little monster that he was. Call me unchristian, I thought, but they deserved to be robbed by the Baron.

Before I could successfully depart, however, I was delayed again, this time by a dumpy woman of middle age with a vaguely familiar face.

"Madame!" she exclaimed in French. "We meet again. How are you?"

"I am well, thank you."

She must have guessed from my puzzled expression, that I had difficulty placing her.

"Hortense Devaux," she said. "From the train, you know. A good friend of dear Valentina."

"Ah yes." I recalled her at last. La Muratova's greatest devotee. "How nice to see you again."

As I recalled, she had no time for me then. I tried to move on,

"You no doubt attended that ill-fated performance of *Medea*," she persisted.

"I did, indeed."

"What a way to treat such a diva!" She had lowered her voice to a whisper, forcing me to lean forward to hear her.

"Most unfortunate," I said.

"More than unfortunate. Much more, Madame. An insult to the greatest actress of our time... One who is greater, in my humble opinion, than Sarah Bernhardt herself."

"I am afraid I cannot comment on that, never having seen Bernhardt. However," registering the fanatical glint in the other's eye, "what I witnessed of La Muratova's performance was enough to convince me that I was in the presence of a very powerful talent."

I thought the woman was going to embrace me.

"Oh yes, yes, yes. So powerful. You should have seen her, Madame, in *La Dame aux Camelias*. I shall never forget it. Never. I was in tears... What she could have achieved with *Medea* if only they had let her! It was a crime against Art."

In the throes of her passion, she had raised her voice, and people were looking at us. I saw Lady Barnard whisper to her husband, and then titter.

I tried to hush the woman, conscious that her words might land her in trouble.

"Do not worry about me, Madame. I would be happy to say the same thing to his face. I mean the Sultan of Turkey himself. That Philistine!"

Then, to my horror, her eyes welled up, and the devotee veritably flung herself on my breast. Lady Barnard was now laughing openly, and pointing, as were some of the other people present.

"Come, come, Madame Devaux," I said, trying to calm her. "This is not the place. Let you and me go somewhere more quiet."

Lamb-like then, she allowed herself to be led away to the side of the room, where I sat her down on a divan.

"Is your husband here?" I asked, hoping to shift the problem onto other shoulders, mine having become quite soaked from the outpourings of the lachrymose lady.

"What husband? You think I have a husband...?"

"I really do not know."

She reared up a little then. "I am wedded to Art," she said. "I write poetry, Madame. I have neither the time nor the energy for anything else."

"I see," I replied. "Most interesting."

I inquired then what had brought her to Constantinople. She looked at me as if I were mad.

"Valentina, of course."

"You came all this way to see her perform!"

"Now you understand my disappointment."

From a passing attendant, she took one of those nutty little cakes oozing syrup, and popped it, whole, into her mouth.

"Oh, not just to see Valentina." she continued, munching, "You see, Madame, I am an adventuress in the amphitheatre of Life. I travel wherever the whim takes me, searching out inspiration..." Her wide face, blotched unflatteringly from those recent tears, took on a seraphic expression. "I should like very much to show you my poetry."

I was almost frantic with frustration. How could I get away from this tiresome person, whose eyes burned into mine and who, by now, had a tight hold on my wrist?

"That would be an honour," I said, "but just now I am afraid I have to leave."

I stood up, shaking off her grip.

"Go," she sighed, adding enigmatically. "My life is one long series of departures and goodbyes."

Feeling guilty at abandoning her – but only a little – I hurried back to my room, hoping there would be a message from Mr. H. However, I was to be disappointed. Not only was there no message, there was no Madeleine, just when I wished the girl to perform an errand for me and seek out Naime. Trusting she would return in a short while, too weary to go in search of either of them, I lay down on my bed and closed my eyes.

How it happened, I do not know, but I must have fallen into a deep sleep, for I awoke to find a full hour had passed. Vague recollections of a dream returned to me, in which the Baron as Schmidt Pasha was holding tight to my hand, whispering "Marta,

Marta," and laughing. I shook my head to dispel the unpleasant image.

In the usual course of events, now would be time to bathe in preparation for dinner, with Madeleine to assist me. But the wretched girl was still absent, presumably off gossiping with her new friends. Crossly, I divested myself of my day dress and put on my shift and robe, to go to the bath house and search out my maid.

Not only was she not there, but none of the girls had seen her all afternoon. Whatever was the minx up to?

"Maybe she went to the French class," Cemile said.

"Why should she do that?" I replied. "She has no need to learn French."

The girl shrugged. "Just something to do."

"But the French class must be well over by now."

It was a thought, though. Madeleine knew Jeanne-Claude. Perhaps they had got chatting about Paris and lost track of time. I expressed the thought aloud.

"Madame Cordelier is a kind lady," Zehra said.

They all agreed.

"Didn't she sit up all night with Kumru after the monkey bit her," Cemile remarked.

"And she was quite frantic when Usul had her accident."

"What do you mean?" I asked.

"Madame Cordelier was in the carriage, too."

"She was so upset. You see, everything happened too quickly for her to do anything."

"It must have been so horrible for her."

The girls were all speaking together, while I sat in shock. Jeanne-Claude was in the carriage! She had attended Kumru after the monkey bite. A chilling notion came to me.

"Was Madame Cordelier present at any of the other times the girls had their accidents?" I asked.

They were not stupid. They guessed what I was suggesting.

"She can't have had anything to do with any of it," Cemile said. "Madame Cordelier is kindness itself."

My mind fizzed. Jeanne-Claude present at least at two of the deaths. She might well carry a pretty little gun. And, given how much the girls liked her, it would be easy enough for her to lure them to rooftops or bathrooms. Such were the monstrous imaginings crowding my brain.

"Does she teach you all French?" I asked. "She knows you all well?"

They nodded. "Such a nice lady," they said again.

"She often does errands for us, brings us things from the bazaar, lends us books, gives us little presents."

A nice lady, or a madwoman? No, no. The last was impossible. Such delightful chats I'd had with her. There was no madness there. And if not mad, what reason could she possibly have for killing the girls? No, it was wild to think of it. All the same, I recalled the words of Mr. H regarding Eliza Dodds, when I protested her innocence. "How well can you claim actually to know her?" he had asked. "Someone you have met only a handful of times."

I asked the girls to tell Madeleine, if she made an appearance, to go to my room and on no account leave until I arrived.

"What are you going to do, madame?" Beylem asked. They sensed my fears. That something bad had happened to Madeleine.

I hardly knew. To go and look for her in all the places she might be, I supposed. The harem was not so very big.

Just as I stood up, about to leave, a disreputable-looking old gypsy woman approached me, and babbled something in a strange tongue. I looked for help to the girls.

"She says she has a message for you, madame," said Cemile. "From Madeleine?"

Cemile asked further and the old woman nodded, adding a few words.

"From a lady. To meet her."

"What lady?"

The gypsy woman looked at me with rheumy eyes. She gave a toothless grin, and held out her hand.

"A generous one."

I ignored the gesture.

"To meet me where?"

The old woman chewed at her lips, and gave me a sly look, her hand still out.

"She forgets." Cemile said. "A coin will prompt her memory."

I had brought nothing of the sort with me, and felt like shaking the woman.

Beylem said something to the gypsy in a sharp voice. The crone grimaced, and then reluctantly muttered something.

"On the bridge nearest the harem gate," Beylem told me. "I had to threaten her to get her to speak, but said she would be rewarded if she told the truth. I hope that is all right, madame."

I nodded, my mind spinning. There was no time to lose. I rushed from the place back to my room, hastily putting on my dress, coat, boots and hat. What lady? Jeanne-Claude? Lady Barnard? Perhaps it had nothing at all to do with Madeleine. Maybe – I thought hysterically – Hortense Devaux wants to read me some of her poems.

I hurried to the front door, only to find the old gypsy woman loitering there, smiling obsequiously, her hand still out. I rummaged in my pocket and drew out a coin. Thank goodness it was enough. She bowed and shuffled off.

It was beginning to get dark as I made my way to the bridge. I could tell a figure was standing there, but when I got close, perceived that it was no woman. The Baron! Transformed once more from Schmidt Pasha into a European gentleman, in a fur coat, top hatted and leaning on a cane.

"Marta, my dear," he said, taking my arm whether I wanted him to or no. "How good of you to come. I was turning into a block of ice, standing here. Let us walk and talk, to restore the circulation."

"What is all this about?" I tried to shake him off, but he had me fast, forcing me to accompany him along the snowy path.

"What an inconvenience you are, Marta dear. You know, I really cannot allow you to involve Mr. Sherlock Holmes in my philanthropic schemes."

"It is a little late for that," I said. "Mr. Holmes has already been appraised of your scoundrelly activities."

"Has he? Has he really?" He smiled broadly, and the little light there was abroad glinted on that gold canine.

"Yes. I sent him a letter..." I faltered then, for he continued to smile.

"Alas, the postal service here isn't quite as reliable as it is in London," he said.

"I gave it to Madame Cordelier."

"So you did."

A horrid realisation dawned and my earlier fears confirmed. "Jeanne-Claude," I said. "She is part of your swindle!"

"My swindle! You don't mince your words, do you, Marta?" His face burst into a broad smile. "But you are quite wrong. It is no swindle of mine. Madame Cordelier herself came up with the plan, the clever girl. Living here, do you see, realising how very fearful Abdul Hamid is regarding his security. How superstitious. How easy to lead by that very long nose of his."

"I suppose," I said scornfully, "she is yet another of your conquests."

He laughed. "Hardly that. No, Janneke's devotion stems from the fact that blood is thicker than water, as they say. That and the money involved, of course."

"Janneke?" I gaped at him.

"Her Flemish name. But after my little contretemps with dear Sherlock, the notoriety forced her to change her identity. She went to Paris and became more French than the French. Yes, you may well look surprised. She is my sister."

I could see little similarity between the pair. For one thing, their colouring was quite different, he so fair, she so dark, until I remembered thinking she coloured her hair, blackened her brows. Yes, now I saw it. Something similar about those pale eyes. There was no doubt in my mind that this, at least, was the truth.

"Unlike myself whom am somewhat fastidious," the Baron continued, amused by my discomfiture, "Janneke has no reservations about getting her hands dirty. At the moment, your lovely little maid is being well looked after by her, but…"

"What!" I struggled to free myself, in a fury.

"Ooh, tigress!" he said, throwing up his hands. "Please don't bite me."

"Leave Madeleine alone."

"Calm yourself, Marta, please. Nothing will happen to the girl as long as you keep silent about my affairs." He sighed. "What a headache you have been to me. Thank goodness, Janneke was on the spot to keep a sharp eye on you."

So all those seemingly chance meetings were orchestrated by this demonic pair! How foolishly naïve I felt.

"And dear Sherlock still hanging about… What a nuisance! I was hoping at every moment for him to go away and leave me in peace, but no such luck. Yet I could not delay any longer putting my scheme into practice. Abdul Hamid, do you see, was getting impatient."

"Mr. Holmes will soon put a stop to your deceptions."

"Alas for poor Madeleine if that is the case. But, you know, Marta, it is better to leave Sherlock out of it. He may not be as devoted as you are to the pretty little girl. In fact, her fate may, in his view, be incidental."

"I cannot believe it," I said, while, in fact, imagining it only too well. He would be sorry for her, perhaps, but the greater good would mean more to him.

I recalled my recent suspicions.

"All those deaths..." I began.

"You mean the slave girls. Nothing to do with me, dear lady. How could it when, as you well know, I wasn't even in Constantinople at the time?" He chuckled. "Abdul Hamid was already utterly panic-stricken on learning of the assassination, by an anarchist, of Elizabeth of Austria, simply because she wore a crown. A subsequent series of lucky accidents in the harem terrified the life out of the Sultan, and encouraged him to seek help in strengthening his security. I merely facilitated it."

"Nothing to do with you, you say, Baron? But what of your sister? I am told she was present when these deaths happened."

"I cannot speak for dear Janneke, although, as I said, she has fewer qualms than I do about using any means possible to achieve her end... In fact, it seems she has got a something of a taste for blood recently. Ha ha!" He had me pressed against the railing of the bridge. Never mind his sister, the man was capable of anything, and the water below us was icy and deep. "But come, dear Marta, let us reach an understanding. I like you, most sincerely, and should hate anything bad to happen to you. All you have to do is keep quiet just for a few more days. That's all. That's all I need."

I could feel his hot breath on my face, so close he was. And although he was smiling, there was menace in that smile.

"A few days," I repeated, "and then you will be gone?"

"I swear it. I will disappear, as if I was never here." He made a theatrical little swirl, thankfully releasing me. "Now you see me, now you don't... A good trick, you must agree."

"Taking the Sultan's money with you, I suppose."

He laughed merrily. "Of course, dear lady, and that of many others, too, lining up to press absurd sums into my hand. Rich people can be so stupid, Marta. They deserve me."

Precisely my thoughts regarding Lord and Lady Barnard. Now I regretted them. No one, however unpleasant, deserved the Baron. However, my chief concern was not for them, but for Madeleine. I had to agree to the Baron's terms, or at least pretend to. Putting on a pleading voice, I said, "Swear that no harm will come to my maid if I do as you say."

"Most certainly, dear lady. I swear it on my mother's grave." He raised my hand to his abominable lips, and kissed it.

Was his mother even dead, I wondered. Had he ever had a mother?

"And was La Muratova also part of your plan?" I asked.

"Valentina! As if I would confide in such a leaky vessel." He laughed. "No, no. Valentina was just an *amuse-bouche*, so to speak. Though I admit that it suited me to pack her off out of the way in case she let slip some inconvenient pillow talk."

I blushed. I could not stop myself.

"Dearest Marta," he said. "You English are so easily shocked. Have you ever even experienced passion, I wonder? If you were younger, I might even take on the challenge myself."

I broke from him then and hurried back to the relative safety of the harem, his booming laugh echoing after me.

Chapter Twenty-two

Back in my room, I threw off my coat and sat on my bed, shaking somewhat from the encounter. Ignoring the Baron's final disgraceful insult, however, I had to ponder what to do next. Clearly, for Madeleine's sake, I could confide in no one, least of all Mr. H. As for the Sultan, he, I was sure, would never believe a mere woman beside the seductive assurances of Schmidt Pasha. No, I should have to try to find the girl myself. But where to start looking? Was she secreted somewhere within the palace complex or had Jeanne-Claude – I could not begin to think of her as Janneke – somehow managed to spirit her out? In that case, how would I ever find her in the labyrinth that was Constantinople?

Without explaining anything other than that my slave was missing, I reckoned I could still enlist the assistance of the other girls, and resolved to do so instantly.

At that moment, a tap sounded on my door. My heart jumped. It could not be Madeleine herself, who would simply have entered. It was Naime.

"I wondered, Madame Hudson," she said, "if you were unwell, since you missed dinner."

Good heavens, I had not even thought of it. How much could I now tell her? I decided to explain that I was worried about my missing slave, since, in any case, Madeleine's absence would soon be generally known.

"How very provoking for you," Naime said. "I can send one of the other slaves to you, if you like."

Was that all it was to her, a mere inconvenience? I was about to refuse her offer but then realised how useful the presence of one of the girls could be.

"Thank you," I said, "that is most kind. Perhaps Beylem or Cemile, if they have no other duties at the moment."

"I shall see to it," she replied. "Please do not worry too much, Madame Hudson. I am sure nothing bad has happened to her."

In view of the fate of the other girls, not to mention poor Gulsima, I wondered that Naime could be so sanguine. Was she completely indifferent to the fate of the slave girls? Then I realised that it was probable she only made the remark in order to comfort me.

"Shall I get some food sent to you?" she asked. "You must be hungry."

Again, I was about to refuse, but after all, I needed to keep up my strength.

"I shall tell the others that you have a headache," she continued. "People were most surprised to see your empty chair."

Oh dear, I had doubtless made a terrible faux pas in absenting myself from yet another meal. But events had swept all other considerations from my head.

"Please apologise to the Valide Sultan on my behalf," I said. "In fact, it is true that I have a headache, so once again you do not need to lie for me, Naime."

She smiled. "But when are we going to have our English class? Tomorrow maybe?"

"Certainly."

Promises, promises.

It was the plump Cemile who arrived shortly after, bearing a tray piled high with food, and clearly delighted to have been asked to assist the English lady. I explained my continuing worries about Madeleine.

"I cannot think where she could have gone," I said. "Perhaps she went exploring and has had an accident."

Cemile looked sceptical at this suggestion.

"She has probably been made to disappear, like Gulsima," was her less than encouraging response.

"Why should she? She has broken no rules."

The girl shrugged.

"Maybe she has just run away."

"She wouldn't do that... No, I want to know if there is anywhere someone could have taken her."

Cemile looked at me, puzzled.

"Taken her?"

"A hiding place."

Her eyes lit up. "Oh, you mean to *have* her. Because of her hair." The horrid thought brought a smile to her face.

"Her hair?"

"It is much admired. Such an unusual shade of red."

"But who would have seen it, other than us? No men enter the harem."

Cemile laughed.

"Oh, madame. The eunuchs have tongues, don't they. To report on us. Word gets around. A pretty little French slave has arrived."

'I see." Dismaying news, indeed.

"She could be anywhere. It wouldn't be the first time. But don't worry. They send them back afterwards."

I shook my head, to convince myself as much as her. "No, it couldn't be that. Madeleine is my slave, after all. It would be a serious breach of etiquette to abduct her."

Cemile clearly did not understand me. Slaves, as she understood it, had no rights. As for my rights, who was I to insist on them?

"Can you help me to look?" I asked.

"Of course, madame. I am yours to command."

We scoured the place, but I soon realised how hopeless was the enterprise. There was nowhere to hide in the harem. We could not enter certain rooms, but that was because they belonged to the Valide Sultan and the wives of Abdul Hamid, where, in any case, Madeleine would hardly be.

"Here's our classroom," Cemile said, opening a door.

I had hopes, unlikely ones to be sure, but, since this was where Jeanne-Claude would have met the girls, maybe there would be at least some clue within it to where they could have gone. Sadly, the room was as empty as the others: no doors apart from the one we had entered by, no possibility of hiding places.

"We learn to sing and dance, here, as well as speak French and Turkish," Cemile said, doing a graceful little twirl.

Of course, I thought. She would not be Turkish herself. Like most of the wives and concubines, fair-complexioned as she was, she would probably be Circassian.

"What about elsewhere in the palace?" I was thinking of all those pavilions. With a sinking heart of the thousand upon thousand of rooms, of the rooms where the Baron and other male guests dwelt.

Cemile knew nothing of any of that. How could she, when she so seldom left the harem?

"And the tunnels?" I asked finally. "Aren't there parts of them where Madeleine could be held against her will?"

She fidgeted and looked furtive. "I know nothing about any tunnels, madame."

What a pity Beylem had not been sent instead of this useless ninny.

"Cemile," I replied severely, "I am perfectly well aware that you girls use the tunnel from the kitchen sometimes. Beylem showed it to me. That's how Gulsima went in and out." And most probably where she met her end.

"But madame, it is dangerous. If you get caught…"

"I know." The Sultan had, after all, forbade me from entering the tunnels again. "But tell me anyway," I continued, adding, "I am not asking you to search the tunnels with me."

She considered.

"There are places down there," she admitted finally, eyes wide with excitement. "We aren't supposed to know about them. Rooms which can only be opened when you say the magic word. Rooms where wonderful treasures are stored. Heaps of gold and silver coins, jewels, rubies and emeralds as large as hens' eggs."

No, she had not seen these riches for herself, and, while it was most likely that Abdul Hamid had hidden wealth, I could not help but wonder if Cemile happened to have heard of Ali Baba and the Forty Thieves, since her account so closely mirrored that of the tale. All the same, could Madeleine really be hidden somewhere in the tunnels, in the cold and dark? I shuddered at the thought of venturing down there again. Needs must, however.

First, we returned to my room. I cannot exactly say why I decided on this particular occasion to don the garment Naime had lent to me and turn myself into a scurrying beetle. Perhaps because it made me anonymous, perhaps because the black cloth would enable me to blend in with the darkness of the tunnels, if anyone else happened to be down there, perhaps because it was warm, perhaps because it smelt comfortingly and pleasantly of the Princess herself – her characteristic sandalwood perfume – perhaps and possibly most importantly, because I could wear loose clothes underneath it, thereby allowing me freer movement.

Cemile giggled a little, helping me into the thing. No doubt she thought me completely mad. Since I could not quite remember the way to the kitchen, she conducted me there, somewhat fearfully, it must be said, in case we should be seen. However, it was very late by now, and, as on my first illicit foray, the denizens of the harem were abed, if not asleep. Cemile still looked about herself.

"What's the matter?" I whispered.

"I have heard, madame, that sometimes the Sultan himself walks these passages at night when he cannot sleep. What if we meet him. Whatever would we say?"

"I'll think of something," I replied.

It seemed unlikely that we would stumble on Abdul Hamid in his nocturnal ramblings. All the same, I kept both my eyes and ears open in case. It would be difficult to account for our presence. I could hardly say that I craved a snack, dressed as I was, and with so much to eat in my room already.

Thankfully, we reached the kitchen without encountering the Sultan or anyone else.

"Do you wish for me to come down with you?" Cemile asked in a small voice.

Of course, I should have preferred a companion, but decided not to put the girl in danger. Instead, I told her in a low voice to return to my room, and tell anyone who might come looking for me that I was asleep.

"I could place pillows under the covers," she said, "to make it look as if you are lying there."

Perhaps I had misjudged her and she was sharper than I had thought.

"That's a very good idea, Cemile."

She looked pleased. I wondered if this were the ruse used by the girls when they themselves ventured out, to fool any spy or snooping eunuch.

"Don't get lost, Madame."

I have to say that this was my greatest fear. Still recalling fairy-tales, I thought of Hansel and Gretel in the woods, and how they had left pebbles and then crumbs of bread as a trail to lead them out. The kitchen had no pebbles, but was well furnished with bread, and I supposed there were no birds in the tunnels to eat them. I explained my thoughts to Cemile.

"Oh, do not think of it, madame. The rats will have a feast day."

Rats! Oh dear, whatever was I doing?

Cemile brought me a jar of dried white broad beans.

"Take some of these, Madame. These will show up well, and the rats and mice won't touch them."

Hoping she was right, I duly plunged my hand into the jar, taking a considerable number to fill the pocket of my gown.

I embraced the amazed girl before squeezing into the entrance to the tunnel with the lamp that she had lit for me, and started down those steep steps most cautiously. I did not want to come a cropper before I had even begun.

It was chill and damp, and smelt of decay. I could not help thinking of those rats, and listened most carefully for any rustling noises, but all I could hear was the occasional drip, drip, drip of water from somewhere. The way out into the park, I remembered, lay straight ahead so when I came to the first turning, I took it instead, making sure to leave a bean conspicuously positioned.

How long I wandered those horrid tunnels, I cannot say, with no sign at all of Madeleine or any place where she might have been imprisoned. Sometimes I came to a way out, either into the palace or out into the park, and had to turn back. A very long passage, indeed, brought me into a coach house which I suspected might even be outside the palace walls. It made sense if the Sultan wished to outsmart, and escape from, any attackers.

Back I trudged, the pointlessness of my search starting to fill me with despair. Were the Baron and his appalling sister really going to get away with theft and murder? I was about to give up altogether and retrace my steps with the help of the beans, when I thought I heard voices further along the tunnel I was in.

I stood perfectly still. Yes, not only were there voices, but a faint flickering could be seen on the curved wall of the tunnel ahead of me. Leaving my lamp on the ground, I cautiously advanced towards whatever was there, most glad of my black disguise.

Creeping round the bend, an astonishing sight met my eyes. A cave had been opened in the side of the tunnel, usually blocked by a stout wooden door which now hung open. Within, lining the walls, were numerous safes and chests, some of them open, and, illuminated by the lamplight, my nemesis, the Baron, together with his duplicitous sister, Jeanne-Claude, was busy stuffing sacks with whatever they could find, the very gold and silver and jewels that Cemile had spoken of. No sign at all, however, of Madeleine.

My thought was to return as swiftly as I could and summon help. Surely, with such indisputable evidence in front of him, the Sultan would at last recognise Schmidt Pasha for the imposter and rogue that he was.

I turned to go but the careless movement must have alerted the sharp-eyed Jeanne-Claude, for she cried out a warning. And although I was as black as the tunnel walls, my lamp, though at a distance, must have let out a faint glow, which outlined my form.

I tried to run, but the Baron leapt forward and grabbed me, pulling back my veil.

He burst out laughing.

"Of course. The unstoppable Marta Hudson disguised as a concubine... Oh, you foolish foolish woman. Why could you not leave well alone?"

Jeanne-Claude stepped forward and slapped me hard on the face. I instinctively reciprocated in kind, whereupon she spat out some sort of imprecation in a guttural language I did not understand. Dutch or Flemish, I supposed.

"Where is Madeleine?" I demanded.

"Not here, evidently," the Baron replied. "Still safe for now. Although..."

Jeanne-Claude interrupted with a barrage of words in that same strange tongue. The Baron frowned, looked thoughtful, and, then with a sigh, nodded his head.

"I am sorry, Marta," he said. "But my sister is right. You are too much of a liability to be allowed to live."

With a swift movement, he stepped towards me, raised his cane, and all went black.

Chapter Twenty-three

Where was I? It was dark, but no longer the pitch blackness of the tunnels. I was lying on my back on what seemed to be stony ground. Stars glinted coldly above me, and the air was frosty. Outside, then. Outside in a place where low grunts and squeaks broke the stillness, where overpowering animal odours made my sore head spin. The menagerie.

Two figures, their backs to me, were busying themselves with something I could not see. I tried to wriggle away, to stand up. In vain. They noticed.

"Oh no, you don't," the Baron exclaimed, pulling me to my feet.

But I had grabbed a stone, and smashed it into his face.

He cursed me roundly, and roughly dragged me to what I now saw with horror was the tiger's cage.

"This beast will make short work of you, Madame Hudson," Jeanne-Claude said, opening the door. 'How silly of you to think of entering it.'

Although I struggled with all my strength, the two of them soon overpowered me and thrust me in to the cage, slamming shut the door behind me.

The noise had roused the beast, who padded towards me, sniffed me. Then, to my astonishment, gently nuzzled into me. Perhaps Guzellik wasn't hungry.

"What's the matter with the creature? Isn't the woman fat enough for it?" That was Jeanne-Claude.

It seemed not. I caressed Guzellik's head. Her tongue licked at my dress.

The expletive emitted by the Baron does not bear repetition.

"We'll see about that!" he exclaimed, and tried to poke at Guzellik through the bars with his cane, but we were too far out of his reach.

He opened the cage door.

"Careful, Reynaert," Jeanne-Claude said.

"I know what I am doing, Janneke. Look at the beast. It's a pussy-cat, not a tiger... We can't leave her here to be found like this."

He entered the cage and approached us, the stick brandished in front of him. I felt Guzellik stiffen, the hairs on her back bristling.

What happened next will be imprinted on my memory forever. Snarling, the tiger suddenly leapt forward and sank her teeth into the outstretched arm of the Baron. She tossed him up and over, smashing his head on to the ground, his body on the back wall of the cage, lifting him high in the air, blood spraying everywhere. I watched horror-struck, even though the Baron and his diabolical sister had planned the same fate for me. But, my God, his squeals of agony were the most frightful sound I had ever heard. Then, even more ghastly, a rattling moan, followed by silence. Silence broken then by the hysterical screeching of Jeanne-Claude outside the cage. The bellows and barks, the howls and roars, the excited yelps of the other animals.

All this noise roused the keeper, evidently sleeping in an adjacent building. He came running, still pulling his jacket on, but stood gawping stupidly for several seconds, before pulling himself together. Speaking in a calm firm voice to Guzellik, who was slathering over her prey, he edged towards me and led me out. In truth, I could hardly stand, my legs trembling beneath me.

"Get my brother out too," Jeanne-Claude shouted at the keeper.

He shrugged as if to say, what is the point. The man is dead.

"She did it!" Jeanne-Claude screeched, pointing at me. "Why did the tiger not attack her?... I'll tell you why. She's a witch."

The keeper shrank away from me then. Indeed, I had no explanation as to why Guzellik behaved the way she did.

Suddenly, Jeanne-Claude started to run.

"You will never find Madeleine now!" she yelled, as she went. "Never."

"Stop her," I shouted, but the keeper stayed where he was. He evidently did not take orders from a witch. I sank down in despair.

Now other people, roused by the unusual noises, started to arrive, and, for the first time since I arrived in Constantinople, I was glad to see the eunuch, Bashir.

"The Baron tried to kill me," I babbled.

"Who?"

I pointed to the remains of the man inside the cage. "Schmidt Pasha."

Bashir presumably had seen terrible sights in his life, some of which, quite possibly, perpetrated by himself. But now the shock on his face was indisputable.

"That is not Schmidt Pasha," he said.

"But it is," I insisted. "The man's real name is Baron Maupertuis. If you can get word to Mr. Sherrinford at the Pera Palace hotel, he will tell you."

A huge weariness suddenly overcame me, a dizziness I could not fight. I sank to the ground. Bashir picked me up in his arms as if I weighed nothing, and, muttering something to the keeper, carried me back down to the harem, and to the welcome space of my room.

Cemile had been sleeping on the floor. On seeing us enter, her big eyes nearly filled her whole face.

"Madame" she exclaimed. "Whatever has happened to you?"

Bashir said something to the girl. Then turned to leave.

"Do not forget," I cried after him. "A message to Mr. Sherrinford at the Pera Palace hotel. It is urgent."

I was not sure if he heard me, since he made no sign.

What a pity, I thought, not for the first time, that Sultan Abdul Hamid was so unreasonably terrified of telephones that he would not permit their use in Yildiz. The time it would take for a carriage to be sent for Mr. H, and to return with him, would allow Jeanne-Claude ample opportunity to deal with Madeleine and to flee.

"Your face, madame…" Cemile said anxiously. "Did you fall?"

I felt my cheek. It was swollen and sore where the Baron had struck me senseless.

"Help me undress," I said.

All I wanted was to lie down, even though this was no time to sleep. At least I could rest until Mr. H arrived.

Cemile drew the black gown over my head with gentle care, then cried out in horror. The garment was covered in blood. 'Are you wounded, madame?"

"No," I reassured her weakly. "It is not my blood."

Before I could explain further, a loud rapping was heard on the door. Cemile hastened to open it. A eunuch, not Bashir, marched in. It was a summons to attend Abdul Hamid himself.

I supposed he wanted to thank me, although, in all honesty, he might have waited until the morning. The eunuch waited impatiently while I dressed, for I could hardly be received by the Sultan in my shift. Then, attended by Cemile, for I was still wobbly on my feet and needed her support, I followed the eunuch to the same room where – it seemed a lifetime ago now – Mr. H and I had our first audience with the Sultan. And there he was once again, a small figure on a sofa, fidgeting with his worry beads amidst the oriental splendours that by now I took for granted, the elaborately woven carpets, the embroidered screen, the canaries roused from sleep by untimely visitors. Cemile, I could tell, was quite overcome, and sank to her knees in a gesture of humility, while I stood my ground.

Indeed, I was surprised that the Sultan did not indicate I should sit. Instead, I had to lean on the girl's shoulder, or I should have fallen.

Abdul Hamid regarded me from under hooded eyelids for a considerable time. Finally he said, "An imposter and a thief…"

"Yes, Your Majesty," I started to reply, "You must be shocked…"

He held up a beringed hand to silence me.

"An imposter, a thief, and a witch…"

I gaped at him. Was he accusing me? I did not understand.

"An imposter, a thief, a witch and a murderer."

"No, Your Majesty, it was the Baron, Schmidt Pasha…"

"Silence!"

He looked over my shoulder and beckoned. Someone else had entered. She passed me and sank into a deep curtsey in front of the Sultan. It was Jeanne-Claude.

What was happening here?

"Repeat your accusations, Madame Cordelier," Abdul Hamid ordered.

"Very well, Your Majesty." She half-turned in my direction. "This evening, my beloved brother and I were taking a midnight stroll in your beautiful park. Suddenly we caught sight of a woman – this woman – but dressed in a *charshaf*, and acting most strangely, as if fearing she might be observed. We decided to follow her. Imagine our amazement, when she made her way through a hidden door into what turned out to be a tunnel."

"Lies," I exclaimed.

"Silence. Please continue, Madame Cordelier."

"Thank you, Your Majesty." She made a little curtsey. "As I was saying, we followed this woman into the tunnel, where we eventually found her in some sort of strong room filled with treasures. Your Majesty, she was trying to rob you."

"No, it was you and your brother. I found you…"

"If you do not hold your tongue, madame, I will have it cut out."

I shivered. Was the Sultan really capable of such brutality? I feared so.

Jeanne-Claude continued her fairy-tale.

"On seeing us, she fled along the passage that, as we soon discovered, leads out into the menagerie. I should say, Your Majesty, that at this time we had no idea it was Madame Hudson in disguise. We thought it was one of the slaves."

He nodded, staring at us both from under heavy eyelids.

"The witch then took refuge in the tiger's cage," Jeanne-Claude said, "using her powers to control the beast. My brother…" Here her voice broke with apparent emotion… "My brave brother followed her in, intending to arrest her, whereupon she muttered some magic words in the tiger's ear and it… it savagely attacked my brother, tearing him to pieces, killing him… my dearest Reynaert." She collapsed in tears.

Abdul Hamid turned pitiless eyes upon me. "You have abused my hospitality, woman. You have stayed here under false pretences, using a false identity. You have even somehow managed to fool the greatest detective of our age into trusting your wisdom. Oh, I should have seen through you when you failed to discover how my dear concubines died. Perhaps it was you who cast a spell on them from a distance. I do not know…" He stroked his beard thoughtfully. "You have planned to rob me of my treasure, I who have been more than generous towards you. Even now you are shamelessly wearing the jewels I gave you, the dress from Paris… But far far worse than any of that, you have caused this poor lady's beloved brother to be killed, a man indeed who had become a close friend to myself, and, in doing so, have cruelly killed the genius who was about to install the most complete system of security ever seen around this palace, around me, Sultan of the Ottomans. Luckily enough, Madame Cordelier has told me that she has the necessary plans required to complete Schmidt Pasha's great work."

He sat back.

For the sake of my tongue, I had to stay quiet during this catalogue of absurdities. Surely Mr. H would arrive soon and disabuse this credulous man.

"What punishment can there be on earth to fit your crimes? Should your hands be cut off? Should you be hanged? Should you be burnt to death? What do you say now?"

If I had not Cemile's shoulder to grip, I should have fallen to the ground.

"I am innocent of all this, Your Majesty," I said. "You have been misled. Sherlock Holmes can explain it."

"Sherlock Holmes and Dr. Watson have been sent back to England. I have no need of them, now that my security is guaranteed by Schmidt Pasha's invention."

This was a mighty blow, indeed. But surely my gentlemen would not depart without me. If true, my sorry fate was sealed.

"Take the witch away." Abdul Hamid waved a hand in the air. "I shall think upon a suitable punishment."

The eunuchs stepped forward and wrenched me from the embrace of Cemile. Jeanne-Claude could not suppress a sneer of triumph.

"Ask her, ask Madame Cordelier what she has done with my maid, Madeleine," I cried, as they dragged me away. "Where is Madeleine?"

They chained me to the wall by my ankle. The cell was underground, and, like the tunnels, dank and musty, and doubtless home to legions of mice and rats. I was wearing the stylish garment I had donned in order to meet the Sultan, a Paris dress in truth, as chosen by Madame Celestine, the pearl grey silk that offered no warmth. Dim light filtering under the door of my cell from the passageway without, was all that saved me from absolute darkness. A jug of brackish water had been left within reach, but nothing else. Perhaps I was to be left starve or freeze to death. If so, a quick execution would prove the preferred alternative.

However, I have been in seemingly hopeless situations before, and have always refused to give in to despair. I still could not believe that Mr. H would abandon me. And surely I had other friends who would speak up for me. Naime, for instance.

I was angry, too. Angry at Sultan Abdul Hamid for his crass obstinacy, his obsession with his own survival. He had not, I now realised, cared one jot for the fate of the slaves except insofar as it affected his own safety. Jeanne-Claude had read him well. I was angry, too, of course, at the woman herself for her lies and duplicity. In due course, the Sultan would find this out to his cost, but, in all likelihood, too late for me. Above all, I was raging at myself, for my naivete, to have trusted Jeanne-Claude as far as I did. Had Mr. H not warned me not to trust anyone?

The illogical nature of my incarceration could not, all the same, but bring a bitter smile to my face. Were I really the witch they accused me of being, with the power to control a tiger, surely the chains and locks of a mere dungeon could not hold me? But no one was there to harken to my reasoning.

Recalling the tiger, led me to ponder again on Guzellik's puzzling behaviour. Why had she spared me and yet set upon the Baron so viciously? Suddenly, huddled in the chill of the dungeon, wishing I could wrap something warm around myself, it came to me. I had been wearing Naime's *charsaf*, a garment redolent with the scent of a woman who had reared the tiger from a cub. Guzellik had taken me for her beloved friend, and, when the Baron had entered wielding his cane, it was Naime she was protecting.

Would I ever have a chance to explain this to Abdul Hamid? Would he even listen?

In this hour of need there was one thing at least that I could do, and I knelt on the stony floor and prayed as I had never prayed before, not just for myself but also for poor little Madeleine. Dear God, let her at least be spared.

Thus prostrated, it was a long long time before I heard anyone approaching, and I was beginning to think I had been abandoned there to rot. Hoping the newcomer would prove to be a saviour, I was sorely disappointed when he turned out to be nothing more than a prison guard with a bowl of slop for me to eat. I tried to talk to him – a very young soldier – but he did not understand French. Miming a shawl for my shoulders, I hoped he would be able to provide me at least with something to keep me warm, but he shook his head. Then he squinted sideways at me, or rather at the ring still incongruously worn on my finger, a ruby set in diamonds. I took it off and offered it to him. He hesitated, took it, then left me alone again.

Would I ever see him or my ring again? Perhaps he would return with a warm blanket, and I could use my remaining jewels to buy other privileges, even – though this was hardly likely – to buy an escape. Meanwhile I swallowed the disgusting soup and waited. What else could I do?

I had quite given up on the young soldier, when – it must have been some hours later, he returned – with another bowl of the same watery gruel as before, and, God be praised, a ragged scrap of woollen material that smelt rank, but comforted, all the same. I thanked him and offered him a diamond brooch, in crescent form. As he took it, I thought how lucky it was at least that I had dressed myself up for that ill-fated interview. How lucky, too, that I was not wearing the amethyst ring gifted to me by dearest Henry. It would have quite broken my heart to part with it.

I cursed myself, all the same, for leaving my fob watch behind, since, without it, I lost all awareness of time. Was it night or day? Was the next inevitable bowl of gruel breakfast, lunch or dinner? I could no longer tell. I know I dozed fitfully, woken with a start when something scurried across my lap. At least the young soldier had started to bring me hunks of bread with my soup, perhaps in exchange for the diamond brooch, hardly a fair exchange, although he was kind enough. Another might not have been.

I still possessed a necklace for bargaining. Pointing to the shackle on my ankle, I hoped that he might rid me of the thing that chafed badly, and made impossible any hope at all of escape. The lad shook his head. That would have been a privilege too far: He had to think of his own life and freedom. Although I had expected as much, it was a grave disappointment. I had already tried to see if I had anything to loosen the shackle. In vain. It was of iron and unbendable.

Still, when I mimed washing myself – for I felt very dirty, something I am not used to, being most particular in my toilette – without any reward, he started bringing me a bowl of water and a rough cloth. It was something. I thanked him, pointed to myself and said "Martha." After a pause, he did the same. "Emin" was his name.

Did my guardian have others to watch and look after? At first, I thought I was all alone in that subterranean dungeon. Then I became aware of a rumbling of low groans, and, once, a shriek that, no sooner emitted, was silenced by a blow. It was either late on the second day or early on the third that something truly dreadful occurred. Blood-curdling screams from an adjacent cell indicated that someone was being tortured there. This was followed by the thud, thud, thud of footsteps along the passageway, together with the sound of something or someone being dragged. When Emin came to me later with my soup, he looked pale and shaken, and did not linger. I could not but ponder that Abdul Hamid was still deciding what frightful punishment he would mete out to me. Perhaps later today or tomorrow, the dungeons would echo to my own screams.

To prevent myself dwelling on possible future unpleasantness, I, instead, closed my eyes and tried to conjure up happy times. To say that dear Henry visited me in that hell-hole would be an exaggeration – I am no believer in the return of the dead to earth, for heaven must surely be far more attractive to the departed. Yet the memory of my late husband consoled me. It was as if he spoke to me, saying "One way or another, Martha dear, this must soon be over."

Communing thus with him, recalling our life together, I told him about our two lovely daughters and their families, Judith in Edinburgh with her three children, and Eleanor, so recently visited by me in Kent, and the new mother of a lovely boy, named Henry for his grandfather, and not, as his silly paternal grandmother, Henrietta, had surmised, for herself. The thought of what Henrietta, with her snobbery and unwavering reverence for royalty and blue blood, would make of my present situation even brought a fleeting smile to my lips.

I was engaged thus, one morning, afternoon or evening – impossible to know – reliving the heady times I had spent in Paris with my sister, when a sudden explosion of noise brought me crashing back to my miserable cell. Angry voices were approaching. Was this it, then? I braced myself as my door swung open. Someone was holding a lamp which, after days spent in darkness, quite blinded me.

"Mrs. Hudson! Martha!" exclaimed a delightfully familiar voice. It was Mr. H, shocked at what he observed.

The next moment, a second man, hurried over to me. Dear Dr. Watson. I am afraid I quite succumbed, and burst into a torrent of tears. He hugged me close.

"You are safe, now," he said. "We are here."

"Free this woman immediately," Mr. H ordered.

Emin, trembling behind him, did not move. The poor boy had no idea what to do, what was going on.

Mr. H then snapped out something in a language I recognised to be Turkish, but still Emin remained transfixed. Then, suddenly, he ran off.

"This is outrageous," Mr. H announced angrily. "We have been trying to find you for three days, Mrs. Hudson, after your maid came looking for us."

"Madeleine?" I looked up at him hopefully.

"No... some slave girl."

"Cemile?"

'That's the one."

I did not understand.

"Cemile came to the hotel?" How was that possible?

"She was in a dreadful state," Dr. Watson said. "We could make no sense of what she was telling us. It seemed so utterly bizarre that I am afraid we took her for a mad woman at first."

How the girl had managed to leave the harem and make her way to the Pera Palace, even to have the sense to ask there for Mr. H, was at that moment quite beyond me. But God bless her for it.

Apparently, Mr. H and Dr. Watson had received none of my earlier messages and had had no inkling that I had been trying to contact them. That puzzled me. I understood that Jeanne-Claude had appropriated the one I had given her, the one that alerted the Baron to the fact that I was on to his scheme. However, what of the one Naime had sent inviting Mr. H and Dr. Watson to Schmidt Pasha's demonstration? No, they had not received that either. So was Naime part of the plot? Impossible. Someone must have intercepted that message too. I could not begin to work it out.

Now Emin returned with a burly, rough looking fellow, a bunch of keys hanging from his waist. Presumably the warden of the dungeons and a man who looked quite capable of inflicting the horrors I had overheard latterly. When Mr. H addressed this individual, again in Turkish, no doubt again demanding my release, he frowned and shook his head and growled out some words in decidedly unfriendly tones, a pig-headed expression on his ugly face.

I did not see Mr. H's move, so sudden it was, but, as a result, the warden crashed senseless to the ground. Mr. H snatched the keys from the man's belt and showed them to a terrified Emin, presumably asking which one would fit my shackles.

The boy took them from his hand and, with shaking hands, unbolted my ankle. Then, while Dr. Watson raised me gently and carried me from the place, Mr. H dragged the still comatose warden across to the wall and tied him up with the shackle in my stead. After which he said something to Emin, who nodded, nervously. Mr. H, to my shock and horror, then knocked him out, too.

He locked the two of them in the cell.

"We'll give that blackguard a taste of his own medicine," he said with satisfaction.

"The young soldier was kind to me," I told him.

"That is precisely why I did what I did, and why I am locking him up too. So that, with luck, he will not be too severely punished."

I felt like a baby as Dr. Watson carried me along those dark corridors and up the slimy stone steps that brought us out of the dungeon. Beside the heavy doors, another two guards lay slumped into oblivion.

"They will be fine," Dr. Watson whispered. "Just a couple of sore heads when they wake up."

Until the Sultan removes those heads from them as punishment, I thought. Still, I could not waste pity on them. I just hoped that Emin would be spared the royal wrath.

The misty half-light that hung over the park indicated to me that it was either late afternoon or very early morning. When I asked Dr. Watson which it was, he was somewhat startled.

"It is evening, my dear," he said.

We hurried through the semi-darkness away from the dungeons to where a carriage was awaiting us near one of the pavilions. The driver must have been paid well for his discretion, for he did not look at the mad woman he was to drive out of the palace grounds. At any moment I expected a hue and cry, but all stayed quiet.

"It is dinner time," Dr. Watson said. "Everyone is engaged in ritual feasting."

I shrank into the shadows within the carriage as we arrived at the gates. Would I be discovered at this last barrier to my freedom? Thankfully not. Mr. H waved in friendly fashion to the guards there, calling out a few words in Turkish, and soon we were rattling down the hill towards the city.

At times, during that journey back, I confess that I wondered if I were dreaming. Was I really out of that dreadful place? Was I really saved? Were my two saviours flesh and blood, or spirits conjured up by a disturbed mind?

"The Sultan told me that he had sent you back to England," I managed to mutter.

"Yes," Mr. H replied, "he told us that we should leave. In fact, he was in such a hurry about it that I inferred something was amiss. Especially when he added that Madame Hudson wished to remain. Delightful though harem life must be, it hardly seemed likely."

"He will come after me." I exclaimed "Mr. Holmes, Abdul Hamid believes I have done terrible things. That was why he threw me into that dungeon." I started to shake uncontrollably. "He will not forgive me, or you, unless you can persuade him of the truth of what I have said."

"Calm yourself, Mrs. Hudson," Dr. Watson said. "Our first duty is to get you clean, warm, fed and rested. Then we will decide what to do."

"We must find Madeleine," I cried. "Madeleine…"

Chapter Twenty-four

We swept into the Pera Palace hotel, Dr. Watson carrying me wrapped in his own thick cloak, both for warmth and to disguise the abject nature of my condition.

"I am a doctor. This lady has had an accident," he called to the receptionist, as he made for the lift.

I suppose they were used to the eccentricities of foreigners, for no one tried to stop us, and soon we reached the haven of the gentlemen's rooms. Dr. Watson ran me a proper bath – by which I mean it was in the style to which we Europeans are used, and not the marble fountain arrangements of the harem.

To say I was shocked at the sight of myself in the big mirror of the bathroom was a considerable understatement. I was filthy, despite my attempts at washing in the cell. The large bruise on my face, from where the Baron had struck me, had turned vile shades of sulphur yellow and purple. Gladly I shed my Paris gown, now reeking, stained and torn, and, after sponging off as much of the grime as I could, stepped into the hot bath, paradoxically shivering there, for I was frozen to the bone.

I did not linger, however, much as I should have loved to wallow in the sweet-scented water, for there was much to discuss, and so, soon, clad in a clean nightshirt of the Doctor's, modestly covered by his robe, I joined my gentlemen in their comfortable bedroom-cum-living room, where I was delighted to find that a good strong pot of tea was awaiting me.

"Since you have been deprived of nourishing food for a while," the Doctor said, "You should not shock the system too quickly with a heavy meal, Mrs. Hudson. Instead, here are some dry biscuits you may take for now."

What a disappointment! Never mind any shock to the system, I had been hoping for a big plate of chops, mashed potatoes, cabbage and gravy, the anticipation of which had often left me salivating in my dungeon. However, I bowed to superior medical advice and nibbled on the biscuits, somewhat tastier and more easily swallowed, as I found, when dipped in the strong sweet tea.

Meantime, I described, as succinctly as possible, what I had discovered regarding the Baron's plan to swindle the Sultan and his guests.

"He was very convincing," I told them. "If I had not seen Mr. Maskelyne perform a similar trick, I too might have been completely taken in."

"I very much doubt that, Mrs. Hudson," said the Doctor, smiling.

"You claim the deaths of the concubines was all part of his scheme?" Mr. H asked.

"By killing off the Sultan's favourites one by one and thereby playing on his superstitious mind, Jeanne-Claude knew that Abdul Hamid would be much more open to the Baron's supposedly infallible security system. Indeed, it seems that she was the instigator and perpetrator of the whole business, rather than her brother. She was already here on the spot, after all, and, apparently, even took a perverted pleasure in the murders. However, before I could unmask her, she had cunningly persuaded the Sultan that it was I, rather than the Baron and herself, who was the villain."

I described finding them filling sacks with looted treasure, having broken into a tunnel strongroom. How they had discovered me and thrown me into the tiger's den.

"Instead of killing me, Guzellik behaved like a pet kitten."

The two of them stared at me aghast.

"So easy, then," I continued, "for Jeanne-Claude to accuse me of witchcraft."

"The tiger spared you but tore the Baron to pieces!" exclaimed Dr. Watson. "Maybe you are a witch, after all, Mrs. Hudson."

Even Mr. H looked bemused.

I explained my theory, then, that Guzellik had taken me for Naime, who had reared him from a cub, since I happened to be wearing her robe, infused with her favourite perfume.

"Yes, I see, I see." Mr. H drummed his fingers on the arm of his chair. "But I fear you are still in grave danger, Mrs. Hudson. If the Sultan's men find you here, they are likely to drag you back to that hell hole without a moment's pause. I cannot rely on my own relationship with Abdul Hamid in this case. He no doubt thinks you have bewitched me too." He smiled grimly, while I could not but chuckle a little wildly at the thought. "We must move you to another place," he continued.

"Another room in the hotel?" the doctor suggested.

"No, they would find her in an instant. Somewhere else. But where? Another hotel would also be too dangerous. Too public."

"The Orient Express?"

I shook my head.

"I will not leave without finding what has happened to Madeleine."

"In any case," Mr. H said, "the next train isn't until Friday. Three whole days away."

A sudden notion came to me.

"If Eliza Dodds is still in Constantinople, I could perhaps lodge with her." I paused, and then added, somewhat mischievously. "I'm sure she would agree, especially if she knew that you were looking into Cecelia's situation."

Mr. H clapped his hands together. "Of course, Mrs. Hudson. What a splendid notion! After all, it is not as if I have anything better to do. Like clearing your good name and opening the eyes of the Sultan of Turkey to the gigantic fraud being perpetrated upon him."

"Now, now, Holmes," Dr. Watson said. "Just consider. Surely, it would be an ideal solution for Mrs. Hudson to stay with Miss Dodds. Who would look for her there? Meanwhile I myself could visit the sister, or whoever she truly is, in her new situation, and see if she wishes to stay there. If she does, then there is little Miss Dodds can do. If not... well... I can endeavour to extract the wretched girl from the situation in which she has placed herself. It would leave you free to pursue your more important business."

Mr. H nodded thoughtfully. "A good idea, Watson. But do we know where Miss Dodds is lodging now? She is hardly still with the Barnards."

"I know where," I said. "She is staying in their city apartment." But then I realised that the address written out by Lady Barnard was still in my reticule back at Yildiz, along with all my other possessions.

Luckily, this did not prove an obstacle, since Mr. H was in possession of the address from his previous interview with Lord Barnard.

"A clod," he commented drily.

There was no time to be lost. At any moment, the imprisoned guards could be discovered and the alarm raised. Thus, once again bundled into Dr. Watson's cloak, I was brought down to the hotel entrance hall.

"I need a conveyance urgently to take this lady to the hospital," Dr. Watson said. "I cannot deal with her injuries here."

This lie was in case anyone came asking.

The receptionist sprang to assistance, while at the same time trying to peer at my face, which I kept buried in the fabric of the cloak. Cabs were usually waiting outside the door, and, thankfully, this was the case now.

Why we went to a hospital instead of directly to Eliza's dwelling puzzled me, until Mr. H explained that our ruse would be of no avail if the cab driver revealed our destination to the Sultan's men.

From the hospital we took another cab – and if I were truly badly injured, I am sure the rattling of my bones, as the cab bumped over the cobbled streets, would have done me no good at all. This time, again in order to foil any pursuers, Mr. H stopped it at an hotel near enough to Eliza's abode. Mr. H entered the establishment, and then, when the cab had driven off, came out again, and we walked the last part, I was pleased to feel my strength returning, even though I was still grateful for the doctor's strong arm.

Thank God that Eliza was home. Although she opened the door only a fearful crack when Mr. H hammered upon it, after taking one look at me she flung it wide. I regretted my sometimes unkind thoughts about her, for she was all solicitude, particularly in view of the horrid bruise on my face, which I explained as the result of a fall. The look she gave me suggested she did not believe a word of it, though she let it pass. Of course, we did not go into details concerning my need for somewhere to stay, but I am sure her penchant for sensational literature sent her imagination spinning. A lady arrives at night, seeking sanctuary! How thrilling was that! However, the full truth of my situation would, I think, have astounded even her. I just hoped we had not put her in danger, too.

"Imagine," she said, after Mr. H and Dr. Watson had hurried away, "your gentlemen taking an interest in poor me." For Mr. H been charmingly attentive – as he could be when he wanted – and had promised to have news of Cecelia before Eliza's departure.

"The Barnards are paying for your return trip, I hope," I said.

"Grudgingly, and only third class. But you know, Martha, I shall be so happy to return to Norwood, to civilisation. If Mr. Holmes manages to persuade dear Cecelia to come with me, my happiness will be complete."

Her broad face, already red, flushed a deeper shade of crimson.

She was of course astonished – and more than a little shocked – to discover that my only apparel consisted of a gentleman's nightshirt and robe, and hastened to provide me with a garment of her own.

"A very poor thing after your Paris style," she apologised, while I assured her that I was much more comfortable in the plain wool dress in a dull shade of brown that she provided for me.

It was a little on the big size, although I could not be called thin, especially after the feasts enjoyed in the harem, and despite the deprivations of the past few days. Still, Eliza was a size or two larger than I was. But better too big than too small.

I suppose I should not have been surprised at the very basic nature of the accommodation provided, although, when Lady Barnard had told me that the erstwhile governess was to be lodged in their city apartment, I had envisaged something much grander than these two poky basement rooms.

"Oh no," Eliza remarked, when I expressed the thought. "This is where their servants stay. The apartment is upstairs, locked." She laughed a little bitterly. "As if they would allow me any luxuries."

"You are well rid of them," I said. "That horrid little boy, in particular."

"Yes, indeed." She lowered her voice, although no one else was listening. "Do you believe in pure evil, Martha?"

Could I say that I did not, after my recent experiences? Yet, if she meant Edward, then I could hardly agree. I saw an over-indulged child in need of sharp discipline, and perhaps affection, too. In my view, his parents were much to blame for the behaviour of their son. I said as much.

"Oh well, I grant they are not nice people, either," she replied. "Still, there is something demonic about that boy. I think he has the evil eye."

So Eliza was already versed in that particular piece of local superstition.

Of course, once we were settled, she could not resist probing my reasons for flight.

"It must have been really urgent, Martha, for you to leave like that without your things."

"It was, Eliza."

I told her nothing of the Baron, nothing of my incarceration, nothing indeed of my miraculous escape from the tiger, although how thrilled she would have been to hear of it. Instead, I simply said that, like her, I had been accused of something of which I was innocent.

"I cannot reveal more at the moment, Eliza," I said, "for your own sake."

"At least tell me who hit you," she pleaded, and, when I paused, added, "No one gets a bruise like that from a fall, Martha."

"It was a man," I replied. "A very wicked man."

She nodded, probably imagining I had fought off a villain with designs on my virtue.

"The beast. I hope he got his just deserts."

One could say that.

There was no way I was prepared to sit quietly tête-à-tête with Eliza Dodds for three days, as instructed by Mr. H. It would have proved a prison almost as unbearable as the other. No, that is too frivolous a comparison. However, to be incarcerated so closely with a woman who never stopped babbling foolishness was hardly tolerable. In any case, I had things to do. I had to find Madeleine.

Since Eliza was such an avid reader of yellow-back novels, I decided to play on that to my advantage, and include her, to a very limited extent in my project. The first thing I needed was for her to acquire for me a *charsaf*, so that I could move anonymously around the city.

"You see," I told her, lowering my own voice to confidential tones, "who knows where my enemies might be lurking?"

Her already bulging eyes nearly popped out of her head with excitement. Unused to inactivity, she had soon become bored, and this was more thrilling than anything she could have imagined happening to her.

"Oh yes, Martha, certainly."

"I also need the address of a Frenchwoman who gives language lessons. Perhaps you could inquire, discreetly, for Madame Jeanne-Claude Cordelier, in the guise of one wishing to become one of her students."

"Where could I do that?"

I pondered. "The French embassy, I suppose." If the woman had been telling me the truth, her husband held some diplomatic role there. In any case, they would surely know the whereabouts of one of their citizens.

"Anything else?"

Could Eliza purchase a gun for me?

I rather thought that would be far beyond her powers, so was astonished when she replied, "Ah, but I already have a pistol, Martha. For my protection, you understand."

When she produced the thing, I was even more taken aback. It was a pretty jewelled trinket of a gun, with an ivory grip, hardly what I should have expected her to possess.

"Where ever did you get this?" I asked.

"I found it in the drawer of the schoolroom where I gave Edward his classes. Presumably, left intended for my use if need be. I decided to bring it with me here, just in case, you know. Though, of course, I have no idea how to us it."

That it was Lady Barnard's missing pistol, I had no doubt. If Eliza had been found it possession of it, all hell, I am sure, would have broken loose again. No wonder the boy was grinning when Lady Barnard mentioned the loss of it.

I examined it.

"Oh, do be careful," Eliza exclaimed, as I looked to see if it was loaded. All six chambers were furnished with bright little bullets. Most satisfactory.

"May I take this then?" I asked.

"Are you going to kill that wicked man with it?" she asked, her imagination already conjuring up the bloody scene.

'I won't be killing anyone, unless they try to kill me first," I promised.

Chapter Twenty-five

Eliza Dodds entered into the spirit of intrigue with a will that surprised me not a little, for someone who had previously shown herself so timorous. Quite likely it was that she saw herself as one of the heroines of the trashy literature she loved so much. At any rate, she readily bustled off to the market, and soon returned bearing a voluminous black *charsaf*.

"The man said it would fit me, so I suppose it will fit you too," she said. And indeed, it covered me from head to toe with quite a quantity of fabric to spare.

Moreover, the French embassy had been happy to furnish her with the address of Madame Jeanne-Claude Cordelier, so, all in all, her expedition had been a great success, and I complimented her on it. She blushed with delight.

"But Martha, promise me you will be careful. These people are dangerous."

No need to tell me that, of course, but I promised anyway.

Madeleine was most likely being held, I reckoned, at Jeanne-Claude's residence, so I resolved to start there. The last thing I wanted, however, was to confront the she-devil herself too soon and alert her to my search. Early the next morning, therefore, having made my way to the apartment block in question, I decided to wait nearby, in the hope that Jeanne-Claude would emerge, and leave the coast clear. Luckily for me, no one paid much attention to a black-clad woman sitting out in the rare winter sun. I hunched my shoulders as if to seem old and feeble and in need of a rest. One woman, indeed, stopped to ask, as I supposed from her kindly tone, if I were all right. I simply shook my head and she passed on. It was tedious and chilly waiting there, all the same, so finally, with no sign of my quarry, I abandoned my watch, took the bull by the horns, and entered the lobby of the apartment block.

The concierge regarded me, in my Turkish garb, with some suspicion, since the building housed only Europeans. However, when I enquired in my imperfect French for Madame Cordelier, he told me that the family had left for their house in Bebek. All that waiting in the cold had been a complete waste of time! Nevertheless, after I insisted that it was a matter of urgency I contact them, the man provided me with the address and directions. He even stepped out with me and summoned a cab.

If he were curious as to who this English woman in Turkish clothes could possibly be, he did not show it. I supposed that some European ladies married into the Moslem faith, with all it entailed. Indeed, had not Cecelia done that precise thing? As the cab carried me out of the city, I wondered if Dr. Watson had managed to meet her.

Bebek proved to be a pleasant and prosperous coastal suburb of Constantinople, with splendid views over the Bosphorus. Narrow streets led from the edge of the sea up the side of a steep hill to my destination. Once again, I realised, with a sinking heart, that I had omitted to inform anyone where I was going. Such a lapse had all but caused my demise in Kent in the previous year, so one might imagine I had learnt not to rush foolishly in where angels fear to tread. Alas, no. My hand closed over the reassuring grip of Eliza Dodds's little gun. At least this time I was better prepared.

The happy thought then occurred to me to send the cab-driver back to the Pera Palace with an explanatory note to Mr. H, paying the man generously for his trouble out of money with which Dr. Watson had furnished me. Still, it was with many misgivings that I watched the cab take off back down the hill to the city. Perhaps the driver would not bother to deliver the message, and just pocket the coins.

My heart in my mouth at what lay ahead, I turned to regard the country residence of the Cordeliers. It was a modest enough wooden house, quite secluded, set as it was in a garden of trees and thick shrubs: an ideal place, in fact, to keep a prisoner hidden. I had high hopes of finding Madeleine within, although exactly how I could effect her escape was another matter. Would I really be prepared to shoot someone in the attempt?

This time, there was no point waiting outside. Who knew how long it would be before I saw anyone emerge? I rang the bell at the gate and a Turkish manservant soon emerged from the house to find out what I wanted. He first addressed me in his own language, taken in by my garb, until I explained in French that I was a friend of Madame Cordelier's. A friend!

"I regret that Madame is not here just now," he replied, adding, with a strange look on his face, "Monsieur is within, if you would like to see him."

"Yes, thank you," I replied. All the better.

"As you will. Who shall I say is calling?"

I had not thought that far ahead. With no idea how involved M. Cordelier might be in his wife's machinations, to give my own name might raise suspicions.

"Eliza Dodds," I replied, the first name that came to me.

The servant led me into the house and up some stairs, I casting my eyes around me, as much as I could within the confines of the headdress, to get my bearings. If Madeleine were on an upper floor, it would prove all the more difficult to escape. But perhaps she was being held in some basement room, if indeed she was here at all.

"Madame Leeza Doss to see you, Monsieur," the servant murmured, showing me in. For some reason, he seemed in a hurry to leave, closing the door behind me with a slam.

The room dazzled with light from the window. I blinked in an effort to see, then blinked again for I could hardly believe what it was that I saw. A hugely fat man overflowed from an armchair by the window, his hair curling in greasy ringlets over his shoulders, his face waxy white, his eyes the pink of an albino. But what horrified me even more was the sight of my poor Madeleine, crouched on the floor beside him, hands and feet bound, her neck encircled by a dog collar at the end of a lead tied to the leg of the chair. The man's pale and podgy hands were caressing her red curls.

"I have to be so careful," the man squeaked in abnormally high-pitched voice. "The creature bites, you know." He giggled horribly.

"M. Cordelier?" I asked uncertainly. He was most certainly not the man I had seen with Jeanne-Claude at the opera.

"The very same," he replied. "And you are...? I missed your name."

"Eliza Dodds. I am a friend of your wife's."

At the sound of my voice, Madeleine jerked in surprise.

"Down," Cordelier hissed. Then chuckled again. "So pretty it is, but such a naughty wild animal."

"Is it necessary to keep her tied up like that, the poor little thing?" I asked. It was a vain hope, but I had to try.

"You think I could chase after, if it ran away? What a notion, madame! No, I am afraid my chasing days are long gone." He giggled as if at a great joke. "But why are you here? Not to discuss my little pet, I think."

He looked at me enquiringly through those pink eyes that were mere slits in the flesh of his face.

"Actually, I am curious. Who is this child and why is she here?"

He shook his head.

"You must answer my question first, madame. It is only polite."

"I was hoping to see your wife."

"Why?"

Why indeed.

"Er... Well, you see, I recently attended a most interesting demonstration by one Schmidt Pasha regarding domestic security. I am a widow woman, M. Cordelier, and, living in this city, often feel threatened. It was most distressing to learn of Schmidt Pasha's sudden death, but I understand your wife has a connection with him, and, indeed, intends to continue his good work."

He was staring at me most disconcertingly while I fumbled through an explanation that had only occurred to me while I was speaking.

"Ha!" he said at last. "Well, I know nothing of any of that. I am an invalid, as you can see, stuck here while my lady wife… well, she conducts herself as she sees fit. Always has done…All I can say is thank God for little distractions." He buried his fingers in Madeleine's hair and pulled on it hard. She gave a cry of pain.

"Enough," I said, throwing back the black hood to free myself from its confining folds. "I am going to release her. It is unconscionably cruel to treat a child that way."

"You will do no such thing, madame. The thing belongs to me. It is my creature. To play with." He pulled Madeleine's hair again.

"Try to stop me," I warned, advancing upon him.

He reached for a bell on a table beside him, but I knocked it out of the way, and drew out Eliza's gun, pointing it at him.

"What!" he cried, trembling like a blancmange. "What is this? You are no friend of Jeanni's to threaten a poor sick man." He raised his squeak to a squark. "Help! Osman!"

"Be quiet." I spoke in as menacing way as I could muster. "Or," waving the gun, "I'll have to use this."

To add to the absurd horror of the situation, the man started sobbing them, a quivering heap of flesh.

"Don't, please," he said. "Don't hurt me."

Ignoring him, I unclipped the lead from the dog collar around Madeleine's neck.

"No…" he protested. "Don't take my pet away. Please."

"Oh, madame!" Madeleine said. "You came for me!"

"Of course, my dear," I replied, smiling at her. "How could you doubt it?"

It was impossible to fiddle with the knotted ropes at her wrists with one hand, while keeping the other holding the gun pointed at the trembling Cordelier.

"You undo her," I said to him at last. "No tricks, or I will blast you to kingdom come."

Not realising how very unlikely I was to fulfil my threat, the coward did as he was told, thick fingers fumbling the while, tears streaming down his lardy cheeks. Once her hands were free, Madeleine slipped away from him and attended to the ties on her feet.

How to get her out of the house was another matter. The windows were too high above the ground to leave that way. We should have to go down the stairs again, without alerting the servants, and I had a sudden idea how that might be managed. First, however, we had to deal with Cordelier. Madeleine removed the dog collar which was far too small to fit around the man's thick neck, if he even had a neck. He did not resist when I used it to buckle his wrist to the arm of his chair. Then I pulled off his necktie and used it to restrain the other arm in similar fashion. Madeline picked up her headscarf, lying on the floor and tied it tightly around his mouth. As a parting touch she tugged hard on his ringlets, making him wince in agony.

"Now you know what it feels like," she snapped.

Cordelier stared at us through terrified eyes. He was clearly mad, and I felt almost sorry for him. But there was no time for that. I knew the bonds would not hold for long. At least they might give us opportunity enough to make our escape.

I told Madeleine to get under the robe, and climb up on me, piggy-back fashion.

"What?"

"We'll hope to get out of the house under it."

"That's mad."

"Have you a better idea?"

She shook her head.

It was lucky that Eliza Dodds had purchased such a very large garment. Even so, we must have presented a bizarre sight, a black beetle suddenly turned hunchbacked. With any luck, the manservant who had shown me in would be elsewhere during our attempt at egress. We cautiously exited the room on to a landing thankfully empty of people, although I could hear the murmur of voices somewhere towards the back of the house. Saying a silent prayer, I made my heavy way across the carpet. Madeleine might be a little slip of a thing, still, I am not as young as I once was, and she dragged off my shoulders. Could I even manage the stairs with her on my back? Slowly did it, me holding the banister for support the while. I could see the front door ahead of us. Step by difficult step, we drew nearer. Would we really reach it without being accosted? Amazingly, we did! I opened it as silently as I could, and we emerged into the blinding daylight.

"Why, Mrs. Hudson, Martha. Leaving so soon!"

Jeanne-Claude stood before us, her smile hideous.

"When I was told that a European woman disguised as a Turk had been asking for me at the apartment, and that she was making her way here, I knew it had to be you, the fugitive from justice."

"I was rescuing the child you abducted."

"Oh, is the slave there too, I thought you had just got fat from the delights fed you in prison."

Madeleine was now extricating herself from under the *charsaf*.

"Let us pass," I said.

"So sorry, my dear murderer," Jeanne-Claude purred. "The Sultan's soldiers even now await you outside the gate, to take you back to prison. But unfortunately, or perhaps fortunately – for who knows what the Sultan's plans are for a witch like you – I cannot let that happen. The Bosphorus is hungry for new flesh."

She drew a gun from her reticule, the jewelled sister of my own. Mine was already in my hand and, the safety catch released, I pulled it out too, pointing it back at her.

"Snap," she said, laughing. "Isn't that a child's card game? Sadly for you, no game this."

She stared at me, considering. I stared back in silence.

"You never fail to surprise me, Martha," she said finally. "But you should know it is dangerous to play with guns. As little Ayla could attest."

"You shot her."

"Did I? I cannot recall. Well, if I did, she deserved it. Ayla was a spoilt brat and refused to learn her French conjugations."

Jeanne-Claude was very collected to jest at such a time. As for me, I was trying not to tremble.

"I do hope no harm came to my poor husband," she continued. "Dear Felix is such a sensitive soul."

"Get behind me, Madeleine," I said.

"Don't do it." Jeanne-Claude's voice was suddenly sharp.

"I wasn't going to," the girl replied. Instead, she stepped in front of me.

"No," I said.

Jeanne-Claude laughed again, taking careful aim. "The little minx has spirit, what a shame she…"

I shot her.

Chapter Twenty-six

No, dear reader, rest assured I did not kill the woman. I aimed for the shoulder of the arm that held the gun and, thank God, the bullet hit its target. Thank God, as well, for those dear brothers of mine who so long ago had equipped me with the skill to shoot straight and true.

Jeanne-Claude stared at me for an unbelieving second, before dropping to the ground. We ran around her, Madeleine kicking her gun well out of reach, before making for the gate, for whatever awaited us outside.

Not a uniform to be seen. Jeanne-Claude had been bluffing, although I had to believe that soldiers might be on their way. Moreover, the shot must have been heard and we had very little time to escape. In my black robe, I had a degree of anonymity, but Madeleine was striking enough to turn heads, especially now that she had left her headscarf behind. On top of that, shouts from the house could already be heard. Cordelier must have been discovered. Our troubles were far from over.

People turned to look at us in amazement as we scurried down the hill, but made no move to stop us. Then, I caught sight of a carriage coming the other way. A cab. Could I hail it? Would it stop? I raised my arm, and, approaching us, it slowed down. To my incredulous relief, I recognised the driver, the same one who had brought me here. The one to whom I had given the note for Mr. H. It was nothing less than a miracle! The cab came to a halt beside us, and we climbed into it.

"I would never have known you, Mrs. Hudson." Another surprise for there was Mr. H himself, lounging back on the seat, making a steeple of his fingers, tapping them together. "Luckily, Madeleine is instantly recognisable… How are you, my dear?"

His voice actually betrayed emotion, although I could not tell to which of us he had addressed the uncustomary endearment.

"Madame was so brave!" the girl exclaimed. "She shot the French woman."

"You what?" He turned to me, astounded.

"Not dead," I replied. "Jeanne-Claude will live to face the Sultan's wrath… If, that is, he believes my version of events at last."

"You may have no fear on that score, Mrs. Hudson. The evidence mounts up." Mr. H frowned. "I have already suggested to Abdul Hamid that the Baron's supposed security measures are nothing more than an illusion."

"How did he take that?"

"Badly, at first. But then, having been permitted to examine the Baron's box of tricks, I informed His Majesty that I myself would attempt to reproduce the effect using mere sleight-of-hand. The show will take place tomorrow afternoon. I hope you will be recovered enough by then to attend."

"I would not miss it for the world," I replied. "So long as the Sultan doesn't take it into his head to throw me back into the dungeons."

"Wear that thing and you will be incognito," he said, adding as he observed my expression. "I jest, Mrs. Hudson. You will be perfectly safe."

He had said that to me before.

Dr. Watson had arranged a two-bed room for Madeleine and myself at the Pera Palace, and it was with the greatest of relief that we took occupancy of it. Despite Mr. H's impatience, I insisted that the first priority was for my little maid to take a good hot bath, to help her recover from her ordeal, even though, of course, we needed, as soon as possible, to find out from her exactly what had transpired. For my part, I was most concerned that she might have been harmed in some way. However, as I told Mr. H, the doctor agreeing with me, she should be allowed some peace, quiet and rest before the interrogation.

I had underestimated the almost boundless resilience of the young. Madeleine, bruised from M. Cordelier's pinches but otherwise not obviously injured, could hardly wait to recount her adventure, her eyes glittering. Thus it was that, wrapped in a huge towelling robe, she was soon reclining on her bed holding court, sipping a sherbet drink, the three of us around her, avid to hear all.

"Madame Cordelier came to our room in the harem, madame. She said you needed me to join her on a trip to the city." Madeleine looked at us with her big eyes. "Why should I doubt her? She was your friend, as I thought, and all the girls kept saying how nice and kind she was. She led me out through a back door, which I found strange, but she said that was where the carriage was waiting for us. When I climbed in, she grabbed me, pressing a sweet-smelling cloth to my mouth. I remembered nothing more until I woke up in the house where you found me, madame."

"Chloroform, without a doubt," said Dr. Watson, frowning.

"Did they hurt you in any way?" I asked.

"Apart from being tied up and having my hair pulled and my skin pinched by that horrid toad, do you mean, madame? No, but Madame Cordelier told me I would be beaten or worse if I wasn't a good quiet girl. All the same," she grinned at the memory, "I really did bite his horrid hand if it came too near."

She had been lucky. Still, I would ask Dr. Watson to examine her in case she had been subjected to anything untoward while unconscious.

"The old man was loony," the girl continued. "Madame Cordelier told him she had brought him a pet to play with. That was me! A pet!" Madeleine was most offended. "'Look at her lovely red hair, Felix,' she told him. 'I know how much you will like that.' And he did. You saw for yourself how he couldn't stop touching it, madame." She ran her fingers through her damp curls. "How loony is that?"

A knock on the door at that moment announced the arrival of a waiter with a trolley of cakes and pastries. Madeleine set upon the goodies with a will, but I had no appetite. In fact, unlike my maid, I was suddenly overcome with fatigue, dizziness and nausea. The good doctor noticed this and insisted that he and Mr. H leave us in peace for a few hours. Mr. H might have liked to ask more questions, of me, in particular, but reluctantly acceded to his friend's direction.

Can there be anything more reviving than a good sleep? When I awoke, it was already evening. Madeleine, for all her high spirits, had also succumbed to slumber, and was breathing softly and regularly. I regarded her with affection. Thank God I had been able to track her down in time, for I had no doubt that Jeanne-Claude would not have hesitated in disposing of her, as she had done with the other poor girls.

I found myself suddenly hungry, not for the remaining sweetmeats that sat piled on the bedside table, but for some hot soup. I hoped the establishment could run to that, and rang down to place the order. That woke up my companion, and so I ordered a portion for her as well.

We picnicked in the bedroom, I musing that a nourishing bowl of tripe soup was worth all the rich feasts provided at Yildiz. Madeleine was less enthusiastic about the dish, but, urged on by me, managed most of hers as well. A gentle tap sounded on the door as we were finishing. It was Dr. Watson.

"Mr. H was wondering, Mrs. Hudson, if you would at last be up to reporting on your adventure, from the time that we left you with Miss Dodds."

Eliza! Good heavens! She was surely imagining all sorts of terrible fates had befallen me since I had gone off, wearing the black robe and armed with her gun. It was quite unforgivable of me to forget her, especially since I had availed of her identity to gain egress into the house in Bebek. I said as much to Dr. Watson, who smiled reassuringly.

"Not at all," he replied. "She already knows you are safe and well. I called upon her to let her know, and also to tell her of my interview with her sister."

"You are so good, Doctor," I said. "What news of Cecelia?"

"The husband was reluctant to let me talk to her but finally agreed, when I told him I was visiting on behalf of Miss Dodds. The girl finally emerged covered from head to toe in those robes like the one you were wearing."

"A *charsaf*," I said.

"Indeed… Well, I am afraid that Cecelia expressed no desire to return to her earlier life. I wondered at first if this were because of the presence of her husband, sitting scowling at me, but it seemed not. 'Yusuf looks after me so well,' she said. 'He gives me everything I want.' I gained a strong feeling that a life of idleness and self-indulgence with a prosperous merchant – for such is the husband – suits the foolish girl down to the ground. Of course, once he tires of her, it may become another matter, but she certainly showed no inclination to return to Eliza, or even, since I asked about this, to see her again. 'Let her return quickly to Norwood,' Cecelia said, her dislike of the place, and perhaps even of her sister, evident in her tone."

"Of course, Eliza is not really her sister," I said.

"No? So Holmes was correct in his surmise?"

"I think not. Eliza told me that the girl was more in the nature of a ward, the child she never had."

"Well then, if they are not related, perhaps Cecelia is not quite as hard-hearted as I thought."

"Oh, I think she is. Poor Eliza."

She would surely have taken the rejection hard.

"I tried to sweeten my account," Dr. Watson continued, "by saying that it seemed Cecelia was truly in love with this Yusuf, and he with her."

"I wonder if that made it better or worse."

He shook his head. "She was most relieved to hear that you and Madeleine are safe, adding that she would love to meet you to hear what happened."

"I shall make sure she does," I replied. "Anyway, I must return her gun."

"Oh!" exclaimed Madeleine, who, even with her scant knowledge of English, understood that much. "Can you not keep it, madame? In case you ever need it again."

I laughed at that. "I certainly hope I shall not," I said.

Chapter Twenty-Seven

The French have an expression, *déjà vu*, to signify a condition in which one feels one has undergone the same experience on a previous occasion. Taking my seat in the same hall of the palace where, only a few incredible days before, Schmidt Pasha had mesmerised the Sultan and audience with his demonstration, I understood what they meant. Now, however, it was the turn of Mr. H, eschewing the razzamatazz of the late Baron, and dressed as usual in a sober suit. To my mind, it was all the more effective for that.

I was seated in a back row with Dr. Watson, somewhat fearful, I have to say it, at the presence of so many armed guards. Despite Mr. H's assurances that the Sultan would not imprison me again, I could not be sure. A command from the head of the Ottoman Empire would surely overcome any objections by some Baker Street detective, no matter how distinguished. I could only pray that Mr. H's presentation would convince Abdul Hamid that it was the Baron who was the villain all along.

It somewhat startled me to observe the presence in the audience of that same distinguished grey-haired gentleman who had accompanied Jeanne-Claude to the performance of "Medea", until Dr. Watson whispered to me that he was the French ambassador, assuredly someone above suspicion, the innocent companion of the she-devil.

My sense that we had all been here before continued as Mr. H started his display. The same map with its criss-crossed lines hung on a screen – Mr. H explaining their significance as if he believed what he was saying about protective magnetic forces. Then he laid his hand upon the large and intriguing-looking box beside him, causing it to emit that familiar long, thin, ray of blue light. At a sign from Mr. H, a soldier ostentatiously wearing the famous amulet walked safely through the same beam.

Then, to my astonishment, I saw my old jailer, Emin, step forward, Mr. H instructing him also to cross through the beam, though without the protection of the amulet. Looking nervous, he obeyed, only to fall and writhe in agony as he encountered the beam. Everyone gasped. The Sultan rose up.

"You promised, Sherlock Bey, to expose a fraud," he said. "But you have only proved its validity."

Mr. H smiled. "So then, Your Majesty, I trust you will award me the huge fee you promised to Baron Reynaert Mauterpuis, otherwise Schmidt Pasha, to install the system at Yildiz." He turned to the audience. "And you, who also wished to avail of these miraculous measures, perhaps you too would like to provide me with sackfuls of your gold. However," he paused, a dramatic moment, "you would be well advised to hold on to your wealth."

He walked across the stage, through the beam with no ill effects.

"I am not wearing an amulet," he said. "And young Emin here was merely acting, is that not so?"

The young guard leapt to his feet grinning and nodding.

Abdul Hamid scowled. "What sport is this! Are you trying to make a fool of me, Sherlock Bey?"

"Not at all, Your Majesty. My aim has always been to stop you being fooled."

"And yet," the Sultan continued, "when Schmidt Pasha performed the experiment, the unprotected soldier on the last occasion was struck down in front of us all. He was clearly suffering great pain."

"On the contrary, he was bribed handsomely into acting as he did, but then, foolishly, boasted about it to my informant."

"Where is the wretch?" Abdul Hamid roared. "Bring him to me. He shall regret he was ever born."

I shivered. After all, I knew something of the Sultan's revenge.

"Don't worry, Mrs. Hudson," Dr. Watson whispered to me. "The man has fled."

"There is no scientific marvel here, no powerful magnetic force field," Mr. H continued, opening the box to show the Sultan and the audience. "Just the source of an ordinary beam of light." He waved his hand through it. "The rest is illusion."

The Sultan had sat himself down again, deep in thought. We all waited. What next?

Finally, he spoke in low tones. "Come with me, Sherlock Bey."

He stood, a small old man, after all, and hurried from the room, his entourage scurrying after. The rest of the audience, unsure and uneasy, muttering to each other, stayed seated until ushered out by the soldiers.

"Of course," I overhead a large man saying to his bony wife: Lord and Lady Barnard, "I knew all along that German chappie was a fraud, Lettie. It was all too good to be true. He wouldn't have seen a penny of *my* money, I can tell you."

Lady Barnard glanced at me at that moment, and maybe noticed my cynical smile, for she tossed her head, took her husband's arm and stalked out.

Back at the hotel, I was surprised to find a note from Naime, expressing the hope that I would be free to join the ladies of the harem for dinner before returning to England. So she knew even before I did that my departure was imminent!

I felt no great enthusiasm, to say the very least, for returning to that gilded cage. However, to see the Princess one more time, to thank her for her kindness and trust when I was shunned by all the others, was surely worth the sacrifice. I also wished, if possible, to see Cemile and to thank her, too. Without her bravery and gumption, I might still be rotting in that dungeon. I showed the invitation to Dr. Watson, and he agreed that it would be a courtesy to accept.

"But wait until we hear from Holmes," he suggested. "He will know better what to do."

It was late afternoon before the detective returned. Indeed, although I said nothing to Dr. Watson, I was starting to become anxious at the delay. Was the Sultan so incensed at the revelation that he had been duped, that he decided to shoot the messenger?

Not at all. When Mr. H finally made an appearance, he was all smiles. Not only had he convinced the Sultan of the villainy of the Baron in this and other regards, he had provided sufficient evidence, by drawing on the information I had given him, against the sister for the deaths of the slaves.

"She is now under arrest," he told us.

"In the dungeons where I was held," I asked hopefully.

He shook his head. "I understand representations have been made on her behalf for mercy by the French ambassador, who is a friend of hers."

"A misguided one," I said.

"Indeed. But be that as it may, she is currently in hospital receiving treatment for the wound you inflicted on her, Mrs. Hudson. An armed guard at her door, at least. After which she will be confined under house arrest at the Sultan's pleasure."

"I almost wish I had killed her. The harridan deserves no mercy. She should be made to pay for the deaths of those poor girls."

"She is pleading innocence, stating how she was taken in by her brother. Moreover, the ladies of the harem are apparently vociferous in their defence of her. Such a lovely, kind woman, they say. She couldn't have done such awful things, unless under a spell."

"So she will escape justice?"

He sighed. "It is difficult for Abdul Hamid to accept that a woman could be so devious and cruel."

Not in my case, I thought.

"However," Mr. H continued, "a search of the house in Bebek has revealed incriminating documents, as well as a hoard of the Sultan's gold, silver and jewels removed from the safes in his tunnels. And her husband is leaking like a sieve in his attempts to wriggle out of any involvement."

I reared up. "He must at least be held accountable for what he did to Madeleine."

Mr. H shook his head wearily. "I am afraid that she, in the eyes of the Sultan, is a slave with no rights."

Just as Gulsima was. I had to accept now that that sweet girl had been killed, simply for the crime of falling in love with the wrong person. I could not wait to leave this accursed place, to go home.

"I shall refuse the invitation to dinner at the palace," I said.

"Oh no, Mrs. Hudson," Mr. H replied. "You must not do that. In any case, the next Orient Express is not for two days. You can fulfil your obligation tomorrow."

"I have no obligation to these people," I said. "An apology to me would be more appropriate."

Mr. H smiled. "I think I can promise you that," he said. "The Sultan is most thankful to you for all that you have done."

At long last.

Meanwhile, I sent an invitation to Eliza Dodds, requesting that she join me at the hotel at her convenience. Perhaps, if were not too late, for dinner that very evening.

It was not too late. Rather than replying by messenger, the lady herself arrived almost by return, an attendant informing me that she was awaiting me in the hotel lobby. Luckily, I was already dressed and ready, and descended to meet her. Eliza had obviously made an effort to fit in with the style required in such a splendid hotel, but, sadly, in her best brown serge outfit, she only managed to look a little less dowdy than usual beside the birds of paradise that fluttered through the doors of the establishment. For my part, I was almost ashamed that all I had to wear were the fine and fashionable gowns selected by Madame Celestine: it was if I was showing up the poor governess. In truth, I too would have been more comfortable in plainer clothes, and quite intended to leave all my finery behind when I departed.

Perhaps it was this evident contrast in our appearances that caused her to feel at a disadvantage.

"You are very good to waste time with such as me, Martha," she said.

"Not at all," I replied embracing her. "I owe you so much."

The finality of the news regarding Cecelia must have depressed her spirits, for she looked drawn and tired.

"I am sure we shall both be glad to return to England. It will be such a relief for me to be at home again in my little house," I said, leading her into the dining room, so luxurious it seemed to belie my words. "I am sure you feel the same."

Perhaps she suspected I was patronising her, for she said nothing in reply. It was only after she had, warily, accepted a glass of wine – and had taken the merest sip of it – that she started to relax and return to her usual garrulous self. How full she was of the wrongs inflicted on her by the Barnards, especially mother and son, and by her betrayal by the ungrateful Cecelia – "After all I did for her, Martha." It proved impossible to stem the flow, between a harangue against Turkish men who took advantage of pretty young women, the unholy religion they all practised here, the spicy food that gave her indigestion, the queer customs and clothes. Only when she broke from her rant to consume her chicken with rice, carefully picking out the strips of red and green capsicums and laying them to one side, was I able to regale her with my adventures. She was all attention, then, her mouth hanging open while I told of Madeleine's ordeal, how she was held prisoner, and how, while helping her escape, I had been forced to make use of the gun to shoot Madame Cordelier.

"Dead?" she exclaimed in horror, tinged with a ghoulish fascination.

"No, no," I assured her. "I hit her shoulder. She will recover."

Eliza was hardly less shocked. "How could you do such a thing, Martha? I should have been too terrified to move, let alone fire a dangerous weapon."

"The virago had a gun of her own and was threatening Madeleine," I said. "I had no option but to act."

Eliza toyed with a bread roll.

"And is Madeleine all right?" she asked, regarding the crumbs she had made, and rolling them around the plate. "I mean, she was not submitted to any immodesty, I trust."

"No, nothing like that. Just cruelty and captivity."

"Thank God!" Eliza looked wise. "She had a very narrow escape, indeed."

For her, as I understood it, the violation of a girl's virtue was a fate far worse than death.

"I must return your gun," I said.

"Oh no!" She was horrified at that suggestion. "Not if it has shot someone."

I refrained from remarking that shooting was what guns were designed for.

"Then," I said, "I shall return it to Lady Barnard, for I suspect it belongs to her."

At first, I thought to send it anonymously, since I had no desire to engage with that particular female ever again, but then realised that the evidence would point inexorably to Eliza as the one who had taken it. I would send the gun back with a terse note, saying that I thought this must belong to her, adding no further explanation. Let her Ladyship think what she would. That it had indeed been found in the harem.

Just now, despite Eliza's previous disdainful remarks regarding Turkish cuisine, I noticed that she was doing full justice to the fine fare in front of her, and I could not help but wonder if she went hungry, now that she was without a situation and income. When I delicately suggested a loan, however, she told me in sharp tones that she was well able to pay her way, a large crumb of syrupy pistachio from the baklava she was devouring, distractingly clinging to her upper lip as she spoke. Should I tell her about it? Thankfully, she wiped her mouth before I could say anything.

She declined the offer of coffee.

"I cannot abide the way they serve it here," she said. "It is even worse than the slop we bought in Vienna. Remember that, Martha? Before we had any notion of what awaited us here."

A faraway look came into her eyes, and then a large tear rolled down her cheek. To comfort her, I put my hand on hers, but she shook it off as if I had given her an electric shock. Suddenly she was in great hurry to leave, her excuse being the need to return to her apartment before it got too late.

"For, you know, Martha," she explained, "I do not like to travel through the city at night."

I was glad enough to have seen her, lonely woman that she was, and – I am sorry to admit it – more glad again when she departed in the cab I insisted she must take, paying for it when she was already inside. Watching it rattle off away from the hotel, I found myself fearing, somewhat unkindly, that she might be on the same Orient Express that was to carry my two gentlemen and me back to London. If so, I anticipated long dreary sessions in the ladies' saloon, listening to her further bemoaning her fate.

The next day I spent packing. Madeleine was horrified that I meant to leave the fine French gowns and valuable jewellery behind.

"I have no use for them in London," I said. "In any case, I do not wish to be beholden in any way to Abdul Hamid."

"What about this?" Madeleine picked up the plate bearing the Sultan's image.

I was inclined to tell her to drop it, but had second thoughts.

"That I shall bring with me and find an appropriate place in the house to display it, where there is no need often to look upon it." It would prove a conversation piece, if nothing more. The other plate, featuring the moonlight scene on the river, I made sure to wrap most carefully. It was beautiful, and I should cherish it along with the memory of she who had given it to me.

Madeleine was now toying with a gold bracelet set with rubies and diamonds.

"Are you quite sure about the jewellery, madame?"

"Yes. It is all far too fancy for me," I replied. "But you may choose a piece or two if you wish."

Of course she wished, slipping the bangle on to her slim wrist.

"It's too big," she complained.

In the end, she selected a silver necklace set with turquoise stones, along with a diamond and sapphire brooch in the form of an exotic bird. I had never had occasion to wear either of them.

"Will you not keep something, madame?" she persisted. "You liked to wear this silver brooch."

I wavered. It was a pretty thing with a filigree design that reflected the Arabic alphabet, and not as showy or, indeed, as valuable as the others.

"I shall think on it," I replied at last.

It occurred to me then that I should like to bring something back as gifts for my daughters, as well as for my loyal maids, Clara and Phoebe, although such jewellery as I had here was rather too extravagant for them. In any case, I should prefer that the gifts came from me and not from the Sultan.

"You are sure to find something in the bazaar, madame," Madeleine suggested, when I voiced my intention.

"An excellent idea. Let us go there forthwith."

Taking a cab that carried us from the hotel over the Golden Horn, we eventually arrived at the Grand Bazaar. How very pleasant it was to wander freely down those aisles, without Bashir, or some other eunuch, brooding company on our heels! Madeleine and I lingered by pungent stalls piled high with brightly coloured spices, with dried fruits and nuts, with that sweetmeat we call Turkish Delight. For my maids, I purchased a box of the latter, which they could share, as well as two pretty silk scarves, selected by my companion, and, for fun, two of those blue, white and black glass beads in the form of pendants, to ward off the evil eye.

For my daughters, Eleanor and Judith, I selected two more richly patterned silk scarves and two exquisitely woven rugs, small enough to fit in my trunk, now that it would be empty of dresses. More Turkish Delight for the children and more blue beads. For myself, advised by the stallholder, I bought a selection of brightly coloured spices. I could regale my gentlemen with Turkish dishes when we returned, whether they wished it or no. It was, I confess, the most enjoyable and relaxing activity I had experienced since arriving in Constantinople.

That evening found Madeleine and I travelling, for the last time, by carriage up to Yildiz. The winter weather had softened almost into mildness and a powder blue mist hung over the Bosphorus. Mosques and towers stood silhouetted against the sky. Dogs howled at the moon. Strange to think that in a few days all this would seem as a fevered dream. One promise I made to myself then and there was to stay home safely in future. No more adventures for me. Or, at least, not for a good long while...

Bashir welcomed me almost with a smile.

"I am happy to see you are unharmed, madame," he said.

To say I was astonished at this was an understatement: I was quite flabbergasted. That this huge negro eunuch could prove himself, with those simple words, so much more than a mere gatekeeper of the Sultan's. I understood then that Bashir was not a bad man. A cruel fate had made him what he was, and dictated what he had to do.

Just now he suggested that, while I was feasting with the ladies of the harem, Madeleine might like to visit the slaves, to say her farewells. She agreed willingly, having brought with her a selection of my discarded jewels to distribute among them, to Cemile in particular, in case I had no opportunity to thank the girl in person. For their part, I imagined the slaves would be all agog to hear of Madeleine's adventure.

Bashir then led me through familiar passageways to the dining hall, where the wives and daughters were already seated. All eyes turned towards me as I entered. I felt most conspicuous, and was pleased when Naime beckoned me to take the empty seat next to her. A servant approached with the usual scented water and towel, for me to wash my hands before eating.

The meal was as awkward as I had anticipated, the embarrassed glances, the fixed stares, the stilted conversation. Were it not for the presence of the Princess, I doubted that I could have borne it. How many of them knew of that which I had undergone? Did the aged Valide Sultan realise that I had been subjected to the full horrors of her stepson's dungeons, threatened with torture and death? I rather suspected that she, at least, did not, for she simply smiled, nodded and winked knowingly at me the while, pressing more and more little dishes upon me, until I had to shake my head politely and indicate that I really could not eat any more of the too rich fare. Indeed, I felt quite nauseous.

Bedrifelek and the other wives, for their part, once they decided to broach the subject, were all insincere concern.

"How terrible it must have been for you! Of course, we were all completely taken in by Schmidt Pasha and that dreadful French woman."

"She is Flemish," I said.

"Precisely, passing herself off as French, the miserable whore."

For reasons either of delicacy or diplomacy, they probed no further into my ordeal, and soon took to chatting among themselves about their usual idle concerns, the latest sensational novel by one Paul de Kock apparently furnishing them with great entertainment.

I started to wonder why on Earth I had been invited. At least, Naime, sitting close, squeezed my hand from time to time in an expression of solidarity.

The Sultan was absent. His excuse, relayed by Bedrifelek, was that affairs of state had regrettably taken precedence over His Majesty's desire to thank me in person for all I had done in clearing up the mystery of the deaths of the slaves, and so on. My own reading of his non-appearance was somewhat different. The coward could not face me.

Thus, I was most taken aback when, towards the end of the meal, the Valide Sultan stood up with difficulty and some ceremony, and beckoned me to her side. With Naime translating, the Queen Mother informed me that the Sultan was pleased to confer upon me the Order of the Chefakat. She stared at me expectantly, a smile hovering over her lips.

I was bemused and not sure quite how to react.

"It's a great honour," whispered Naime, "given to very few European women, most of them princesses or duchesses, for their charitable work."

I had to bite my lip then to stop myself from laughing out loud. Was that what I had done? Charitable work!

The Valide Sultan, still smiling and nodding, presented me with the Order. I looked at the thing, a five-pointed enamelled star, resting on a wreath set with what looked to be diamonds and rubies and hanging from another smaller star.

"The highest class," Naime said, encouragingly.

I was clearly required to express my boundless gratitude, and dutifully bowed my thanks while the wives applauded.

"I was just glad to be of help," I said somewhat weakly, wondering at the same time what on Earth to do with the medal. Call me unforgiving, but I wished for nothing at all from this cruel man, except possibly the apology that I was never now likely to receive.

At last, the dinner was done. I embraced Naime with some emotion. She was the only person I would miss from Constantinople.

"May you find a good man to be your husband," I told her, "and may your children bring you joy."

All I had with me of a personal nature, apart of course for the amethyst ring, from which I hoped never now to be parted, was a gold locket I was wearing next to my skin, containing images of my two daughters. It was a small thing, but I presented her with it anyway, as a memento.

She hugged me with tears in her eyes.

"I shall cherish it for ever," she said, adding, "Please Mrs. Hudson, do not forget me."

I promised, of course, and we wept together.

"And Naime," I said, after I had composed myself, "please make a big fuss of Guzellik the next time you visit her. She saved my life and killed a bad man."

The princess laughed merrily then.

"You know," she said, "my father wanted Guzellik shot and made into a rug. It was all I could do to stop him. Then, when Schmidt Pasha was revealed to be a scoundrel, my father awarded Guzellik with a medal a bit like yours."

I joined in her laughter, although the thought of being considered on the same level as a wild beast was perhaps not very flattering.

Thus, it was that, in pretence at least of good humour, we rejoined Madeleine at the gates of the harem. Bashir having summoned the coach driver, we mounted the vehicle. Naime waved us off, I leaning from the window of the carriage until I could see her no longer.

"You will miss her, madame," Madeleine said.

"Yes, it is hard to think of such a lovely and talented young woman having to spend her life locked away from the world. Such a waste."

"But it is their way," Madeleine replied wisely. "You and I would not like it – and, as for me, I hope to leave that accursed convent as soon as possible – but it is what they are all used to. They would feel strange living as we do."

"You are right, my dear. Thank you for that."

"You know," she went on, "it was Princess Naime who sent Cemile to the Pera Palace hotel after you disappeared. She was sure that you were not guilty, but had to act in secret, to avoid her father's anger."

On hearing that, I nearly ordered that the carriage be turned around so that I could embrace my good angel again.

"Cemile was so pleased with her gifts. They all were, madame, thanking you and wishing you well."

As we continued the journey back to the hotel, Madeleine, as usual, cheered me with her lively chat. As I had thought, and in contrast to the Sultan's reticent wives and daughters, the slave girls had been hungry to hear every single detail of her and my ordeal.

"Their hair quite stood on end when I told them about being treated like a dog, tied to that horrid man." She smiled. "They wanted to know exactly what he had done to me and seemed a bit disappointed when I said that he had just pulled my hair and pinched me. But their jaws dropped completely when I told how you rescued me, and how you shot Madame Cordelier before she could shoot us."

"You were lucky," Cemile had told her. "She might have murdered you, like she did all the others. It must have been your hair saved you. She always liked your red hair."

"I never really cared for that Madame Cordelier," Beylem had insisted. "There was always something cold about her."

"How she could say that with a straight face, I do not know." Madeleine laughed merrily. "Beylem was always the one hottest in her defence of the woman. Nevertheless, madame," she continued,

'I think they still suspect you of having magic powers, after you tamed the tiger and all."

'Well, maybe I have, Madeleine," I told her. 'Maybe I have."

Epilogue

Christmas is coming on fast and I am sitting in my kitchen in Baker Street. It is late. Clara and Phoebe have gone to bed, and Mr. H and Dr. Watson are above in their rooms. I can hear the faintest murmur of voices, but that is all.

It is a week now since we returned from Turkey. I slept for most of the journey back, being utterly worn out and not wishing for more company than that of those near and dear to me. I mostly ate in my cabin, while the thought of having to make polite conversation in the ladies' saloon discouraged me from venturing there. If Eliza were on the same train, I did not see her, but perhaps, after all, she had stayed longer in Constantinople, in the vain hope that Cecelia might have a last-minute change of heart.

In Paris, another heart-rending separation took place, when I had to bid farewell to Madeleine. She had proved such a faithful little maid, and I loved her dearly. The best news awaited her, however. Katy, now living with her father on the family estate in the Midi, had begged that her friend might come to live with them as her companion, and Papa had, apparently, been only too pleased to indulge his daughter. No more convent life, then, for the spirited little miss.

Valentina Muratova – as Dr. Watson informed me, having read of it in *The Times of London* – had meanwhile set off on a tour of America, presumably to perform *La Dame aux Camellias* and *Medea* in their original, unbowdlerised versions.

Abdul Hamid had rewarded Mr. H most handsomely for clearing up the mystery of the slave deaths, and for saving him from the machinations of Baron Mauterpuis. I was not resentful. I suppose the Sultan reckoned that the Order of Chefakat – which I have thrown into a drawer, though tempted to throw into the Thames – was enough recompense for a mere woman. In any case, as I informed Mr. H, when he offered to pass some of the reward money on to me, I had no wish to receive anything at all from a man I abhorred.

"But you would be receiving it from me, Mrs. Hudson," he replied with a smile. "I sincerely hope that you do not abhor me in equal measure."

Of course, I did not, but still stood stubbornly on my principles, even if my principles did not extend to the pretty little silver brooch, which I have after all retained. Naime told me that the curling Arabic letters over the filigree spelt out the word LOVE, something, after all, to hang on to in a world often all too short of that emotion.

If I refused a share in the Sultan's munificence, Dr. Watson hinted, privately, that I might expect a larger than usual Christmas gift from Mr. H, to which I replied, somewhat tartly, that any gift at all would fit that particular bill, since Mr. H was not in the habit of presenting me with anything at the festive season.

"Oh," he replied. "That is just his way. But you must know, Mrs. Hudson, that, while Holmes may not have said it in so many words, he is boundlessly grateful to you for all that you have done. Without your insights and assistance, he was unlikely ever to have been able to get to the bottom of the matter. And of course, he is extremely remorseful for subjecting you to such a terrible ordeal. He had no idea, when we set out, that it would come to that. We both thank God that you came through it unscathed."

The wind is howling down the chimney, as if a devil is trying to gain access, but I am cosy in my little kitchen, sitting by the dying glow of the stove. Am I unscathed? Not completely, perhaps, since I sometimes wake in the night, thinking myself back in that cold, dark, damp prison, hearkening to the groans and shrieks of my fellow damned. But let me dwell on that no longer. The joyful festival that is Christmas will, it is to be hoped, dispel frightful memories. Eleanor. son-in-law George, and baby Henry will be traveling up from Kent to spend the holiday with me and I can hardly wait. Already today I prepared the dried fruits for the plum pudding, setting them to soak overnight in brandy. Tomorrow, Clara and I will start the mixing and boiling, adding in a silver sixpence and other little charms, while Phoebe, well away from trouble, will be tasked with polishing the cutlery in the scullery, where she cannot break or spill anything.

It was there, in the scullery, in fact, that I hung the plate bearing the image of Abdul Hamid, but then had to turn his face to the wall, because Phoebe said it gave her nightmares. Perhaps I shall present it to George for his silly mother, Henrietta, since she adores any contact with royalty, however remote. Although, on second thoughts, I should not wish that hooded glare even on my worst enemy.

Notes

While researching this novel, I drew on many sources, both printed and digital. Above all, the biography of Abdul Hamid II, *The Sultan*, by Joan Haslip (1958), proved invaluable, as did *Harem: The World Behind the Veil* by Alev Lytle Croutier (1989) and *An Englishwoman in a Turkish Harem* by Grace Ellison, first published in 1915. *Orient Express History* by Arjan de Boer, full of historical photographs and eye-witness accounts, brought that part of Mrs Hudson's journey to life, as did a TV documentary that had David Suchet, who has portrayed Agatha Christie's Poirot so memorably, travelling on the refurbished train between Venice and Prague, even though the décor would have been somewhat different in the 1890s. A Turkish film series, *Midnight at the Pera Palace hotel*, is, as I write, being shown on Netflix and provided more useful background, as did Orhan Panuk's *Istanbul* and Graham Greene's *Stamboul Train*. The entertaining memoirs of the French journalist, Henri de Blowitz, recounting his meeting with Abdul Hamid in 1883, illustrates the baroque intrigues of the Ottoman court and the paranoia of the Sultan. The website of Yildiz palace set the scene for me there, and various websites detailing kitchen customs and food of the Ottoman period, helped me plan the menus.

More vivid insights into harem life, largely unchanged over the centuries, can be found in the letters of Lady Mary Wortley Montagu, her husband being the ambassador to the Sublime Porte, as the central government of the Ottoman Empire was called, between 1717-1718. Regarding the inoculations that she witnessed against smallpox ("engrafting," as Lady Mary calls the practice), she writes of it in vivid detail to a friend in a letter of 1717:

Apropos of distempers, I am going to tell you a thing, that will make you wish yourself here. The small-pox, so fatal and so general amongst us, is here entirely harmless by the invention of ingrafting, which is the term they give it. There is a set of old women, who make it their business to perform the operation, every autumn, in the month of September, when the great heat is abated. People send to one another to know if any of their family has a mind to have the small-pox; they make parties for this purpose, and when they are met (commonly fifteen or sixteen together) the old woman comes with a nut-shell full of the matter of the best sort of small-pox, and asks what vein you please to have opened. She immediately rips open that you offer her, and with a large needle (which gives you no more pain than a common scratch) and puts into the vein as much matter as can lie open the head of her needle, and after that, binds up the little wound with a hollow bit of shell; and in this manner opens four or five veins...

Every year thousands undergo this operation; and the French ambassador says pleasantly, that they take the small-pox here by way of diversion, as they take the waters in other countries. There is no example of any one that has died in it; and you may believe I am very well satisfied of the safety of this experiment, since I intend to try it on my dear little son.

In a work of fiction of this type, certain liberties have of necessity to be taken. To include and describe more than I have done the many wives and children of the Sultan would have over-burdened the narrative with unnecessary detail. However, Bedrifelek was indeed the Sultan's first consort in the late 1890s and Naime his favourite daughter. She, indeed, had a colourful life afterwards, marrying a man who, it was said, subsequently plotted with his mistress to murder her. Luckily for her the plotters were exposed before any harm could be done. Naime remarried, but was exiled in 1924, following the fall of the Ottoman Empire, finally settling in Albania, where she died, possibly in a Nazi concentration camp, in 1945. As for Abdul Hamid himself, he was deposed in 1909 and sent into exile in Thessaloniki. He returned to Constantinople in 1912, to be confined in the Beylerbeyi palace on the Bosphorus until his death in 1918.

Abdul Hamid was a huge fan of the Sherlock Holmes stories of Sir Arthur Conan Doyle and had them translated as soon as they were published. When the author and his new wife, Jean, honeymooned in Constantinople in 1907, the Sultan bestowed on him the Order of the Medjidie (second class) and on Jean the Order of the Chefakat, the same as that presented to Mrs. Hudson. Conan Doyle recalls this in his *Memories and Adventures* of 1923:

> *It was Ramadan, and the old sultan sent me a message that he had read my books and that he would gladly have seen me had it not been the Holy month. He interviewed me through his Chamberlain and presented me with the Order of the Medjidie, and, what was more pleasing to me, he gave the Order of Chevekat to my wife. As this is the Order of Compassion, and as my wife ever since she set foot in Constantinople had been endeavouring to feed the horde of starving dogs who roamed the streets, no gift could have been more appropriate.*

Any errors, historical or cultural, in the narrative are mine alone, or perhaps Mrs. Hudson's, for she writes of the Ottoman world from the ignorant perspective of a Victorian matron, with all the prejudices of her class. That said, she is still more open-minded than most, and I trust no one will be offended by her account.

Acknowledgements

Thanks as ever to my readers, Ann O'Kelly, Phyl Herbert, Pete Morriss, Bernie McCormick and particularly Pat Jackson, for her meticulous copy-editing.

Grateful thanks to the Karakulak family, for their hospitality and invaluable suggestions.

Thanks to the great team at MX books, the ever-supportive and enthusiastic Steve Emecz, Richard Ryan, and Brian Belanger who always produces such striking covers.

About the Author

Susan Knight is the author of three previous Mrs Hudson novels: *Mrs Hudson goes to Ireland*, *Mrs Hudson goes to Paris* and *Death in the Garden of England*, as well as a short story collection, *Mrs Hudson Investigates*. Since 2019, she has contributed to the *MX books of new Sherlock Holmes short stories*. Some of these stories have been published in a collection entitled *Sherlock Holmes Investigates: The Strange Case of the Pale Boy and other mysteries*.

Her other works include the novels *The Invisible Woman*, *Grimaldi's Garden* and the short story collection, *Out of Order*, as well as a non-fiction book of interviews with immigrant women living in Ireland, *Where the Grass is Greener*.

She lives in Dublin, Ireland.